THIS BOOK IS THE PROPERTY OF
The American Legion Post No. 209
AKRON, OHIO
BOOKS ARE FOR LOAN ONLY AND MUST
BE RETURNED WITHIN TWO WEEKS FROM
DATE

YELLOWSTONE NIGHTS

YELLOWSTONE NIGHTS

By
HERBERT QUICK

AUTHOR OF
ALLADIN & CO.
VIRGINA OF THE AIR LANES, ETC.

GROSSET & DUNLAP
PUBLISHER - NEW YORK

COPYRIGHT 1911
THE BOBBS-MERRILL COMPANY

YELLOWSTONE NIGHTS

YELLOWSTONE NIGHTS

CHAPTER I

IT was August the third—and the rest of it. Being over Montana, and the Rockies, the skies were just as described by Truthful James. In the little park between the N. P. Station and the entrance to Yellowstone Park a stalwart young fellow and a fluffy, lacy, Paquined girl floated from place to place with their feet seven or eight inches from the earth—or so it seemed. They disappeared behind some shrubbery and sat down on a bench, where the young man hugged the girl ferociously, and she, with that patient endurance which is the wonder and glory of womanhood, suffered it uncomplainingly. In fact she reciprocated it.

Note that we said a moment ago that they disappeared. From whose gaze? Not from ours, for we saw them sit and—and what followed. Their disappearance was from the view of a slender man of medium height who was off toward the station, inspecting the salvias, the phloxes, the cannas, the colei, the materials with which the walks were paved, and the earth in the flower-beds. He looked the near things over with a magnifying-glass, and scrutinized the far landscape with field-glasses. When he removed his traveling cap, one saw that he was bald, though not so bald as he seemed—his weak and neutral hair blended so in color with the neutral shades of his face and garb.

As he looked at things near and far, from the formal garden of the little park to the towering peak of Electric Mountain, which flew a pennon of cloud off to the west, or Sepulcher Mountain, half lost in an unaccustomed haze to the south, but displaying above the blue its enormous similitude of a grave, with the stone at head and foot, he made notes in his huge pocket-book, and in making notes he approached closer and closer to the big boy and little girl on the bench. In fact, he stopped on the other side of the bush, and as the lovers kissed for the tenth time, at least, he stepped round toward them, peering into the top of the bushes, pencil poised to jot down the cause of the chirping sound which had greeted his ears.

"I think I heard young birds in this bush," said he.

"You did," responded the young man, blushing.

"This park is full of them," said the girl, rather less embarrassed.

"Did you note the species?" queried he of the glasses. "I seem quite unable to catch sight of them."

"They are turtle-doves," said the girl.

"Gulls!" said the man.

The girl giggled hysterically. The naturalist was protesting that gulls never nest in such places, and the young man was becoming hopelessly confused, when a fourth figure joined the group. He was clad in garments of the commonest sort—but the girl was at once struck by the fact that he wore a soft roll collar on his flannel shirt, and a huge red silk neckerchief. Moreover, he carried a long whip which he trailed after him in the grass.

"Local color at last!" she whispered to her lover. "I know we're going to have a shooting or a cowboy adventure!"

"Well," the new-comer said, "do you go with us, or not, Doc?"

"Go with you?" asked the ornithologist. "Go where?"

"Tour of the Park?" replied the man with the whip. "I'm having hard work to get a load."

"I think," said the person addressed, "that I can finish my inspection of the Park on foot. It is, in fact, surprisingly small, and not at all what I had expected. I have been pacing it off. There are very few acres in it—"

"I'll be dog-goned," said the man with the whip, "if he don't think *this* is the Yellowstone Park! Stranger, look at yon beautiful arch, erected by Uncle Sam out of hexagonal blocks of basalt! That marks the entrance to the Wonderland of the World, a matchless nat'ral park of more'n three thousand square miles, filled with unnat'ral wonders of nature! This is the front yard of the railroad station. It'll take you days and days to do the Park—an' years to do it right."

"Oh, in that case," responded the investigator, "of course you may rely upon my joining you!"

"I want two more, lady," said the driver. "What say?"

"No," said the young man. "We've decided to cut the Park out."

"I've changed my mind, I believe," said the girl. "Let's go!"

"But I thought—"

And so the party was made up. It was like one of those strange meetings that take place on shipboard, on the wharves of ports—wherever fate takes men in her hands, shakes them like dice, and throws them on the board—and peeps at them to see what pairs, threes, flushes and other harmonies make up the strength of the cast.

There were seven of them. In the rear seat of the surrey sat two young men wearing broad-brimmed Stetsons, and corduroys. Their scarfs were pronouncedly Windsor, and the ends thereof streamed in the breeze as did the pennon of cloud from the top of Electric Peak off there in the west. The one with the long hair and the Dresden-china complexion starting to peel off at the lips, was the Minor Poet who eked out a living by the muck-raker's dreadful trade. He spoke of our malefactors of great wealth as "burglars" and grew soft-eyed and mute as the splendors of the Yellowstone Wonderland grew upon him. With him was a smaller man, shorter of hair, and younger in years—which youth was advertised by its disguise: a dark, silky Vandyke. He was an artist who was known to the readers of *Puck, Judge* and *Life* for his thick-lipped "coons" and shapeless hoboes, and who was here in the Park with the Poet for the purpose of drawing pictures for a prose poem which should immortalize both. So much for the rear seat.

The next seat forward was sacred to love. That is, it was occupied by the Bride and Groom, who called each other by the names of "Billy" and "Dolly," and tried to behave as if very mature and long-married—with what success we have seen. It was in pursuance of this scheme that they deliberately refused to take the rear seat when it was pointedly offered them by the Poet and the Artist. They were very quiet now, the Bride in stout shoes, mountain-climbing skirt and sweater, the Groom in engineer's boots and khaki. In the next seat forward sat the man of note-books, field-glasses, magnifying-glasses and drabs. The driver called him at first "Doc"; but soon adopted the general usage by which he was dubbed "Professor." He was myopic; but proud of his powers of observation. So wide was his reading that he knew nothing. His tour of the Park was made as a step toward that mastery of all knowledge which he had adopted as his goal. At once he saw that the rest of the party were light-minded children, frittering life away; and at once they took his measure. This made for mutual enjoyment. Nothing so conduces to good relations as the proper niching of the members of the party.

With him sat Colonel Baggs, of Omaha, who smoked all the time and quoted Blackstone and Kent for his seat-mate's Epictetus and Samuel Smiles. Whenever time hung heavy on the party for sheer lack of power to wonder, Colonel Baggs restored tonicity to their brains by some far-fetched argument to which he provoked Professor Boggs, wherein the Colonel violated all rules and escaped confusion by the most transparent fakir's tricks, solemnly regarding the Professor with one side of his face, and winking and grimacing at those behind with the other.

In the driver's seat sat Aconite Driscoll, erstwhile cow-boy, but now driver of a Yellowstone surrey, with four cayuses in hand, and a whip in place of the quirt of former years. When you tour the Yellowstone may he be your guide, driver, protector, entertainer and friend.

So they were seven, as I remarked. The Bride

counted out as for I-spy, " 'One, two, three, four, five, six, seven; All good children go to heaven!' " The Minor Poet said, " 'We are seven.' " The Artist quoted, " 'Seven men from all the world' "—and looked at the Bride. " 'Back to Docks again,' " she continued, knowing her Kipling, " 'Rolling down the Ratcliffe Road, drunk and raising Cain.' Thanks for including me as a man." The Artist bowed. "Anyhow," said the Poet, " 'We are seven.' "

They were all in the surrey and Aconite had the reins in hand, his whip poised, and his lips pursed for the initiatory chirrup, when there put his foot on the hub the Hired Man, who looked the part and presently explained that he worked on farms as a regular thing, and who was to be number eight. "If this seven business is eatin' yeh so bad," said he, "kain't I make a quadrille of it? I never pay fare, nowheres; but I kin cook, 'n drive, 'n rustle firewood, 'n drive tent-pins—an' you seem to have an empty seat. What say?" Aconite looked back into the faces of his load. All looked at the Bride as commander-in-chief—the Bride nodded. "Shore!" said Aconite. "Hop in!"

They rolled through the great arch at the entrance, and bowled along the road in breath-taking style as they crossed bridge after bridge, the walls of Gardiner Cañon towering on each side with its left-hand copings crumbling into pinnacles like ruined battlements, on which sat fishing-eagles as sentinels, their eyes scanning the flashing stream below. The wild roses were still in sparse bloom; the cottonwood groves showed splotches of brilliant yellow; the cedars gloomed in steady and dependable green. Autumn leaves and spring flowers, and over all a sky of ultramarine.

"See there!" exclaimed the Bride, pointing at the huge stream of hot water where Boiling River bursts from its opening in the rocks, and falls steaming into the Gardiner. "What in the world is it—a geyser?"

"That there little spurt," said Aconite, "is where the sink-pipe dreens off from Mammoth Hot Springs. Don't begin bein' surprised at things like them!"

The Professor made notes. Colonel Baggs asserted that hot water is hot water, no matter where found or in whatever quantities, and couldn't be considered much of a wonder. The Professor took up the gage of battle, while the carriage wound up the hill, away from the river; but even he forbore discourse, when the view opened, as the afternoon sun fell behind the hills, on the steaming terraces and boiling basins of Mammoth Hot Springs.

They scattered to the near-by marvels, and returned to camp where Aconite, assisted by the Hired Man, had prepared camp fare for the party. The Bride and Groom announced their intention to take pot luck with the rest, though the great hotel was ready for their reception.

"We are honored, I am sure," said Colonel Baggs. "Would that we had a troupe of performing nightingales to clothe the night with charm fit for so lovely a member of the party."

"Oh, thank you ever so much," said the Bride, "but I've just proposed to Billy a plan that will be better than any sort of troupe. We can make this trip a regular Arabian Nights' entertainment. Tell them, Billy!"

"We're to make a hat pool," said Billy, "and the loser tells a story."

"Good thought!" said the Poet.

"I don't understand," protested the Professor.

"Well, then, here you are!" said Billy. "I write all our names on these slips of paper—Driver, Poet, Artist, Professor—and the rest of us. I mix them in this Stetson. I pass them to the most innocent of the party, and one is drawn—"

"Well, let me draw, then!" said the Bride.

"Not on your life!" said Billy. "Here, Professor!"

Amid half-hidden chuckling, the Professor took a slip from the hat and handed it to the Groom.

"On this ballot," said he, "is written 'The Poet.' That gentleman will now favor the audience, ladies and gentlemen, with a story."

The moon was climbing through the lodge-pole pines, and the camp was mystic with the flicker of the firelight on the rocks and trees. The Poet looked about as if for an inspiration. His eyes fell on the Bride, so sweet, so cuddleable, so alluring.

"I will tell you a story that occurred to me as we drove along," said he. "If you don't like tragedy, don't call on a poet for entertainment in a tragic moment."

A TELEPATHIC TRAGEDY

BEING THE STORY TOLD BY THE MINOR POET

He sat reading a magazine. Chancing upon a picture of the bronze Sappho which, if you have luck, you will find in the museum at Naples, he began gazing at it, first casually, then intently, then almost hypnotically. The grand woman's head with its low masses of hair; the nose so high as to be almost Roman, so perfect in chiseling as to be ultra-Greek; the mouth eloquent of divinest passion; the neck, sloping off to strong shoulders and a bust opulent of charm—it shot through him an unwonted thrill. It may have arisen from memories of Lesbos, Mytilene, and the Leucadian Rock. It may have been the direct influence from her peep-hole on Olympus of Sappho's own Aphrodite. Anyhow, he felt the thrill.

Possibly it was some subtle effluence from things nearer and more concrete than either, for as he closed the magazine that he might rarefy and prolong this pulsing wave of poetry by excluding the distracting pages from his sight, his vision, resting for an instant upon the ribbon of grass and flowers flowing back beside the train, swept inboard and was arrested by a modish hat, a pile of ruddy hair, a rosy ear, the creamy back and side of a round neck, and the curve of a cheek. A most interesting phenomenon in wave-interference at once took place.

The hypnotic vibrations of the Sapphic thrill were affected by a new series, striking them in like phases. The result was the only possible one. The vibrations went on, in an amplitude increased to the height of their superimposed crests. No wonder things happened: it is a matter of surprise that the very deuce was not to pay.

For the hair combined with the hat in a symmetrical and harmonious whole, in an involved and curvilinear complexity difficult to describe; but the effect is easy to imagine—I hope. The red-brown coils wound in and out under a broad brim which drooped on one side and on the other curled jauntily up, as if consciously recurving from the mass of marvelous bloom and foliage under it. Dark-red tones climbed up to a climax of quivering green and crimson in a natural and, indeed, inevitable inflorescence. But, engrossed by sundry attractive details below it, his attention gave him a concept of the millinery vastly more vague and impressionistic than ours.

The sunburst of hair was one of the details. It radiated from a core of creamy skin from some mystic center concealed under fluffy laciness. The ear, too, claimed minute attention. It was a marvel of curves and sinuosities, ivory here, pearl-pink there, its lines winding down to a dainty lobe lit by a sunset glow, a tiny flame from the lambent furnace of the heart. Cold science avers that these fairy convolutions are designed for the one utilitarian purpose of concentrating the sound-waves for a more efficient impact upon the auditory nerve; but this is crudely false. They are a Cretan labyrinth for the amazing of the fancy that the heart may be drawn after—and they are not without their Minotaur, either!

"Pshaw!" said he to himself. "What nonsense! I'll finish my magazine!"

This good resolution was at once acted upon. He turned his eyes back along the trail by which they had so unwarrantably wandered—along the line of coiffure, window, landscape, page, Sappho; describing almost a complete circle—or quite. As he retraced this path so virtuously, the living picture shifted and threw into the problem—for a problem it had now become—certain new factors which seemed to compel a readjustment of plans. These were a fuller view of the cheek, a half profile of the nose, and just the tiniest tips of the lips and chin. He forgot all about Sappho, but the Sapphic vibrations went on increasingly.

The profile—the new one—was, so far, Greek, also. It was still so averted that there was no danger in amply verifying this conclusion by a prolonged gaze.

No danger?

Foolhardy man, more imminent peril never put on so smooth a front! Read history, rash one, and see thrones toppled over, dungeons filled with pale captives, deep accursed tarns sending up bubbling cries for vengeance, fleets in flames, plains ravaged, city walls beaten down, palaces looted, beauty dragged at the heels of lust, all from such gazes as this of thine. And if you object to history, examine the files of the nearest *nisi prius* court. It all comes to the same thing.

Would she turn the deeper seduction of those eyes and lips to view? Seemingly not, for with every sway of the car they retreated farther behind the curve of the cheek. This curve was fair and rounded, and for a while it satisfied the inquiry. What if another cheek be pressed against that tinted snowy fullness! And what if that other were the cheek we wot of!

Clearly, said the inward monitor, this will never do! This Sappho-Aphrodite-Sunburst Syndicate must be resisted.

At the same time—the half concealed being traditionally the most potent snare of the devil—would it not be in every way safer, as well as more satisfactory, to have a full view of the face? Were there any truth in the theory of telepathy the thing might be accomplished. A strong and continuous exercise of the will acting upon that other will, and the thing is done.

You see the extent to which the nefarious operations of the syndicate have been pushed? Unaffected by the malign influence of those waves meeting in like phases, he would have felt himself no more at liberty to do this thing than to put his rude hand under the dimpled chin and ravish a look from the violated eyes.

For all that, he found himself fixing his will upon the turning of that head. He fancied he saw a rosier glow in the cheek and ear. Surely this can be no illusion—even the creamy neck glows faintly roseate. And still he sent out, or imagined he sent out, the thought-waves commanding the face to turn. And mingled with it was the sense of battle and the prevision of victory.

Slowly, slowly, like a blossom toward the sun, the head turned, the eyes directed upward, the lips a little apart. The mouth, the chin, the Greek nose, the violet eyes, enthralled him for a moment, and swung back out of sight again. He had won, and, winning, had lost. The neck was rosy now. He felt himself tremble as once more she turned her head until the fringed mystery of those upturned eyes lay open to his gaze, though her glance never really met his. He saw, in one intense, lingering look, the blue irises, the lighter border about the pupils, the wondrous rays emanating from those black, mystic flowers; he saw the fine dilated nostrils, the rosy, perfect lips; he saw the evanescent quiver of allurement at the corners of the mouth, the white teeth just glinting from their warm concealment. He saw—

"Oak Grove! All out for Oak Grove! Remember your umbrellas and parcels!"

Thus the brakeman raucously rescuing the victims of wave-interference. Thus Terminus baffling Aphrodite. Yet not without a struggle do the sea-born goddess and the sea-doomed poet surrender their unaccomplished task. He rose, stepped into the aisle, and passed her; then he turned, looked gravely for a moment into her eyes, and sadly whispered, "Good-by!"

If surprised, she did not show the fact by the slightest start. Soberly she dropped her eyelids, seriously she raised them, and with the manner of one who, breaking intimate converse at the parting-place, bids farewell to a dear companion, she breathed, "Good-by!"

Said the lady who drove him from the station, "My dear, is it a guilty conscience or the fate of the race that makes you so—abstracted?"

"A guilty conscience," he laughed, laying a hand on hers. He looked after the flying train, and smiled, and sighed. "After all," he added, "I believe it's the fate of the race!"

"Is that all?" asked the Hired Man.

The pipes went on glowing and dying like little volcanoes with ephemeral periods of activity and quiescence. The campers rose one by one and went to their tents.

"Wasn't that a curious tale?" asked the Bride

when they were alone. "What do you suppose made him think of it as we drove along?"

"Dunno," returned the Groom, kissing the back of her neck. "Don't you think we'd better take the rear seat to-morrow?"

CHAPTER II

"I SHALL never, never be able to feel anything like astonishment again!"

So said the Bride as the party took the road again after two days at Mammoth Hot Springs. Bunsen Mountain had been circumnavigated. Cupid's Cave had charmed. The Devil's Kitchen had stimulated a flagging faith in a Personal Adversary, dealing with material utensils of vengeance. The Stygian Cave, whose deadly vapors had strewed its floor with dead birds, had been pronounced another of his devices and satanically "horrid." The iridescent springs, each of which has built up its own basin, like hanging fountains, were compared to the hanging gardens of Babylon, and pronounced far more worthy of place among the wonders of the world. The lovely Undine Falls had comforted them with prettiness after wildness; and the ogreous Hoodoo Rocks had turned them back to the realm of shivers. The Professor's note-books were overflowing with memoranda; and Colonel Baggs alone went unastounded.

"If the place only had a history," said the Minor Poet, "like the Venusberg, or almost any spot in Europe—"

"Well," said the Colonel, "it's got some history, anyhow. When I was here before—"

"When was that?" asked the Artist, adding a line or two to a surreptitious sketch of the Colonel.

"It was thirty-three years ago the latter part of this month," said the Colonel. "I carried a knapsack in the chase after Chief Joseph and the Nez Percès. There were pretty average lively times right in this vicinity with the first tourists, so far as I know, that ever came into the Park. Some fellows had been up in the Mount Everts country, and to the lower falls. The Nez Percès rushed them. A fellow named Stewart found himself looking into the muzzle of the rifle of a Nez Percè, and made the sign of the cross. The red with the gun, being a pretty fair Christian as Christians go—the tribe had been converted for thirty years—as conversions go—refrained from shooting when he saw the sign. Stewart had a horse that was wild and hard to catch — was wounded and had no idea he could get within reach of the steed; but when he called, the horse came to him and stood for him to climb on, for the first and last time in the history of their relations. Stewart got off with his life."

"Very remarkable," said the Professor, jotting down a note. "Now, how do you account for that on any known scientific law?"

"It simply wasn't Stewart's time," said the Colonel. "Or there's an intelligence that operates on other intelligences—even those of beasts—for our protection. Or we have guardian spirits that can tame horses. Take your choice, Professor. And right here—maybe where we are camped—another bit of history was enacted that in the childhood of the race might ripen into one of those legends the artists deplore the lack of. The campers here had a nigger cook named Stone—Ben Stone—I arrested and confined for giving thanks to the Lord after we picked him up. He was here at Mammoth Hot Springs when a fellow—I forget his name—was shot. The Nez Percès went by one day and saw him here. Next day they came back more peeved than before and shot the man. Ben, the cook, ran, and they after him. He shinned up into one of these trees—maybe that one there. The Indians lost sight of him, and stopped under the tree for a conference. Stone nearly died of fright for fear they would hear his heart beating. He said it sounded like a horse galloping over rocks. They gave him up and went away. The coast being clear, a bear—probably an ancestor of these half-tamed beasts that the Bride photographed last evening—came along and began snuffing about the trees. Ben's heart began galloping again. The bear reared up and stretched as if he meant to climb the tree. Ben's heart stopped. After a while the bear went away. After a day or so the cook came into our camp and went about giving thanks to the Lord continually, and howling hallelujahs until nobody could sleep. So we put him under guard, and I watched him under orders to bust his head if he bothered the throne of grace any more."

"The army is an irreverent organization," said the Professor.

"It isn't what you'd call devout," assented the Colonel.

"Confound this modern world, anyway!" complained the Poet. "Five hundred years ago, we'd have evolved a cycle of legends out of those occurrences!"

"The tales are just as astonishing without legends," insisted the Bride, "as anything in the world, no matter how deep in fable."

Faring on southward, they passed toward Norris Basin in unastonished quietude. A flock of pelicans on Swan Lake created no sensation. A trio of elk in Willow Park crossed the road ahead of the surrey with no further effect than to arouse the Artist to some remarks on their anatomical perfection, and to bring to the surface the buried note-book of Professor Boggs. They stopped at Apollinaris Spring for refreshment, where the Groom held forth on the commercial possibilities of the waters, if the government would get off the lid, and let the country be developed.

"Nix on this conservation game," said he; and nobody argued with him.

At Obsidian Cliff, Mr. Driscoll whoaed up his cayuses to call the attention of his fares to the fact that here is the only glass road in the world.

"Glass?" queried the Professor, alighting, microscope in hand. "Really?"

"Shore," assured Aconite. "They cracked the road out of the cliff by building fires to heat the glass and splashin' cold water to make the chunks pop out—jelluk breakin' a tumbler washin' up the dishes."

"Oh, I see," said Professor Boggs. "Merely obsidian."

"Merely!" repeated Aconite. "Some folks always reminds me of the folks that branded old Jim Bridger as a liar becuz o' what he told of this here region eighty or ninety years ago. He built Fort Bridger, and Bridger's Peak was named after him, and he discovered Great Salt Lake, and I guess he wouldn't lie. He found this glass cliff and told about it then—and everybody said he was a liar. An' he found lots o' things that ain't on the map. We see a little thread o' country along this road, but the reel wonders of this Park hain't been seen sence Jim Bridger's time—an' not then. W'y, once back in this glass belt, he saw an elk feedin' in plain sight. Blazed away an' missed him. Elk kep' on feedin'. Blazed away ag'in. Elk unmoved. Bridger made a rush at the elk with his knife, and run smack into a mountain of this glass so clear that he couldn't see it, and shaped like a telescope glass that brought things close. That elk was twenty-five miles off."

"Giddap!" said Colonel Baggs to the horses. "Time to be on our way."

"After all," said the Poet, "we may not have lost the power to create a mythology."

"Bridger for my money," said the Artist, with conviction.

"Jim Bridger said that," asserted Aconite, "an' I believe him. They found Great Salt Lake where he said it was, all right, an' Bridger's Peak, an' the few things we've run across here. You wouldn't believe a mountain would whistle like a steam engine, would yeh? Well, I'll show you one—Roarin' Mountain—in less'n four miles ahead—in the actual act of tootin'."

"I believe all you said, Mr. Driscoll," said the Bride as they sat about the fire that night. "The glass mountain, the elk and all. After those indescribable Twin Lakes, the Roaring Mountain, and the Devil's Frying Pan, stewing, stewing, century after century—that's what makes it so inconceivable —the thought of time and eternity. The mountains are here for ever—that's plain; but these things in action—to think that they were sizzling and spouting just the same when Mr. Bridger was here ninety years ago, and a million years before that, maybe— it flabbergasts me!"

"Yes'm," said Aconite. "It shore do."

"You're it, Bride!" said the Hired Man, handing her a slip with "Bride" written upon it.

"I'm what?" asked the Bride.

"They've sawed the story off on you," returned the Hired Man. "I hope you'll give a better one than that there Poet told. I couldn't make head nor tail to that."

"It *was* rotten," said the Poet, looking at the Bride, "wasn't it?"

"I'm still living in a glass house," said the Bride. "Don't you know there's only one story a bride can tell?"

"Tell it, tell it!" was the cry—from all but the Poet and the Groom.

"I think I'll retire," said the Groom.

"Off with you into the shadows," said the Poet. "I'll contribute my last cigar—and we'll smoke the calumet on the other side of the tree where we can hear unseen."

About them the earth boiled and quivered and spouted. Little wisps of steam floated through the treetops. There were rushings and spoutings in the air—for they were in the Norris Geyser Basin. And here the Bride, sitting in the circle of men, her feet curled under her on a cushion of the surrey laid on the geyser-heated ground, fixed her eyes on the climbing moon and told her story.

THE TRIUMPH OF BILLY HELL

THE STORY TOLD BY THE BRIDE

Now that so many of the girls are writing, the desire to express myself in that way comes upon me awfully strongly, sometimes.

She looked at the Poet, who nodded encouragement and understanding.

And yet a novel seems so complex and poky in the writing, as compared with a play, which brings one ever so much more exciting success. Louise Amerland says that all literature is autobiographical. If this is so, why can't I use my own romance in making a play? I think I could, if I could once get the scenario to—to discharge, as Billy says. He calls me a million M. F. condenser of dramatic electricity, but says that it's all statical, when it ought to flow. But the scenario must be possible, if I could only get the figures and events juggled about into place. There's Billy for the hero, and Pa, and the Pruntys, and me for the heroine, and comic figures like the butler and Miss Crowley and Atkins, and the crowds in Lincoln Park. I want the statue of Lincoln in it for one scene.

"That would be great," said the Artist.

After I was "finished" at St. Cecilia's I went into Pa's office as his secretary. He wasn't very enthusiastic, but I insisted on account of the sacredness of labor and its necessity in the plan of woman's life having revealed themselves to me as I read one of Mrs. Stetson's books. Pa fumed, and said I bothered him; but I insisted, and after a while I became proficient as a stenographer, and spelled such terms as "kilowatt," and "microfarad," and "electrolyte," in a way that forced encomiums from even Pa. Upon this experience I based many deductions as to the character of our captains of industry, one of which is that they are the most illogical set in the world, and the more illogical they are the more industry they are likely to captain.

Take Pa, for instance. He began with a pair of pliers, a pair of climbers, a lineman's belt, and a vast store of obstinacy; and he has built up the Mid-Continent Electric Company—for we are an electric family, though Billy says magnetic is the term.

"Spare me!" prayed the Groom.

But how does Pa order his life? He sends me to

St. Cecilia's, which has no function but to prepare girls for the social swim, and is so exclusive that he had to lobby shamefully to get me in: and all the time he gloats—simply *gloats*—over the memory of the pliers, the climbers, the lineman's belt, and the obstinacy—no, not over the obstinacy, of course: that is merely what makes him gloat. And he hates Armour Institute graduates and Tech men poisonously, and wants his force made up of electricians who have come up, as he says, by hard knocks, and know the practical side. As if Billy Helmerston— but let me begin at the beginning.

I was in the office one day superintending Miss Crowley, the chief stenographer, in getting together the correspondence about an electric light and power installation in Oklahoma, when, just at the door of the private office, I met a disreputable figure which towered above me so far that I could barely make out that it had good anatomical lines and a black patch over one eye.

I will here deceive no one: it was Billy. He explained afterward that he possessed better clothes, but had mislaid them somehow, and that the cut over his eye he got in quelling a pay-night insurrection in his line-gang out in Iowa, one of whom struck him with a pair of four-hole connectors. I am sorry to confess that I once felt pride in the fact that Billy knocked the linemen's heads together—and yet Pa talks of hard knocks!—until they subsided, the blood, meanwhile, running all down over his face and clothing and theirs. It was very brutal, in outward seeming, no matter what plea of necessity may be urged for it.

I almost fell back into the doorway, he was so near and so big. His way of removing his abominable old hat, and his bow, gave me a queer little mental jolt, it was so graceful and elegant, in spite of the overalls and the faded shirt.

"I was referred to this place as Mr. Blunt's office," said he. "Can you direct me to him?"

Now Pa is as hard to approach as any Oriental potentate; but I supposed that Billy was one of the men from the factory, and had business, and I was a little fluttered by the wonderful depth and sweetness of his voice; so I just said: "This way, please" —and took him in to where Pa was sawing the air and dictating a blood-curdling letter to a firm of contractors in San Francisco, who had placed themselves outside the pale of humanity by failing to get results from our new Polyphase Generator. (Billy afterward told them what was the matter with it.) I saw that my workman had picked out an exceedingly unpsychological moment, if he expected to make a very powerful appeal to Pa's finer instincts.

"Well," roared Pa, turning on him with as much ferocity as if he had been a San Francisco contractor of the deepest dye, "what can I do for you, sir?"

"My name is Helmerston," started Billy.

"I'm not getting up any directory," shouted Pa. "What do you want?"

"I'm just through with a summer's line-work in the West," answered Billy, "and I took the liberty of applying for employment in your factory. I have—"

"The blazes you did!" ejaculated Pa, glaring at Billy from under his eyebrows. "How did you get in here?"

I was over at the filing-cases, my face just burning, for I was beginning to see what I had done. Billy looked in my direction, and as our eyes met he smiled a little.

"I hardly know, Mr. Blunt," said he. "I just asked my way and followed directions. Is it so very difficult to get in?"

I saw at once that he was a good deal decenter than he looked.

"Well, what can you do?" shouted Pa.

"Almost anything, I hope," answered Billy. "I've had no practical experience with inside work; but I have—"

"Oh, yes, I know!" said Pa, in that unfeeling way which experience and success seem to impart to the biggest-hearted men—and Pa is surely one of these. "It's the old story. As soon as a dub gets so he can cut over a rural telephone, or put in an extension-bell, or climb a twenty-five without getting seasick, he can do 'almost anything.' What one, definite, concrete thing can you do?"

"For one thing," said Billy icily, "I think I could help some by taking a broom to this factory floor out here."

"All right," said Pa, after looking at him a moment. "The broom goes! Give this man an order for a broom. Put him on the pay-roll at seven dollars a week. Find out who let him in here, and caution whoever it was against letting it occur again. Call up Mr. Sweet, and tell him I want a word with him on those Winnipeg estimates. Make an engagement with Mr. Bayley of the street-car company to lunch with me at the club at two." And Pa was running in his groove again.

"I'm sorry," he whispered, as he passed me going out.

"Thank you," I answered. "It's of no consequence—"

And then I noticed that he was looking into my eyes in a wistful and pathetic way, as if protesting against going out. I blushed as I showed him to the door: and he wasn't the first whose eyes had protested, either.

"You mustn't violate the rules, Dolly," said Pa, as we crossed the bridge in the bubble, going home. "You know perfectly well that I can't say 'no' to these tramps—"

"He wasn't a tramp," said I.

"A perfect hobo," answered Pa. "I know the type well. I have to let Burns handle them."

"He was very graceful," said I.

"Any lineman is," replied Pa. "They have the best exercise in the world. If he steals anything, you're responsible, my dear."

I supposed the incident to be closed with my statement that he had nice eyes, and Pa's sniff; but, in a few days, Pa, who watches the men like a cat, surprised me by saying that my graceful hobo was all right.

"He gathered up and saved three dollars' worth of beeswax the other men were wasting, the first day," said Pa. "Melted and strained and put it in the right place without asking any questions. And then he borrowed a blow-torch and an iron, and began practising soldering connections. He looks good to me."

"Me, too," said I.

"Blessed be the hobo," said the Colonel, "for he shall reach paradise!"

It seems strange, now, to think of my hearing these things unmoved. The dreadful humiliation to which Billy was subjected, the noble fortitude with which he bore it, and the splendid way in which he uplifted the menial tasks to which he was assigned, have always reminded me of Sir Gareth serving as a scullion in Arthur's kitchen. It is not alone in the chronicles of chivalry—but I must hasten this narrative.

I must not delay even to inform you of the ways in which it was discovered that Billy could do all sorts of things; that there was no blue-print through which his keen eye could not see, and no engineering error—like that in the Polyphase Generator—that he couldn't detect; or how he was pushed up and up by force of sheer genius, no one knowing who he was until he found himself, like an eagle among buzzards, at the head of a department, and coming into the office to see Pa quite in a legitimate way.

"Hooray! Hooray!" came from behind the tree.

"Shut up, Poet!" commanded the Artist, "or I'll come back there!"

I didn't know these things personally, because I had left the office. I had found out that there seemed to be more soul-nurture in artistic metal work than in typewriting, and had fitted up a shop in the Fine Arts Building, where Louise Amerland and I were doing perfectly enchanting stunts in hammered brass and copper—old Roman lamps and Persian lanterns, after designs we made ourselves. Pa parted with his secretary with a sigh, the nature of which may be a question better left unsettled.

This romance really begins with my visit, after months and months of absence, to the restaurant which I had dinged at Pa until he had instituted for the help. I told him that the social side of labor was neglected shamefully, and for the work people to eat at the same table with their superintendents and employers would be just too dear and democratic, and he finally yielded growlingly. He was awfully pleased afterward when the papers began to write the thing up. He said it was the cheapest advertising he ever got, and patted me on the shoulder and asked me if I wasn't ashamed to be so neglectful of my great invention. So one day I got tired of working out Rubáiyát motifs in brass, and I went over to the café for luncheon, incog. And what do you think? Billy came in and sat down very informally right across from me!

"Hello!" said he, putting out his hand. "I've been looking for you for eons, to—to thank you, you know. Don't you remember me?"

Before I knew it I had blushingly given him my hand for a moment.

"Yes," I replied, taking it away, and assuming a more properly dignified air. "I hope you have risen above seven a week and a broom; and I am glad to see that your head has healed up."

"Thank you," he replied. "I am running the installation department of the dynamo end of the business. And you? I'm no end glad to see you back. Did you get canned for letting me in? I've had a good many bad half-hours since I found you gone, thinking of you out hunting a job on—on my account. You—pardon me—don't look like a girl who would have the E. M. F. in the nerve-department to go out and compete, you know."

I was amazed at the creature's effrontery, at first; and then the whole situation cleared up in my mind. I saw that I had an admirer (*that* was plain) who didn't know me as Rollin Blunt's heiress at all, but only as a shop-mate in the Mid-Continent Electric Company's factory—a stenographer who had done him a favor. It was more fun than most girls might think.

"How did you find out," said I, "that I had been —ah—canned?"

"I watched for you," he replied. "Began as soon as my promotion to the switchboard work made it so I could. After a couple of months' accumulation of data I ventured upon the generalization that the old man—"

"The who?"

"Mr. Blunt, I mean, of course," he amended, "had fired you for letting me in. Out of work long?"

"N-no," said I; "hardly a week."

"Where are you now?" he asked.

"I'm in a shop," I stammered, "in Michigan Avenue."

I looked about to see if any of the employees who

knew me were present, but could see none except Miss Crowley, who wouldn't meet a man in the same office in a year, and a dynamo-man never, and who is near-sighted, anyhow. So I felt safe in permitting him to deceive himself. It is thus that the centuries of oppression which women have endured impress themselves on our more involuntary actions in little bits of disingenuousness against which we should ever struggle. At the time, though, to sit chatting with him in the informal manner of colaborers at the noon intermission was great fun. It was then that I began to notice more fully what a really fine figure he had, and how brown and honest and respectful his eyes were, even when he said "Hello" to me, as if I were a telephone, and how thrilling was his voice.

"I'd like," said he, "to call on you—if I might."

I was as fluttered as the veriest little chit from the country.

"I—I can't very well receive you," said I. "My—the people where I—I stop wouldn't like it."

"I'm quite a respectable sort of chap," said he. "My name's Helmerston, and my people have been pretty well known for two or three hundred years up in Vermont, where we live—in a teaching, preaching, book-writing, rural sort of way, you know. I'm a Tech man—class of '08—but I haven't anything to boast of on any score, I'm merely telling you these things, because—because there seems to be no one else to tell you, and—and I want you to know that I'm not so bad as I looked that morning."

"Oh, this is quite absurd!" cried I. "I really—it doesn't make any difference; but I'm quite ready to believe it! I must go, really!"

"May I see you to your car?" said he; and I started to tell him that I was there in the victoria, but pulled up, and took the street-car, after he had extracted from me the information that I lived close to Lincoln Park. But when he asked if I ever walked in the park, I just refused to say any more. One really must save one's dignity from the attacks of such people. I had to telephone Roscoe where to come with the victoria.

Soon after, quite by accident, I saw him on two successive evenings in Lincoln Park, both times near the Lincoln statue. I wondered if my mentioning the south entrance had anything to do with this. He never once looked at the motorists, and so failed to see me; but I could see that he took a deep interest in the promenaders—especially slender girls with dainty dresses and blond hair. It appeared almost as if he were looking for some one in particular, and I smiled at the thought of any one being so silly as to search those throngs on the strength of any chance hint any person might have dropped. I was affected by the pathos of it, though. It seemed so much like the Saracen lady going from port to port hunting for Thomas à Becket's father—though, of course, he wasn't any one's father then, but I can't think of his name.

The next evening I took Atkins, my maid, and walked down by the Lincoln monument to look at some flowers. It seems to me that we Chicagoans owe it to ourselves to become better acquainted with one another—I mean, of course, better acquainted with our great parks and public places and statues. They are really very beautiful, and something to be proud of, provided as they are for rich and poor alike by a paternal government.

Strangely fortuitous chance: we met Billy!

"Well, *well!*" exclaimed Aconite.

He came striding down the path to meet me—Atkins had fallen behind—his face perfectly radiant with real joy.

"At last!" he ejaculated. "I wondered if we were *ever* to meet again, Miss—Miss—"

"Blunt," said I, heroically truthful, and suppressing one of those primordial impulses which urged me to say Wilkinson—now, as a scientific problem, why Wilkinson? But I did not wish to lose Atkins' respect by conversing with a man who did not know my name.

"Miss Blunt?" cried he interrogatively. "That's rather odd, you know. It's not a very common name."

"Oh, I don't know," said I, uncandid again, as soon as I saw a chance to get through with it—little cat. "It seems awfully common to me. Why do you say that it's odd?"

"Because I happen to have a letter of introduction to Miss Blunt, daughter of the old—of Mr. Blunt of the Mid-Continent—"

"You have?" I broke in. "From whom?"

"From my cousin, Amelia Wyckoff," said he, "who went to school with her at St. Cecilia's."

"Well, of all things!" I began; and then, with a lot of presence of mind, I think, I paused. "Why don't you present it?" I asked.

"Well, it's this way," said Billy. "You saw how

Mr. Blunt sailed into me and put me in the broom-brigade without a hearing? I didn't have the letter then, and when I got it I didn't feel like pulling on the social strings when I was coming on pretty well for a dub lineman and learning the business from the solder on the floor to the cupola, by actual physical contact. And then there's another thing, if you'll let me say it: since that morning I've had no place in my thoughts for any girl's face but one."

We were sitting on a bench. Atkins was looking at the baby leopards in the zoo, ever so far away. Billy didn't seem to miss her. He was looking right at me. My heart fluttered so that I knew my voice would quiver if I spoke, and I didn't dare to move my hands for fear he might notice their trembling. The idea of *my* behaving in that way!

I was glad to find out that he was Amelia's cousin; for that insured his social standing. That was what made me feel so sort of agitated. One laborer ought not to feel so of another, for we are all equal; but it *was* a relief to know that he was Amelia's aunt's son, and not a tramp.

"I must be allowed to call on you!" he said with suppressed intensity. "You don't dislike me very much, do you?"

"I—I don't like cuts over the eye," said I, evading the question.

"I don't have 'em any more," he urged.

And then he explained about the émeute in the line-gang, and the four-hole connectors, and confessed to the violent and sanguinary manner in which he had felt called upon to put down the uprising. I could feel my face grow hot and cold by turns, like Desdemona's while Othello was telling the same kind of things; and when I looked for the scar on his forehead he bowed his head, and I put the curls aside and found it. I would have given worlds to—it was so much like a baby coming up to you and crying about thumping its head and asking you to kiss it well. Once I had my lips all puckered up—but I had the self-control to refrain—I was so afraid.

It was getting dusk now, and Billy seized my hand and kissed it. I was quite indignant until he explained that his motives were perfectly praiseworthy. Then I led him to talk of the rich Miss Blunt to whom he had a letter of introduction, and advised him to present it, and argued with appalling cogency that one ought to marry in such a way as to better one's prospects, and Billy got perfectly furious at such a view of love and marriage—explaining, when I pretended to think he was mad at me, that he knew I was just teasing. And then he began again about calling on me, and seeing my parents, or guardians, or assigns, or *any one* that he ought to see.

"Because," said he, "you're a perfect baby, with a baby's blue eyes and hair of floss, and tender skin, and trustfulness; and I ought to be horsewhipped for sitting here in the park with you in—in this way, with no one paying any attention but Mr. Lincoln, up there."

Then I did feel deeply, darkly crime-stained; and I could have hugged the dear fellow for his simplicity—*me* helpless, with Atkins, and the knowledge of Amelia Wyckoff's letter; not to mention Mr. Lincoln—bless him!—or a park policeman who had been peeking at us from behind a bunch of cannas! I could have given him the addresses of several gentlemen who might have certified to the fact that I wasn't the only one whose peace of mind might have been considered in danger.

I grew portentously serious just before I went home, and told Billy that he must see me on my own terms or not at all, and that he mustn't follow me, or try to find out where I lived, but must walk around the curve to the path and let me mingle with the landscape.

"May I not hope," said he, "to see you again soon?"

"I may feed the elephant some peanuts," said I, "on Thursday evening—no, I shall play in a mixed foursome, and then dine on Thursday afternoon at the Onwentsia—"

"Where?" said he, in a sort of astonished way.

"I believe I could make you believe it," said I with more presence of mind, "if I stuck to it. But I can't come on Thursday. Let us say on Friday evening."

He insisted that Friday is unlucky, and we compromised on Wednesday. This conversation was on Tuesday.

"May I turn for just one look at my little wood nymph," said he, "when I get to the curve?"

Of course I said "Yes"—and he turned at the curve, and came striding back with such a light in his eyes that I had to allow him to kiss my hand again, under the pretense that I had got a sliver in my finger.

I went back Wednesday, and again and again, and

sneaked off once with him to an orchestra concert, and it wasn't long before Billy knew that his little stenographer was willing to allow him to hope. But I refused to let him call it an engagement until he promised me that he would present the letter to the other Miss Blunt.

"Why, Dolly? Why, sweetheart?" he asked; for it had got to that stage now. Oh, it progressed with dizzying rapidity!

"Because," I replied, "you may like her better than you do me."

"Impossible!" he cried with a gesture absolutely tragic in its intensity. "I dislike her very name—'Miss Aurelia Blunt!'"

"That's unjust!" I cried, really angry. "Aurelia is a fine name; and she may have a pet name, you know."

"Only one Miss Blunt with a pet name for little Willie!" said he. "My little Dolly!"

But I tied him down with a promise that before he saw me again he'd call on Aurelia. When I saw him next he looked guilty, and said he had found her out when he called. I scolded him cruelly, and made him promise again. The fact was that when he called I couldn't find it in my heart to sink to the prosaic level of Miss Aurelia Blunt. I had had the sweetest, most delicious courtship that any girl *ever* had, up to this time, and I was afraid of spoiling it all. I was afraid sort of on general principles, you know, and so was "out." And after he went away I stole down into the park in my electric runabout and talked to Mr. Lincoln about it. He seemed to know. When I went away, I left a little kiss on the monument.

Billy was perfectly cringing that next day when he had to confess that he had failed on what he called "this Aurelia proposition." He begged to be let off.

"You see," said he, "she may give me a frigid reception, and take offense at my delay in presenting this letter. Amelia may have written her, and she may be furious. There may be some sort of social statute of limitations on letters of introduction, and the thing may have run out, so that I'll be ejected by the servants, dearie. And, anyhow, it will place me in an equivocal position with Mr. Blunt—my coming to him as a tramp, and holding so very lightly the valuable social advantage of an acquaintance with the family. He won't remember that he jumped on me with both feet and gave me six months on bread and water. It—it may queer me in the business."

I here drew myself up to my full height, and froze him as I have seldom done.

"Mr. Helmerston," said I, "I have indicated to you a fact which I had supposed might have some weight with you as against sordid and merely prudential considerations—I mean my preferences in this matter. It seems, however, that—that you don't care the least little bit what *I* want, and I just know that you don't—care for me at all as you say you do; and I'm going home at once!"

Well, he was so abject, and so sorry to have given me pain, that I wanted to hug him, but I didn't.

Oh, I almost neglected to say that all our behavior had been of the most proper and self-contained sort. I would almost be willing to have Miss Featherstonehaugh at St. Cecilia's use a kinetoscope picture of all our meetings in marking me in deportment. Of course, conversations in parks and at concerts do not lend themselves to transports very well, and the kinetoscopes do not reproduce what is said, do they? Or the way one feels when one is grinding into the dust, in that manner, the most splendid fellow in the whole terrestrial and stellar universe.

"I'll go, by George!" he vowed. "And I'll sit on Aurelia's doorstep without eating or drinking until she comes home and kicks me down the stairs!" I was wondering as I went home how soon he would come; but I was astonished to learn that Mr. Helmerston was in my reception-room.

"Hi informed 'im," said the footman, "that you would 'ardly be 'ome within a reasonable time of waiting; but 'e said 'e would remain until you came, Miss, nevertheless."

I went down to him just as I was, in my simple piqué dress, wearing the violets he had given me. "Mr. Helmerston," said I, "I must apologize for the difficulty I have given you in obtaining the very slight boon of meeting me, and say how good you are to come again—and wait. Any friend of dearest Amelia's, not to mention her cousin, is—"

He had stood in a state of positive paralysis until now.

"Dolly! Dolly! Dearest, dearest Dolly!" he cried, coming up to me and taking—and doing what he hadn't had a chance to do before. "Oh, my darling, are *you* here?"

After quite a while he started up as if he had forgotten something.

"What is it?" said I. "There isn't a promenader or a policeman this side of the park, sweetheart!"

"No," he answered after another interval—for I hadn't called him anything like that before—"but I was thinking that—that Aurelia—is a long time in coming home."

"Why, don't you know *yet*, you goosey," said I. "*I'm* Aurelia!"

And this brings me to the point where dalliance must cease—most of the time—while the drama takes on the darker tinge given it by Pa's cruel obstinacy, and the misdeeds of the Pruntys—whom I should have brought on in the first act, somehow, on a darkened stage, conspiring across it over a black bottle, and once in a while getting up to peek up and down the flies, meanwhile uttering the villain's sibilant "Sh!" I don't suppose it *is* artistic, from the Augustus Thomas viewpoint, but I wanted the honeyed sweets of this courtship of mine without a tang of bitter; and, honestly now, isn't it a lovely little plot for a love-drama?

"Gee!" exclaimed the Hired Man. "I was afraid you was through!"

"I am," said the Bride softly, "for to-night. If

you'll excuse me now. Maybe I'll tell the rest of it at the next camp—if you want me to."

"I assure you," said the Professor, "that your tale does credit to your teachers in elocution."

"We all thank you," said the Artist, "for what we've had—and won't you continue at the next session—Scheherazade?"

"I'll see," said she. "Billy! Where are you!"

"I have mysteriously disappeared," replied the Groom from behind the tree. "Come hunt me!"

CHAPTER III

AT the behest of Aconite, the party refrained from expressions of more than mild interest at the Norris Basin. Aconite assured them that they ought to save their strong expressions for things farther on. The Poet wrote some verses for the purpose of creating a legend to account for the fact that the Monarch Geyser ceased to spout some ten years ago. But when he came to the Growler, and the Hurricane, and the new Roaring Holes, which are really gigantic steam whistles, he dismounted from his Pegasus and threaded his way through the dead forest—killed by escaping steam—in a trance of wonder. But Aconite's advice to economize language until the Lower Geyser Basin should be reached was followed so far as superlatives were concerned. Night found them scattered, and it was only when they took the road once more that the party was whole again. The Artist stopped the surrey at the Gibbon Paint Pots so that he might use some of their bubbling sediment as a pigment with which to paint a souvenir picture for each of the party. Cañons, boiling springs and waterfalls—rocks, mountains, wild beauty on every hand—all these they were assured were inconsiderable parts of the prelude to the marvels awaiting them at the next halt. But when they came to the crossing of Nez Percè Creek, the Bride expressed a desire to wait, to stop, to rest her eyes and quiet her spirits before anything more striking should be imposed upon her powers of observation.

"I fell like Olger the Dane and King Desiderio, when they watched on the tower for Charlemagne; and if we go on, I shall, like Olger, fall 'as one dead at Desiderio's feet!'"

The Poet looked in the Bride's eyes, and nodded sympathetically. Mr. Driscoll pondered the mysteries of the Bride's statement for a while, and threw down his lines.

"If that's the way the Bride feels," said he, "we'll stop here and grub our systems up a little."

"The champion hard-luck story of this or any other age," said the Colonel, as they lighted their pipes after dinner, "was enacted right up this creek in that Nez Percè uprising wherein I fought and bled and died."

"More matter for myths," said the Artist. "Let's have it, e'en though it be as dolorous as the tale of the Patient Griselda."

"I don't recall more of Griselda's story," said the Colonel, "than that she was given the worst of it by her husband, the king. But this Nez Percè Creek story isn't any tale of the perfidy of our nearest and dearest, but of things just unanimously breaking bad for a man from Radersburg, Mr. Cowan. He and his wife and some friends were camped down here a couple of miles at the Lower Geyser Basin, right close by the Fountain Geyser, just beyond the hotel—only there wasn't any hotel yet for thirty years. Chief Joseph and his Nez Percès came through trying to get away from the United States. They picked up the Cowan party, and brought them right along where we now are, and a few miles up this creek, where Joseph, Looking-Glass, and the other chiefs held a conference and decided to let the Cowan party go, after destroying their transportation system by cutting the spokes out of their buggies. This they did, and the Indians went on. Some of the bucks, feeling that it was careless of the chiefs to overlook a bet like this, came back, and in process of correcting their leaders' mistake shot Mr. Cowan in the thigh—which was bad luck Item one. He slipped from his horse, stunned by the shock, and his wife ran to him and tried to shelter him from further harm. But in spite of her efforts another Indian shot him in the head, holding his rifle so close that the powder burned the flesh. He was not killed, however, though all parties to the affair supposed he was, and Mrs. Cowan was removed from the corpse to which she clung, and carried away by her friends. You see, the Indians were not unanimously for these killings, and allowed most of the whites to go. The Indians threw a cord or so of rocks on Cowan's head and went on with a consciousness of good work well and thoroughly done.

"Cowan revived, pulled his head from among the rocks, and drew himself to a standing posture by the limb of a tree. An Indian happening along, shot him with much care in the back, and left him for dead again.

"Cowan, however, refused to die, and though without food, and wounded in the thigh, the head, and the back, and with his head hammered to a jelly by the rocks thrown on it, started to crawl back to camp. He met Indians, and hid from them. He crawled day after day—being unable to walk a step.

He had a chance—for an uninjured man—to catch a Nez Percè pony which had been abandoned, but could not walk. Hard luck, indeed! He met a body of friendly Bannock scouts who would have taken care of him, but he supposed them to be hostiles and hid from them. Harder luck still! After crawling seven or eight miles, which took several days, he reached his old camp and there was reunited to his faithful dog, which at first snapped at and then welcomed him.

"At the camp his first good luck came—he found matches, coffee and some food—not to mention the dog, which I venture to state helped him almost as much as the provisions. Next day he met some scouts sent out to trail the hostiles and incidentally with instructions to bury Cowan—but they praised him instead. They fixed him up as well as they could, and left him by their camp-fire to await the coming of General Howard with the main body of troops. The ground was peaty, and full of dead vegetable matter, and after a nap, Cowan awakened to find that the earth all about him was on fire, and wounded as he was he had to roll out of the fire zone, getting burned scandalously as he rolled."

"Here," said the Hired Man. "You tell the rest of this to marines!"

"I'm telling you," said the Colonel, "the historic truth. General Howard came along and the surgeons gave Cowan all the care they were able to afford him. They took him up to Bottler's Ranch, north of the Park, and there Mrs. Cowan rejoined the remains and fragments of her still living spouse. They went to Bozeman after a while, carrying Cowan in a wagon. At the top of the hill down which they had to go, the neck-yoke broke and the horses ran away, and spilled Cowan out on the rocks and the generally unyielding surface of Montana. A conveyance was brought from Bozeman, and the much-murdered man was taken to a hotel."

"Thank God!" breathed the Poet. "Even a Montana hotel was a sweet boon as bringing the end of these troubles."

"Who said it was the end?" inquired the Colonel. "It wasn't. In the hotel at Bozeman his hoodoo haunted him. People flocked to the hotel to see him. If the vaudeville stage had been invented then in its present form, he could have made a fortune. They crowded into his room and sat on his bed. The bed collapsed, and Cowan was hurled to the floor and killed again. The hotel-keeper, seeing that even a cat's supply of lives must be about used up, ordered the crowd out of the place. He said he thought of throwing Cowan out, too, being afraid his hotel would burn up, or be blown away, or something, with such a Jonah aboard. But Cowan succeeded in getting home. They asked him if he didn't often think of his soul's salvation while enduring all these sufferings and passing through all these perils. 'Not by a damned sight!' said the unreconstructed sinner. 'I had more important things to think of!'"

"And all that took place right here?" asked the Bride.

"Here and hereabouts," answered the Colonel. "I was here about the time, and I know."

"If Jim Bridger," said Aconite, "had narrated them adventures, what would folks have said? And yet, the Colonel's correct. The tale are true!"

"Here's where you can sleep under a roof, Bride," said the Hired Man, as they made camp at the Lower Geyser Basin.

"So you don't want the rest of the story?" she queried.

"Ma'am," said the Hired Man. "We should all be darned sorry to lose you from the camp; but—"

"But me no buts," said the Bride. "I stay with the—with—the what do you call it, Mr. Driscoll, that I'm staying with?"

"The outfit, Miss Bride," said Aconite. "And the outfit's shore honored." And after the tasks of camp had been done, amid the strange and daunting surroundings of the wonderful geyser basin, when the camp reached that lull that precedes slumber, and which over all the world, whether on prairie, in forest, or on desert, is devoted to tobacco, music and tales, the Bride went on with her story.

THE TRIUMPH OF BILLY HELL

THE SECOND PART OF THE BRIDE'S STORY

The Pruntys live near Saint Joe, where they have a town and stockyards and grain-elevators, and thousands and thousands of acres of land all of their own, just like mediæval barons—only instead of having a castle with a donjon-keep with battlements and mysterious oubliettes and drizzly cells and a moat, they live in a great wooden house with verandas all round, and of a sort of composite architecture—Billy says that it is Queen Anne in front and Mary Ann at the rear—and hot and cold water in every room, and with a stone windmill-tower with a wheel on the top that you couldn't possibly put in a picture, it is so round and machiney-looking. Old Mr. Prunty says it cost twenty-seven thousand five hundred and eighty-three dollars and thirty-six cents—says it every chance he gets, without the variation of a cent. The Pruntys are scandalously rich. Their riches bought them a place in this play.

When Pa had begun to forge to the front in Peoria, where he began, he had all the knack he ever possessed for getting business, but he didn't have much money. I don't see any reason why we shouldn't confess this here. So he went to old Mr. Prunty, with whom he had become acquainted while he was putting in a town lighting-plant in the Prunty private village, and showed him how remunerative it would be to put money into Pa's business. This Mr. Prunty did, and I once saw the balance-sheet showing the profits he made. They were something frightful to a mind alive to the evils of the concentration of wealth—and the necessity of dividing with other people; but I shouldn't care so much for *that*, I am afraid, if it hadn't brought us into relations with Enos Prunty, Junior, who was brought up to the business of taking over the Mid-Continent Electric Company, and incidentally, me. The very idea!

I must not be disingenuous any more, and therefore I will admit that at one time I should have consented to the merger if it hadn't been for Enos' perfectly impossible name. Not that I loved him; not at all. But he wasn't bad looking, and he had overcome a good deal of the Prunty *gaucherie*—I should think he ought to, the schools he had been through—and a girl really does like to think of trousseaux, and establishments and the like. One day, though, I hired a card-writer on the street to write out for me the name, "Mrs. Enos Prunty, Jr.," upon looking at which I fled as from a pestilence, and threw it into the grate, and had a fire kindled, although it was one of those awful days when the coroner never can tell whether it was the heat or the humidity.

I had met Billy in the restaurant the day before.

But Pa liked Enos, and sort of treated the matter as if it were all arranged; and when Billy came into the spotlight as our social superior—which the Helmerstons would be by any of the old and outworn standards—I began to pet Pa one evening, and ask him how he liked Mr. Helmerston; whereupon Pa exploded with a terrific detonation, and said he wanted the relations of Mr. Helmerston with the Blunt family confined strictly to the field of business; that he hated and despised all the insufferable breed of dubs—I never could get Pa to say "cad"—who crept into employments like spies, under false pretenses, and called an Institute of Technology a "Tech," and looked down on better electricians who had come up by hard knocks. And Pa insisted that a man must have been pretty tough who had acquired in college circles from the Atlantic to the Missouri the *nom de guerre* of "Billy Hell."

Pa is a good business man, and has exceptional facilities for looking up people's records; but it seemed a little sneaky to use them on Billy, and to know so much, when we were so sure he never suspected a thing. I told him so, too, but all he said was "Huh." I was very angry, and when Mr. Prunty, Junior, came to see me next time I repulsed his addresses with such scorn that he went away in a passion. He said he laid no claim to being a human being, but he was, at least, a member of the animal kingdom, and that my way of treating him would have been inhuman had he been a toadstool. I retorted that I'd concede him a place among the mushrooms—fancy *my* twitting any one of mushroomery! But the old-family attitude of the Helmerstons was getting into my mental system.

Pa, in the meantime, was preparing to shunt Billy off to Mexico to superintend the installation of the Guadalanahuato power plant—a two years' job—at a splendid salary. But our Mr. Burns went over to the Universal Electric Company (after we had made him what he was!) and Mr. Aplin proved quite incapable of running the business, although he was *such* a genius in watts and farads and ohms and the coefficient of self-induction, and Billy was simply forked into the general charge of the main office, against his will, and shockingly against Pa's.

I forgot to say that Pa was ill, and confined to his room for a long time. This touches a tender spot in Pa's feelings, but the truth must be told; and you must understand that all his illness came from an ingrowing toe-nail. He had to have an operation, and then he had to stay in the house because it wouldn't heal; and there he was, using language which is really scandalous for a good church-worker like Pa, while Billy attended to the business.

I heaped coals of fire on Pa's head by staying with him hours and hours every day, and reading to him, until he asked me for goodness' sake to stop until he got the cross-talk out of his receiver. I said I'd be glad to dispense with all his cross talk, and he said: "There, now, don't cry"—and we had a regular love feast. Pa was a little difficult at this period. However, that day he got more confidential than he ever was before, and told me that serious business troubles were piling up, and worried him. We were likely, he said, to be spared the disgrace of dying rich. This was irony, for Pa despises this new idea that one should apologize for one's success.

He went on to tell me that Mr. Prunty had always had the most stock in the Mid-Continent, and that now that Enos had got so conceited about being able to run the business, and not being allowed to, the Pruntys seemed to want the whole thing, and hinted around about withdrawing, or buying Pa out.

I have this scene all in my mind for the play, with me sitting in "a dim religious light" and listening to the recital of our ruin and crying over Pa's sore foot. I did cry a good deal about this, truly, for I knew perfectly well that it was the nasty way I had treated Enos that made them so mean; but I still wished from the bottom of my heart that he would come back so I could search my soul for worse things to do to him. I told Billy about this trouble, and explained that Pa couldn't possibly raise money to buy out the Pruntys, and that they could be calculated upon not to pay Pa anything like what his stock was worth.

"I see," said Billy, "you are being squeezed by the stronger party."

He was looking out of the window in an abstracted sort of way, but he came to when I answered that, personally, I hadn't been conscious of anything of the sort.

When the conversation got around to the business again, Billy told me that Goucher—a Missourian that the Pruntys had injected into the business, and who was perfectly slavish in his subserviency to Enos—had been quizzing around Billy, trying to find out what ailed Pa, and if it was anything serious.

"I didn't like the little emissary," said Billy, "and so I told him that Mr. Blunt was precariously ill, with a complication of Bright's disease in its tertiary stage, and locomotor ataxia. He wrote down the Bright's disease and asked me how to spell the other. I told him that the Bright's disease would probably terminate fatally before he could master so much orthography; and still he didn't tumble! Goucher went away conscious of having performed well an important piece of work. I can't help thinking now that this incident has more significance than I then supposed."

He sat puckering up his brows for a long time, and I let him pucker.

At last he said: "Dolly, I shouldn't a bit wonder if they are trying to take some advantage of a dying man. I can see how they work the problem out. 'Here is a sick man,' they say, 'who has been doing the work of half a dozen for twenty years. He is going to pieces physically. If he has some fatal disease, and knows it, we can settle with him, and make him pay a few hundred thousand dollars for the privilege of getting his daughter's inheritance disentangled from a business which she can't run, and in which she will be at the mercy of—of people with whom her relations are a little strained. But first, we'll find out just how sick he is, and whether he's likely to get well soon, or at all.' And so they send Goucher mousing about; and he reports Bright's disease, and something else he can't spell, and they make an appointment with Helmerston for to-morrow morning to find out more about it, Mr. Goucher not being very clear. And your father's rather fierce manner of hiding what his ailment really is makes them all the more suspicious."

"You tell them," said I, firing up, "that Pa is still able—"

But I saw that Billy had one of those epoch-making ideas which mark the crises of history, and I stopped spellbound. He finally struck himself a fearful blow upon the knee, and said that he had it, and one looking at him could easily believe it. Then he explained to me his plan for discomfiting the Pruntys and hoisting them by their own petard. This is deeply psychological, being based upon an intuitive perception of what a Prunty would do when he believed certain things and had money at stake.

"I must take responsibility in this," said Billy, squaring his shoulders, "and bet my job on my success, and put our happiness in jeopardy. But, if we win, Mr. Blunt can never again say that I am an engineer only, with no head for practical business; and I shall have outlived the disgrace of my Tech training—and the nickname. You must handle your father, and keep me informed of any engagement the Pruntys make with him. I must do the rest. And, if I lose, it's back to climbing poles again!"

I asked Billy if I couldn't do something in line work, and he said I might carry the pliers. And when I said I meant it, he behaved beautifully, and called me his angel, and—and violated the rules, you know—and went away in a perfect frenzy of determination. I felt a solemn joy in spying on Pa and reporting to Billy. It seemed like a foretaste of a life all bound up and merged with his. And this is what took place:

The elder Mr. Prunty called on Billy and said he was appalled at the news Mr. Goucher brought that Mr. Blunt had Bright's disease; and was there any hope that the doctors might be mistaken?

Billy told him that the recent progress in bacteriological science, with which Mr. Prunty was no doubt fully conversant, seemed to make the diagnosis a cinch. By this he meant that they were sure about it.

"I see," said the driver. "I've heared the word afore."

He used a term that Mr. Prunty understood, Billy said, owing to his having done business all his life with reference to it.

Mr. Prunty suggested that people live a long time with Bright's disease, sometimes.

Billy, who is really a great actor, here grew mysterious, and told Mr. Prunty that, being mixed up with Mr. Blunt in business, it seemed a pity that he, Mr. Prunty, should have the real situation concealed from him, and that, as a matter of fact, Mr. Blunt's most pronounced outward symptom was a very badly ulcerated index toe. This of Billy's own knowledge, and Mr. Prunty might depend upon it.

Mr. Prunty studied on this for a long time, and then remarked that he had known several people to recover from sore toes.

Billy then pulled a book—a medical work he had borrowed—from under the desk, and showed Mr. Prunty a passage in which it was laid down that people's toes come off sometimes, in a most inconvenient way, in the last stages of Bright's disease. Mr. Prunty read the whole page, including a description of the way that dread disease ruins the complexion, by making it pasty and corpselike, and then laid the book down with conviction in his eyes.

"From this," said he, motioning at the book with his glasses, "it would seem to be all off."

"If it's Bright's disease," said Billy, "that causes

this lesion of the major lower digit, the prognosis is, no doubt, extremely grave. But while there's life, you know—"

"Yes," answered Mr. Prunty, "that is a comfort, of course. Does he know what ails him?"

"He is fully aware of his condition," said Billy, "but, unfortunately, not yet resigned to it." (I should think not.)

"I see you have been studying this thing out," said Mr. Prunty, "as exactly as if it had been an engineering problem; and I want to say, Mr. Helmerston, that I like your style. If we ever control this business the future of such careful and competent and far-sighted men as yourself—in fact, I may say *your* future—will be bright and assured. Have you any more information for me as to this —this sad affair of Blunt's?"

Billy thanked him, and said he hadn't, at present, and Mr. Prunty went away, trying to look sad. Billy went to the bank in Pa's name and arranged for a lot of money to be used in acquiring the Prunty stock, if it should be needed. The stock was worth twice as much, and the bank people knew it, and couldn't have believed, of course, that we would get it for *that*. Then the Pruntys made an engagement with me for Pa over the telephone, for a certain hour of a certain day, and I told Billy.

"The time has come," said Billy, when the plot began thickening in this way, "for Little Willie to beard the lion in his den. Smuggle me into the room an hour before the Pruntys are due, darling, and we'll cast the die."

I was all pale and quivery when I kissed Billy—in that sort of serious way in which we women kiss people we like, when we tell them to come back with their shields or on them—and pushed him into the room.

I heard all they said. It was dark in there, and Pa thought at first that it was a Prunty. Pa was sitting in the Morris chair, with his foot on a rest.

"That you, Enos?" said he. "Help yourself to a chair. I'm kind of laid up for repairs."

"It's Helmerston," said Billy. "I called to talk to you about this affair with Mr. Prunty. I have some information which may be of value to you."

Pa sat as still as an image for perhaps a minute. I could almost hear his thoughts. He was anathematizing Billy mentally for butting in, but he was too good a strategist to throw away any valuable knowledge.

"Well," said he at last, "I'm always open to valuable information. Turn it loose!"

Then Billy told him all you know, and a good deal more, which I shall not here state, because it is not necessary to the scenario, and I did not understand it, anyhow. There was some awfully vivid conversation at times, though, when Pa went up into the air at what Billy had done, and Billy talked him down.

"Do you mean to say, you—you young lunatic," panted Pa, "that you've told Prunty that he's got a living corpse to deal with, when I need all the prestige I've won with him to hold my own?"

But Billy explained that he'd taken the liberty of thinking the whole thing out; and, anyhow, had merely refrained from removing a mistaken notion from Prunty's mind.

"But," said he, "you can assure him when he gets here that you are really in robust health."

"Assure him!" roared Pa. "He'd be dead sure I was trying to put myself in a better light for the dicker. I couldn't make him believe anything at all. I know Prunty."

Billy said that the psychology of the situation was plain. Mr. Prunty was convinced that Pa was in such a condition that he never could go back to the office, and could no more take sole ownership of the Mid-Continent than a baby could enter a shot-putting contest. What would they do when it came to making propositions? They would offer something that they were sure a case in the tertiary stage couldn't accept. They would probably offer to give or take a certain price for the stock. Believing that Pa wasn't in position to buy, but was really forced to sell, they would name a frightfully low price, so that when Pa accepted it perforce they would be robbing him out of house and home, almost. This was the way with these shrewd traders always, and to whipsaw a dying man would be nuts for a man like Prunty. (I am here falling into Billy's dialect when he was in deadly earnest.) Then the conversation grew mysterious again with Pa listening, and once admitting that "that would be like old Enos."

"But he'll back out," said Pa, "if he's thief enough ever to start in."

"Have him make a memorandum in writing, and sign it," answered Billy.

"But," rejoined Pa, in a disgusted way, as if to ask why he condescended to argue with this young fool, "you don't know Prunty. Unless he has the cash in hand he'll go to some lawyer and find a way out."

"I thought of that, too," said Billy; "and so I took the liberty of going to the bank and getting the cash—for temporary use, you know."

"I like your nerve!" moaned Pa angrily. "Do you know, young man, that you've built up a situation that absolutely forces me to adopt your fool plans? Absolutely infernal nonsense! To imagine it possible to get the Prunty stock at any such figures is—" And Pa threw up wild hands of desperation to an unpitying sky.

"Is it possible to imagine," said Billy, "such a thing as the Pruntys trying to get your stock at that figure? That's the thing I'm looking for and counting on." And when Pa failed to reply, but only chewed his mustache, Billy went on: "I thought the logic of the situation would appeal to you," said he. "And now let us set the stage. The time is short."

And then came the most astounding thing, and the thing that showed Billy's genius. First he took out the electric-light bulbs of the electrolier, and screwed in others made of a sort of greenish glass—just a little green tinge in it. He took some stage appliances and put just a little shade of dark under Pa's eyes, and at the corners of his mouth; and when the green lights were turned on Pa had the most ghastly, ghostly, pasty, ghoulish look any one ever saw. I was actually frightened when I came in: it was as bad as Doctor Jekyll turned to Mr. Hyde. Pa looked rather cheap while Billy was doing this, but the time was getting short, and he was afraid the Pruntys would come bursting in and catch them at it. Billy placed Pa right under the green lights, and shaded them so that the rest of us received only the unadulterated output of the side lamps. Then they arranged their cues, and Billy stepped into the next room. As he went, Pa swore for the first time since he quit running the line-gang, when, he claims, it was necessary.

"If this goes wrong, as it will," he hissed through his livid lips, "I'll kick you from here to the city-limits if it blows the plug in the power-house!"

"Very well, sir," answered Billy—and the footman announced the Pruntys.

I was as pale as a ghost, and my eyes were red, and the look of things was positively sepulchral when they came in, Enos tagging at his father's heels as if he was ashamed. The footman turned on the light, and almost screamed as he looked at poor Pa, with the pasty green in his complexion, and the cavernous shadows under his eyes. Billy had seen to it that the Pruntys had had plenty of literature on the symptoms of Bright's disease, and I could see them start and exchange looks as Pa's state dawned on them.

"I'm sorry to see you in this condition," said Mr. Prunty, after Pa had weakly welcomed them and told them to sit down.

"What condition?" snapped Pa, the theatricality wearing off. "I'm all right, if it wasn't for this blamed toe!"

"Is it very bad?" asked Mr. Prunty.

"It won't heal," growled Pa, and the visitors exchanged glances again. "But you didn't come here to discuss sore toes. Let's get down to business."

Then Mr. Prunty, in a subdued and sort of ministerial voice, explained to Pa that he was getting along in years, and that Pa wasn't long—that is, that Pa was getting along in years, too—and both parties would, no doubt, be better satisfied if their interests were separated. Therefore he had decided to withdraw his capital from the business, and place it in some other enterprise which would give his son a life work along lines laid out in his education and training. He didn't want to sell his stock to the Universal Electric Company as he had a chance to do (Pa started fiercely here, for he was afraid of the Universal Electric); although the old agreement by which neither party was to sell out to a competitor was probably no longer binding; and so they had come as man to man to talk adjustment.

"But," says Pa, "this takes me by surprise. I don't quite see my way clear to taking on such a load as carrying all the stock would be. Mid-Continent stock is valuable."

They exchanged glances again, as much as to say that Pa was evidently anxious to sell rather than buy, and was crying the stock up accordingly, so as to get as much money as he could for me before he died.

"We may not be so grasping as you think," said Mr. Prunty; and then nothing was said for quite a while.

Pa was looking awfully sick, and Mr. Prunty was just exuding love and kindness and magnanimity from every pore.

"You had some proposition thought out," interrogated Pa, feeling anxiously for his own pulse, "or you wouldn't have come. What is it, Prunty?"

"Well," answered Mr. Prunty, gazing piercingly at Pa, as if to ask if such a cadaverous person *could* possibly take on the sole control of the Mid-Continent even if he had the money—"well, we had thought of it a little, that's a fact. We thought we'd make you an offer to buy or sell—"

"Hurrah for Billy!" my heart shouted. For this was just what he said would happen. But, instead of hurrahing, I came to the front and gave Pa a powder. It was mostly quinine, and was dreadfully bitter.

"To buy or sell," went on Mr. Prunty, "at a price to be named by us. If it's a reasonable figure, take our stock and give us our money. If it's too high, why, sell us yours. That's fair, ain't it?"

Pa lay back and looked green and groaned. He was doing it nobly.

"What is fair in some circumstances," he moaned, "is extortion in others; and I—er—yes, I suppose it would be called fair. What's your give-or-take price, Prunty?"

"We are willing," said Mr. Prunty, "to give or take seventy-five for the stock."

Pa was so still that I had to rouse him, and Mr. Prunty repeated his offer.

"I—I'm getting a little forgetful," said Pa, "and I'd like to have you put it in writing, so I can consider it, and be sure I have it right, you know."

The Pruntys consulted again, and again they came forward. Enos wrote down the proposition, and Mr. Prunty signed it. I didn't understand it very well, and the strain was so frightful that I expected to fly all to pieces every instant, but I didn't.

When Enos handed the paper to Pa, Pa cleared his throat in a kind of scraping way, and in stepped Billy with a great box under his arm.

"Mr. Helmerston," said Pa, as calmly as General Grant at—any place where he was especially placid—"I want you and my daughter to be witnesses to the making of the proposition in this writing, from Mr. Prunty to me."

Billy read the paper, and said he understood that it was a give-or-take offer of seventy-five for all the stock of the Mid-Continent. Mr. Prunty said yes, looking rather dazed, and not so sympathetic.

"I accept the proposition," snapped Pa, his jaw setting too awfully firm for the tertiary stage. "I'll take your stock at seventy-five. Helmerston, pay 'em the money!"

Billy had the cash in ten-thousand-dollar bundles;

and I was so fascinated at the sight of so much treasure being passed over like packages of bonbons, that for a while I didn't see how funny Mr. Prunty was acting. When I did look, he was holding his nose in the air and gasping like one of Aunt Maria's little chickens with the pip. He seemed to have a sort of progressive convulsions, beginning low down in wrigglings of the legs, and gradually moving upward in jerks and gurgles and gasps, until it went off into space in twitchings of his mouth and eyes and nose and forehead. Enos had the bundles of money counted, and a receipt written, before he noticed that his father was having these fits, and then *he* seemed scared. I suppose these people have a sort of affection for each other, after all.

"Father," said he— "Father, what's the matter?"

"Matter?" roared Mr. Prunty. "Does the fool ask what's the matter? Don't you see we're done brown? Look at the basketful they brought, that we might just as well have had as not, if it hadn't been for— Blast you, Blunt, I'll show you you can't chisel old Enos Prunty out of his good money like this, I will! I'll put the whole kit and boodle of yeh in jail! That stock is worth a hundred and fifty, if it's worth a cent. Ene, if you'll stand by like a stoughton bottle and see your old father hornswoggled out of his eye-teeth by a college dude and this old confidence-man, you'll never see a cent of my money, never! Do you hear, you ass? He's no more sick than I am! That's false pretenses, ain't it? He's got some darned greenery-yallery business on that face of his! Ain't that false? Blunt, if you don't give me the rest in the basket there I'll law you to the Supreme Court!"

"Hush, father," said Enos; "Aurelia's here."

"When you get everything set," said Pa, with a most exasperating smile, "just crack ahead with your lawsuit. We'll trot you a few heats, anyhow. You'd better take your pa away, Enos, and buy him a drink of something cool."

"I want to compliment you, Mr. Helmerston," said Enos, quite like a gentleman, "on the success of your little stage-business, and especially on your careful forecast of the play of human motives. I can see that a man with only ordinary business dishonesty, like myself, need not be surprised at defeat by such a master of finesse as you."

He bowed toward me. Billy flushed.

"If you mean, sir—" he began.

"Oh, I mean nothing offensive," answered Enos.

"I will be in the office in the morning, and shall be ready, as secretary, to transfer this stock on the books, previous to resigning. Come, father, we've got our beating; but we can still have the satisfaction of being good losers. Good-by, Miss Blunt; I wish you joy!"

Pa came out of the green light as they disappeared, limping on his wrapped-up foot, and shouted that he had always said that Enos was a brick, and now he knew it. I ran up to him and kissed him. Then I threw myself into Billy's arms.

"Aurelia!" said Pa, looking as cross as a man *could* look in such circumstances, "I should think you'd be ashamed of yourself!"

I dropped into a chair and covered up my face, while Pa went on addressing Billy, trying to be severe on him for letting me kiss him, and to beam on him at the same time for helping him with the Pruntys.

"Young man," said he, "I owe you a great deal. This tomfoolery happened to work. Please to consider yourself a part of the Mid-Continent Electric Company in any capacity you choose."

"Yes, sir," said Billy, gathering up the money. "Is that all, sir?"

"I should like to have you take Enos' place as secretary," added Pa.

"Thank you," said Billy. "I shall be pleased and honored. Is that all? Do I still go to Mexico?"

Pa pondered and fidgeted, and acted awfully ill at ease.

"Yes," said he at last. "You're the only competent engineer we've got who understands the plans. You'll have to go for a few months—if you don't mind—anyhow."

"Pa," said I, "I'm tired of metal work, and I need a vacation in new and pleasant surroundings, and—and associations. Billy is awfully pleasant to associate with, and—and be surrounded by; and I've never, never been in Guadalanawhat-you-may-call-it; and—and—may we Pa?"

"Young woman!" glared Pa, "who have you the effrontery to call 'Billy'?"—Pa could never acquire what he calls "the 'whom' habit."

Billy stepped manfully forward.

"You would recognize the name 'Billy,' " said he, "if it were joined with the rather profane surname with which it is, unfortunately, connected, 'from the Atlantic to the Missouri.' Mr. Blunt, you can not be ignorant of the sweet dream in which I have indulged myself with reference to your daughter. I know I am unworthy of her—"

"Oh, cut that short!" said Pa. "Take this grease off my face, and remove these infernal stage lights! There, Dolly—there! Mr. Helmerston, er—Billy—will start for Mexico within a month. If you—if you really want to go with him, why go!"

And so we're going, by way of Yellowstone Park.

CHAPTER IV

"YOU see," said Mr. Driscoll, when, after three days of independent wonder-gazing in the thirty square miles of the Lower Geyser Basin, his seven fares came together for departure, "as I told yeh, this trip is just gettin' good."

"I have seen," said the Poet, "a spring from the bottom of which fires leap in lambent flames, to be quenched by the air when they reach the surface. Let me die, now!"

"I have seen," said the Artist, "the Mammoth Paint Pots from which we may dip our colors in that day 'when earth's last picture is painted, and the tubes are twisted and dried.'"

"I have seen," said the Bride, "a lake perched upon a marble platform, the slopes of which it drapes with a lace of runnels—like the web that was woven by the Lady of Shalott while she looked in her magic mirror."

"In that day when we perfect our mythology," said the Poet, "we shall know of the nymph of this lake, who uses it as a mirror, and will die if she looks away from the image to gaze on the real knight as he passes."

"I question that, really," said the Professor. "In an age of pure science—"

"Scat!' said the Colonel. "I have seen a pool that goes mad when any passing idiot throws gross material into its pure idealism—and I sympathize with it."

"I have seen," went on Professor Boggs, "a natural object—I refer to the Fountain Geyser—which gives us a valuable lesson in steady performance, with no eccentricities. Every four hours it plays for fifteen minutes, shooting its water to a height of sixty feet. Note the mathematical correspondence—the feet correspond to the minutes in the hour—the hours are four—four into sixty goes fifteen times, the number of minutes the geyser plays—I shall work this out in an essay—it seems very significant."

"I have seen," said the Groom, "in the Great Fountain Geyser, a natural power installation. It throws its huge volume of water to a height of one hundred feet. It is on a pedestal like an emplacement for a monument, and its crater looks like the hole in which to set the shaft. That makes the matter of utilizing the power a cinch. I figure—"

"Billy!" said the Bride. "Aren't you ashamed?"

"The Professor and myself," answered the Groom, "represent the spirit of the age. We only are sane."

"You, Billy Helmerston," said the Bride, "are a fraud!"

Nine miles to the Upper Geyser Basin—passing the Midway Basin half-way—and the tourists found their tents already pitched by Aconite who had preceded them with the impedimenta, and returned light for the drive. They took a whole day for the journey, and even so felt as if they were committing an atrocity in negligence. The Jewell Geyser, the Sapphire Pool and the Mystic Falls seemed small by comparison with the gigantic phenomena of the Lower Basin, and smaller still next day compared with the stupendous marvels of the Upper Basin. At the Mystic Falls, the Bride insisted on taking luncheon.

"It's like the really normal loveliness of earth," said she. "It goes better with humanity, and luncheon, and flowers and fairies and gentle things. I want to eat a meal in neither Paradise nor the Inferno—and we seem to be in one or the other most of the time."

At luncheon, Professor Boggs came forward with an original and practical idea with relation to the Yellowstone Nights' Entertainment, as they had come to call their camp-fire stories.

"I hold," said he, "that one is entitled to time for putting his thoughts in order before presuming to deliver an address, even of the narrative sort. I find myself apprehensive of being called upon next, and this interferes with my powers of observation. I suggest that we cast lots for the next tale now, and thus free the minds of all but the narrator, who may retire if he choose, and collate his data."

"It's a good thought," said the Groom. "Poet, perform your office!"

The Poet passed the hat to the Bride, who closed her eyes and felt about discriminatingly, saying she was trying to find Billy in the hat. The Poet read the ballot and handed it to the Artist.

"Groom!" read the Artist, handing the slip of paper to Billy. "You're nominated."

"Stung!" ejaculated Billy.

THE HEART OF GOLIATH

THE STORY TOLD BY THE GROOM

"I often think," said the Groom, in beginning his tale that night, "when this adventure recurs to me, what a different world it would be if we could see into one another's minds, and telepathically search one another's hearts. I don't know whether it would be better or not; but that it would be different, this story proves. It is a tale that came to me when I was traveling about in the Missouri Valley, earning the money for my Tech course, and long before my time with the Mid-Continent Electric Company. It shows how a soul that is pitchy darkness to its nearest and dearest, may be illumined by the electric light of self-revelation to the eye of the chance-met stranger."

I first saw him on the platform just before my train pulled out from Sioux City to Aberdeen. He was a perfect mountain—an Alp, a Himalaya—of man. He must have been well toward seven feet tall;

and so vast were his proportions that as he stooped to the window to buy his ticket he reminded me of a mastiff peering into a mouse's hole. From a distance —one could scarcely take in the details at close range—I studied him as a remarkable specimen of the brawny western farmer, whose score in any exhibition would be lowered by one fact only: lofty as his height was, he was getting too heavy for it.

I had to go into the smoking-car to find a vacant seat, and there I could see but one. I had but just slipped into it when in came the Gargantuan farmer and sat down all over me, in a seemingly ruthless exercise of his undoubted right to half the seat, and his unquestionable ability to appropriate as much more as his dimensions required. Falstaff with his page reminded himself of a sow that had overwhelmed all her litter save one: I felt like the last of the litter in process of smothering. And he was as ignorant of my existence, apparently, as could possibly be required by the comparison.

He wore with bucolic negligence clothes of excellent quality. His hat was broad as a prairie. I have no idea where such hats are bought. I am sure I never saw one of such amplitude of brim on sale anywhere. It was of the finest felt, and had a band of heavy leather pressed into a design in bas-relief.

A few dried alfalfa leaves had lodged in the angle between the crown and the brim, and clung there, even when he took the hat off to wipe his brow, thus giving me a view of the plateau of felt, which I should never have obtained otherwise.

His face was enormous but not puffy; and the red veinlets on the cheek and nose had acquired their varicosity by weathering rather than by indulgence. His hair was clipped short, as though he had had a complete job done as a measure of economizing time. He had a high beak of a nose, with rugged promontories of bone at the bridge, like the shoulders of a hill; and his mouth was a huge but well-shaped feature, hard and inflexible like the mouth of a cave.

His shirt was of blue flannel, clean and fine, and its soft roll collar fell away from his great muscular neck unconfined and undecorated by any sort of cravat. His tun of a torso bulged roundly out in front of me like the sponson of a battleship. Stretched across the immense waistcoat was a round, spirally-fluted horsehair watchguard as big as a rope, with massive golden fastenings; and suspended from it was a golden steer made by some artificer who had followed Cellini afar off, if at all, and which gave the area (one must use geographical terms in describing the man), an auriferous and opulent appearance.

His trousers were spotted with the stains of stables; and his huge boots, like barges, had similar discolorations overlaying a brilliant shine. He carried one of those heavy white sticks with which the drovers and dealers at the Sioux City stockyards poke the live stock and take the liberties accorded to prospective purchasers with pigs and bullocks. On the crook of this he rested his great hands, one piled upon the other, and stared, as if fascinated by them, at four soldiers returning from service in the Philippines, who had two seats turned together, and were making a gleeful function of their midday meal, startling the South Dakota atmosphere with the loud use of strange-sounding expressions in Tagalog and Spanish, and, with military brutality, laughing at the dying struggles of a fellow-man being slowly pressed to death under that human landslide. I resented their making light of such a subject.

My oppressor stared at them with a grim and unwavering gaze that finally seemed to put them out and set them ill at ease; for they became so quiet that we could hear noises other than theirs. Once in a while, however, they winked at me to show their appreciation of my agonies, and made remarks about the water-cure and the like, meant for my ears. My incubus seemed not to hear a word of this badinage. I wondered if he were not deaf, or a little wrong in his intellect. The train stopped at a little station just as I had become quite desperate, and two men sitting in front of us got off. With the superhuman strength of the last gasp I surged under my tormentor—and he noticed me. I verily believe that until that instant he had not known of my presence; he gave such a deliberate sort of start.

"Excuse me!" said he. "Forgot they was any one here—let me fix you!"

He had already almost done so; but he meant well. He rose to take the vacated seat; but with a glance at the soldiers he threw the back over, turned his back to them and his face to me, and sat down. His ponderous feet like valises rested on each side of mine, his body filled the seat from arm to arm. For a while, even after discovering me, he stared past me as if I had been quite invisible. I saw a beady perspiration on his brow as if he were under some great stress of feeling. It was getting uncanny. I understood now how the soldiers, now breaking forth into riot again, had been suppressed by that stony regard. When he spoke, however, it was in commonplaces.

"They're lots of 'em comin' back," said he.

A slow thrust of the bulky thumb over his shoulder indicated that he meant soldiers. I nodded assent. A great many were returning just then.

"Jack's come back," said he; "quite a while."

His voice was in harmony with his physique—deep, heavy, rough. Raised in rage it might have matched the intonations of Stentor, and terrified a thousand foes; for it was a phenomenal voice. The rumble of the train was a piping treble compared with it.

"You don't know Jack, do yeh?" he asked.

"I think not," said I.

"Course not," he replied. "Fool question! An' yit, he used to know most of you fellers."

I wondered just what he might mean by "you fellows," but he was silent again.

"You don't live near here," he stated at last.

"No," said I. "I am just passing through."

"If you lived in these parts," said he, "you'd know him."

"I dare say," I replied. "Who is Jack?"

I was a little piqued at his rudeness; for he returned no reply. Then I saw that he was gazing into vacancy again so absently that I should have pronounced his case one of mental trouble if his appearance had not been so purely physical. He took from a cigar-case a big, dark, massive cigar, clubhouse shape like himself, gave it to me and lighted the twin of it. I thought myself entitled to reparation for his maltreatment of me, and, seeing that it was a good cigar, I took it. As for any further converse, I had given that up, when there rumbled forth from him a soliloquy rather than a story. He appeared to have very little perception of me as an auditor. I think now that he must have been in great need of some one to whom he might talk, and that his relations to those about him forbade any outpouring of expression. He seemed all the time in the attitude of repelling attack. He did not move, save as he applied the cigar to his lips or took it away; and his great voice rolled forth in subdued thunder.

"I've got four sections of ground," said he, "right by the track. . . . Show you the place when we go through. Of course I've got a lot of other truck scattered around. . . . Land at the right figger you've got to buy—got to. . . . But when I hadn't but the four sections—one section overruns so they's a little over twenty-six hundred acres—I thought 'twas about the checker f'r a man with three boys. . . . One f'r each o' them, you understand, an' the home place f'r mother if anything happened. . . . Mother done jest as much to help git the start as I did. . . . Plumb as much—if not more.

"Tom an' Wallace is good boys—none better. I'd about as quick trust either of 'em to run the place as to trust myself."

There was a candid self-esteem in the word "about" and his emphasis on it.

"I sent Wallace," he resumed, "into a yard of feeders in Montana to pick out a trainload o' tops with a brush and paint-pot, an' I couldn't 'a' got a hundred dollars better deal if I'd spotted 'em myself. . . . That's goin' some f'r a kid not twenty-five. Wallace knows critters . . . f'r a boy . . . mighty well. . . . An' Tom's got a way of handlin' land to get the last ten bushel of corn to the acre that beats me with all my experience. . . . These colleges where they study them things do some good, I s'pose; but it's gumption, an' not schoolin', that makes boys like Tom an' Wallace.

. . . They're all right. . . . They'd 'a' made good anyhow."

I could feel an invidious comparison between Tom and Wallace, of whom he spoke with such laudatory emphasis, and some one else whom I suspected to be the Jack who had come back from the Philippines; and his next utterance proved this instinctive estimate of the situation to be correct. He went on, slower than before, with long pauses in which he seemed lost in thought, and in some of which I gave up, without much regret, I confess, the idea of ever hearing more of Jack or his brothers.

"Jack was always mother's boy," said he. "Mother's boy . . . you know how it is. . . . Make beds, an' dust, an' play the pianah, an' look after the flowers! . . . Wasn't bigger'n nothin', either. . . . Girl, I always thought, by good rights. I remember . . . mother wanted him to be a girl. . . . She was on the square with the children . . . but if any boy got a shade the best of it anywhere along the line, it was Jack. . . . I don't guess Tom an' Wallace ever noticed; but maybe Jack got a leetle the soft side o' things from mother. . . . Still, she's al'ays been dumbed square. . . .

"I seen as soon as he got old enough to take holt, an' didn't, that he wasn't wuth a cuss. . . . Never told mother, an' never let on to the boys; but I could see he was no good, Jack wasn't. . . . Some never owns up when it's their own folks . . . but what's the use lyin'? . . . Hed to hev a swaller-tail coat, an' joined a 'country club' down to town—an' him a-livin' in the middle of a strip o' country a mile wide an' four long, wuth a hundred dollars an acre . . . all ourn . . . goin' out in short pants to knock them little balls around that cost six bits apiece. I didn't let myself care much about it; but 'country club!'—Hell!"

He had visualized for me the young fellow unfitted to his surroundings, designed on a scale smaller than the sons of Anak about him, deft in little things, finical in dress, fond of the leisure and culture of the club, oppressed with the roughnesses and vastnesses about his father's farms, too tender for the wild winds and burning suns, with nerves attuned to music and art rather than to the crushing of obstacles and the defeat of tasks: and all the while the image of "mother" brooded over him. All this was vividly in the picture—very vividly, considering the unskilful brush with which it had been limned—

but just as it began to appeal to me, Anak fell quiescent.

"I never thought he was anything wuss than wuthless," he went on, at last, "till he come to me to git some money he'd lost at this here club. . . . Thirty-seven dollars an' fifty cents. . . . Gamblin'. . . . I told him not by a damned sight; an' he cried—cried like a baby. . . . I'd 'a' seen him jugged 'fore I'd 'a' give him thirty-seven fifty of my good money lost that way. . . . Not me. . . . Wallace give him the money f'r his shotgun. . . . An' mother—she al'ays knowed when Jack had one o' his girl-cryin' fits—she used to go up after Jack come in them nights, an' when he got asleep so he wouldn't know it she'd go in and kiss him. . . . Watched and ketched her at it, but never let on. . . . She run down bad—gittin' up before daylight an' broke of her rest like that. . . . I started in oncet to tell her he was no good, but I jest couldn't. . . . Turned it off on a hoss by the name o' Jack we had, an' sold him to make good f'r twenty-five dollars less'n he was wuth, ruther'n tell her what I started to. . . . She loved that wuthless boy, neighbor—there ain't no use denyin' it, she did love him."

He paused a long while, either to ponder on the strange infatuation of "mother" for "Jack" or to allow me to digest his statement. A dog—one of the shaggy brown enthusiasts that chase trains—ran along by the cars until distanced, and then went back wagging his tail as if he had expelled from the neighborhood some noxious trespasser—as he may have conceived himself to have done. Goliath watched him with great apparent interest.

"Collie," said he, at last. "Know anything about collies? Funny dogs! Lick one of 'em oncet an' he's never no good any more. . . . All kind o' shruvle up by lickin', they're that tender-hearted. . . . Five year ago this fall Tom spiled a fifty-dollar pedigreed collie by jest slappin' his ears an' jawin' him. . . . Some critters is like that . . . Jack . . . was!"

He faltered here, and then flamed out into pugnacity, squaring his huge jaw as if I had accused him—as I did in my heart, I suspect.

"But the dog," he rumbled, "was wuth somethin' —Jack never was. . . . Cryin' around f'r thirty-seven fifty! . . . Talkin' o' debts o' honor! . . . That showed me plain enough he wasn't wuth botherin' with. . . . Got his mother to come an' ask f'r an allowance o' money—so much a month. . . . Ever hear of such a thing? An' him not turnin' his hand to a lick of work except around the house helpin' mother. . . . Tom an' Wallace hed quite a little start in live stock by this time, an' money in bank. . . . Jack hed the same lay, but he fooled his away—fooled it away. . . . Broke flat all the time, an' wantin' an allowance. . . . Mother said the young sprouts at the club had allowances . . . an' he read in books that laid around the house about fellers in England an' them places havin' allowances an' debts of honor. . . . Mother seemed to think one while that we was well enough off so we could let Jack live like the fellers in the books. . . . He lived more in them books than he did in South Dakoty, an' talked book lingo all the time. . . . Mother soon seen she was wrong.

"She was some hurt b'cause I talked to the neighbors about Jack bein' plumb no good. . . . I don't know who told her. . . . I didn't want the neighbors to think I was fooled by him. . . . I never said nothing to mother, though. . . . She couldn't f'rgit thet he was her boy, an' she kep' on lovin' him. . . . Nobody orto blame her much f'r that, no matter what he done. . . . You know how it is with women.

"One time purty soon after the thirty-seven fifty deal a bad check f'r two hundred come into my bundle o' canceled vouchers at the bank, an' I knowed in a minute who'd done it. . . . Jack had been walkin' the floor nights f'r quite a spell, an' his eyes looked like a heifer's that's lost her calf. . . . He hed a sweetheart in town. . . . Gal from the East . . . big an' dark an' strong enough to take Jack up an' spank him. . . . It was her brother Jack had lost the money to. Jack jest wrote my name on a check—never tried to imitate my fist much—an' the bank paid it. . . . When I come home a-lookin' the way a man does that's been done that way by a boy o' his'n, mother told me Jack was gone, an' handed me a letter he left f'r me. . . . I never read it. . . . Went out to the barn so mother wouldn't see me, an' tore it up. . . . I'd 'a' been damned before I'd 'a' read it!"

He gloomed out over my head in an expressionless way that aroused all the curiosity I am capable of feeling as to the actual workings of another's mind. He seemed to be under the impression that he had said a great many things in the pause that ensued; or he regarded my understanding as of small importance; for he recommenced at a point far advanced in his narrative.

"—'N' finely," said he very calmly, "we thought she was goin' to die. I asked the doctor what we could do, an' he told me what. . . . Knowed all the boys since he helped 'em into the world, you know—a friend more'n a doctor—an' he allowed it was Jack she was pinin' f'r. So I goes to her, a-layin' in bed as white as a sheet, an' I says, 'Mother, if they's anything you want, you can hev it, if it's on earth, no matter how no-account I think it is!' . . . A feller makes a dumb fool of himself such times, neighbor; but mother was good goods when we was poor an' young—any one of the neighbors can swear to that. . . . She looks up at me . . . an' whispers low . . . 'Go an' find him!' . . . An' I went.

"I knowed purty nigh where to look. I went to Chicago. He'd dropped clean down to the bottom, neighbor. . . . Playin' a pianah . . . f'r his board an' lodgin' an' beer . . . in . . . in a beer hall."

I was quite sure, he paused so long, that he had

told all he had to narrate of this history of the boy who could not stand punishment, and was so much like a collie; and I knew from the manner in which he had lapsed into silence, more than from what he had said, what a dark passage it was.

"Well," he resumed finally, "I hed my hands spread to strangle him right there. . . . I could 'a' done it all right—he was that peaked an' little. . . . He wouldn't 'a' weighed more'n a hundred an' fifty—an' *my* son! . . . I could 'a' squushed the life out of him with my hands—an' it was all right if I hed. . . . You bet it was! . . . Not that I cared f'r the two hundred dollars. I could spare that all right. I'll lose that much on a fair proposition any time. . . . But to take that thing back to mother . . . from where I picked it up from!

"I reckon I was ruther more gentle with Jack goin' home than I ever was before. . . . I hed to be. They was no way out of it except to be easy with him—'r lam the life out of him an' take him home on a cot . . . an' mother needed him in runnin' order. So I got him clothes, an' had him bathed, an' he got shaved as he used to be—he had growed a beard—an' I rode in one car and him in another. . . . When mother seed him, her an' him cried together f'r I suppose it might have been two hours 'r two and a quarter, off an' on, an' whispered together, an' then she went to sleep holdin' his hand, an' begun to pick up, an' Jack went back to his own ways, an' the rest of us to ourn, an' it was wuss than ever. . . . An' when he sold a team o' mine and skipped ag'in, I was glad, I tell you, to be shet of him. . . . An' they could do the mile to the pole in twenty, slick as mice.

"Next time mother and Wallace went an' got him. . . . Mother found out some way that he was dyin' in a horsepittle in Minneapolis. . . . He claimed he'd been workin f'r a real estate firm; but I had the thing looked up . . . an' I couldn't find where any of our name had done nothing. . . . An' it seemed as ef we'd never git shet of him. . . . That sounds hard; but he was a kind of a disease by this time—a chronic, awful painful, worryin' disease, like consumption. . . . An' we couldn't git cured of him, an' we couldn't die. . . . It was kind o' tough. He moped around, an' mother had some kind o' promise out of him that he wouldn't leave her no more, an' he was pleadin' with her to let him go, an' Tom an' Wallace an' me never sayin' a word to him, when this here Philippine War broke out . . . you know what it's about—I never did . . . an' Jack wanted to enlist.

" 'I can't let him go!' says mother.

" 'Let him go,' says I. 'If he'll go, let him!'

"Mother looks at me whiter'n I ever expect to see her again but once, maybe; an' the next morning she an' Jack goes to the county seat an' he enlists. I went down when the rig'ment was all got together. Mother an' me has always had a place where we kep' all the money they was in the house, as much hern as mine, an' she took five twenty-dollar gold pieces out of the pile, an' sewed 'em in a chamois-skin bag all wet with her cryin' . . . an' never sayin' a word . . . an' she hangs it round his neck, an' hung to him an' kissed him till it sorter bothered the boss of the rig'ment—some kind of colonel—because he wanted the men to march, you know, an' didn't seem to like to make mother fall back. . . . She seemed to see how it was, finely, an' fell back, an' this colonel made the motion to her with his sword they do to their superiors, an' they marched. . . . Jack stood straighter than any one in the line, an' he had a new sort of look to him. He everidged up purty good, too, in hithe . . . I don't see much to this soldier business. . . . Maybe that's why he looked the part so well. . . . I give the captain a hundred f'r him. . . . Jack sent it back from a place called Sanfrisco, without a word. 'So much saved!' says I. He was wuthless as ever."

The immense voice labored, broke, stopped—the man seemed weary and overcome. To afford him an escape from the story that seemed to have mastered him, like the Ancient Mariner's, I called his attention to what the four soldiers were doing. They had dressed as if for inspection, and were evidently going out upon the platform. The noticeable thing in their appearance was the change in their expressions from the hilarity and riotousness of a few moments ago, to a certain solemnity. One of them carried a little box carefully wrapped up, as a devotee might carry an offering to a shrine. The huge farmer glanced casually at them as if with full knowledge of what they were doing, and, ignoring my interruption, seemed to resume his monologue—as might the habitué of a temple pass by the question of a stranger concerning a matter related to the mysteries—something not to be discussed, difficult to be explained, or not worth mention. He pointed out of the window.

"Our land," said he; "both sides . . . tiptop good ground. . . . Didn't look much like this when mother an' me homesteaded the first quarter-section. . . . See that bunch of box-elders? Me an' her camped there as we druv in. . . . Never cut 'em down. . . . Spoil an acre of good corn land, too; to say nothin' o' the time wasted cultivatin' 'round 'em. . . . Well, a man's a fool about some things!"

It was a picture of fulsome plenty and riotous fertility. Straight as the stretched cord by which they had been dropped ran the soldierly rows of corn, a mile along, their dark blades outstretched in the unwavering prairie wind, as if pointing us on to something noteworthy or mysterious beyond. Back and forth along the rows plodded the heavy teams of the cultivators, stirring the brown earth to a deeper brownness. High fences of woven wire divided the spacious fields. On a hundred-acre meadow, as square and level as a billiard table, were piled the dark cocks of a second crop of alfalfa. One, two, three farmsteads we passed, each with its white house hidden in trees, its big red barns, its low hog-houses, its feed yards, with their racks polished by the soft necks of feasting steers. And everywhere was the corn—the golden corn of last year in huge cribs like barracks; the emerald hosts of the new crop in its ranks like green-suited lines-of-battle arrested in full career and held as by some spell, leaning onward in act of marching, every quivering sword pointing mysteriously forward. My heart of a farmer swelled within me at the scene, which had something in it akin to its owner, it was so huge, so opulent, so illimitable. Somehow, it seemed to interpret him to me.

"Purty good little places," said he; "but the home place skins 'em all. We'll be to it in a minute. Train slows up f'r a piece o' new track work. We'll git a good view of it."

Heaving himself up, he went before me down the aisle of the slowing train. There stood the soldiers on the steps and the platform. We took our places back of them. I was absorbed in the study of the splendid farm, redeemed from the lost wilderness by this man who had all at once become worth while to me. Back at the rear of the near-by fields was a row of lofty cottonwoods, waving their high crests in the steady wind. All about the central grove were pastures, meadows, gardens and orchards. A dense coppice of red cedars enclosed on three sides a big feed-yard, in which, stuffing themselves on corn and alfalfa, or lying in the dusty straw, were grouped a hundred bovine aristocrats in stately unconcern of the rotund Poland-Chinas about them. In the pastures were colts as huge as dray-horses, shaking the earth in their clumsy play. There were barns and barns and barns—capacious red structures, with hay-forks rigged under their projecting gables; and, in the midst of all this foison, stood the house—square, roomy, of red brick, with a broad porch on two sides covered with climbing roses and vines.

On this veranda was a thing that looked like a Morris chair holding a figure clad in khaki. A stooped, slender, white-haired woman hovered about the chair; and down by the track, as if to view the passing train, stood a young woman who was tall and swarthy and of ample proportions. Her dress was artistically adapted to country wear; she looked well-groomed and finished. She was smiling as the train drew slowly past, but I was sure that her eyes were full of tears. I wondered why she looked with such intentness at the platform—until I saw what the soldiers were doing. They stood at attention, their hands to their service-hats, stiff, erect, military. The girl returned the salute, and pointed to the chair on the veranda, put her handkerchief to her eyes, and shook her head as if in apology for the man in khaki. And while she stood thus the man in khaki leaned forward in the Morris chair, laid hold of the column of the veranda, pulled himself to his feet, staggered forward a step, balanced himself as if with difficulty, and—saluted.

The soldiers on the platform swung their hats and cheered, and I joined in the cheer. One of the good fellows wiped his eyes. The big farmer stood partly inside the door, effectually blocking it, and quite out of the girl's sight, looking on, as impassive as a cliff. The pretty young woman picked up a parcel —the offering—which one of the soldiers tossed to her feet, looked after us smiling and waving her handkerchief, and ran back toward the house. The train picked up speed and whisked us out of sight just as the khaki man sank back into the chair, eased down by the woman with the white hair. I seemed to have seen a death.

"That was mother," said the man of the broad farms, as we resumed our seats—"mother and Jack . . . jest as it always hes been. . . . Al'ays mother's boy. . . . The soldiers comin' from the war al'ays stand on the platform as they go by—if they's room enough—with their fingers to their hats in that fool way. . . . All seem to know where Jack is someway, no matter what rig'ment they belong to. . . . Humph!

"It's something he done in the Philippines . . . in the islands. . . . I don't know where they are. . . . Off Spain way, I guess. . . . They's a kind of yellow nigger there, an' Jack seemed to do well fightin' 'em. . . . They're little fellers something like his size, you know. . . . Some high officer ordered him to take a nigger king on an island once; an' as I understand it, the niggers was too many f'r his gang o' soldiers. So Jack went alone an' took him right out of his own camp. . . . I reckon any one could 'a' done the same thing with Uncle Sam backin' him; but the president, 'r congress, 'r the secretary of war thought it was quite a trick. . . . I s'pose Jack's shootin' a nigger officer right under the king's nose made it a better grandstand play. . . . Anyhow, Jack went out a private, an' come back a captain; an' every soldier that rides these cars salutes as he passes the house, whuther Jack's in sight 'r not. . . . Funny! . . . All kinds o' folks to make a world!"

"Then," said I, for I knew the story, of course,

when he mentioned the circumstances, "your son Jack is Captain John Hawes?"

He nodded slowly, without looking at me.

"And that beautiful, strong girl?" I inquired.

"Jack's wife," said he. "All right to look at, ain't she? Lived in New York . . . 'r Boston, I f'rgit which. . . . Folks well fixed. . . . Met Jack in Sanfrisco and married him when he couldn't lift his hand to his head. . . . She'd make a good farm woman. . . . Good stuff in her. . . . What ails him? Some kind o' poison that was in the knife the nigger soaked him with when he took that there king . . . stabbed Jack jest before Jack shot. . . . Foolish to let him git in so clost; but Jack never hed no decision. . . . Al'ays whifflin' around. . . . If he pulls through, though, that girl'll make a man of him if anything kin. . . . She thinks he's all right now . . . proud of him as Chloe of a yaller dress. . . . Went to Sanfrisco when he was broke an' dyin', they thought, an' all that, an' begged him as an honor to let her bear his name an' nuss him. . . . And she knew how wuthless he was before the war, an' throwed him over. . . . Sensible girl . . . then . . . I—"

He was gazing at nothing again, and I thought the story ended, when he began on an entirely new subject, as it seemed to me, until the relation appeared.

"Religion," said he, "is something I don't take no stock in, an' never did. . . . Religious folks don't seem any better than the rest. . . . But mother al'ays set a heap by religion. . . . I al'ays paid my dues in the church and called it square. . . . May be something in it f'r some, but not f'r me. I got to hev something I can git a-holt of. . . . Al'ays looked a good deal like graft to me . . . but I pay as much as any one in the congregation, an' maybe a leetle more—it pleases mother. . . . An' so does Jack's gittin' religion. . . . Got it, all right. . . . Pleases mother, too. . . . Immense! . . . But I don't take no stock in it.

"The doc says he's bad off."

I had not asked the question; but he seemed to feel a necessary inquiry in the tableau I had seen.

"He used to come down to the track when he first got back an' perform that fool trick with his hand to his hat when the soldiers went by an' they let him know. . . . Too weak, now; . . . failin'. . . . Girl's al'ays there, though, when she knows.

. . . Kind o' hope he'll—he'll—he'll . . . You know, neighbor, from what she's done f'r him, how mother must love him!"

We had come to the end of his journey, now—a little country station—and he left the train without a word to me or a backward look, his huge hat drawn down over his eyes. I felt that I had seen a curious, dark, dramatic, badly-drawn, wildly-conceived and Dantesque painting. He climbed into a carriage which stood by the platform, and to which was harnessed a pair of magnificent coach-bred horses which plunged and reared fearfully as the train swept into the station, and were held, easily and by main strength, like dogs or sheep, by a giant in the conveyance who must have been Tom or Wallace. From time to time, the steeds gathered their feet together, trampled the earth in terror, and then surged on the bits. The giant never deigned even to look at them. He held the lines, stiff as iron straps, in one hand, took his father's bag in the other, threw the big horses to the right by a cruel wrench of the lines to make room for his father to climb in, which he did without a word. As the springs went down under the weight the horses dashed away like the wind, the young man guiding them by that iron right hand with facile horsemanship, and looking, not at the road, but at his father. As they passed out of sight the father of Captain Hawes turned, looked at me, and waved his hand. I thought I had seen him for the last time, and went back to get the story from the soldiers.

"It wasn't so much the way he brought the datto into camp," said one of them, "or the way he always worked his way to the last bally front peak of the fighting line. It takes a guy with guts to do them things; but that goes with the game—understand? But he knew more'n anybody in the regiment about keepin' well. He made the boys take care of themselves. When a man is layin' awake scheming to keep the men busy and healthy, there's always a job for him. . . . And he had a way of making the boys keep their promises. . . . And he's come home to die, and leave that girl of his—and all the chances he's had in a business way if he wants to leave the army. It don't seem right! The boys say the president has invited him to lunch; and he's got sugar-plantation and minin' jobs open to him till you can't rest. . . . And to be done by a cussed poison Moro kris! But he got Mr. Moro—

played even; an' that's as good as a man can ask, I guess. Hell, how slow this train goes!"

As I have said, I never expected to see my big farmer again; but I did. I completed my business; returned the way I came, passed the great farm after dusk, and the next morning was in the city where I first saw him. Looking ahead as I passed along the street I noticed, towering above every form, and moving in the press like a three-horse van among baby carriages, the vast bulk of the captain's father. He turned aside into a marble-cutter's yard, and stood, looking at the memorial monuments which quite filled it until it looked like a cemetery vastly overplanted. I felt disposed to renew our acquaintance, and spoke to him. He offered me his hand, and when I accepted it he stood clinging to mine, standing a little stooped, the eyes bloodshot, the iron mouth pitifully drooped at the corners, the whole man reminding me of a towering cliff shaken by an earthquake, but mighty and imposing still. He held a paper in his free hand, which he examined closely while retaining the handclasp, and in a way I had come to expect of him, he commenced in the midst of his thought and without verbal salutation.

"We've buried Jack!" said he.

"I'm deeply sorry!" said I.

"Well," said he, "maybe it's just as well. . . . He was . . . you know! . . . But mother takes it hard—hard! . . . I'm contractin' f'r a tombstun. . . . He wanted to see me . . . at the last. . . . 'Dad,' says he, jest as he used to when he was . . . was a little feller, . . . 'I want you to forgive me before I die. . . . It's a big country where I'm going, . . . an' . . . you and I may never run into each other—so forgive me! Mother'll find me—wherever I go . . . but you, Dad, . . . for fear it's our last chance, let's square up now!' . . . I . . . I . . ."

He went out among the stones and seemed to be looking the stock over. Presently, he returned and showed me the paper. It was what a printer would call "copy" for an inscription—the name, the dates, the age of Captain John Hawes—severe, laconic. At the bottom were two or three lines scrawled in a heavy, ponderous hand, with the half-inch lead of a lumber pencil. Only one fist could produce that Polyphemus chirography.

"He went out a private," it read, *"and came back a captain."* And then, as if by afterthought, and in huge capitals, came the line: *"And died a Christian."*

"Is that all right?" he asked. "Is the spellin' all right? . . . I don't care much about this soldier business . . . an' the Christian game . . . don't interest me . . . a little bit, . . . but, neighbor, you don't know how that'll please mother! 'Died a Christian!' . . . Someway . . . mother . . . always loved Jack!"

At the turning of the street I looked and saw the last scene of the drama—one that will play itself before me from time to time in retrospect for ever. The great, unhewn, mountainous block was still there, standing among his more shapely and polished brother stones, a human monolith, the poor, pitiful paper in his trembling hand.

CHAPTER V

"I FIND myself," said the Driver, at the next session of the Scheherazade Society, as Colonel Baggs called their camp-fires, "in a whale of a dilemmer. I have never had nothin' happen to me worth tellin'. I have punched cows till this dry farmin' made it necessary to take to some more humble callin', and there's nothin' to cow-punchin' that is interestin'.

"I have showed you here in the Upper Geyser Basin fifteen geysers of the first magnitude, an' a hundred smaller ones; I have showed you Old Faithful, the Giant, the Giantess, the Fan and the Riverside. I have showed you the Grotto Geyser, which is a cross between a geyser and a cave. I have showed you the quiescent spring at its best—the Morning Glory pool with more colors than any rainbow ever had. I've showed you jewels and giants and ogres and sprites, and—"

"Here!" shouted the Groom. "Saw off on that

professional patter! You're not the driver now, but Aconite Driscoll, the Cow-boy, and telling us the story of your life. We have seen more things here than Münchhausen, Gulliver, Mandeville, Old Jim Bridger and the whole brood of romancers ever could imagine. Give us some North American facts, now."

"Well, if I must, I must," said poor Aconite. "But there's nothin' to it. I reckon I'd better narrate to you some of the humble doin's of the J-Up-and-Down Ranch over on Wolf Nose Crick, in the foot-hills of the Black Hills—in the dear, dead past beyond recall—thanks to the Campbell method of dry farmin'."

THE TALE OF TEN THOUSAND DOGIES

THE TALE TOLD BY THE DRIVER

The way I gets into this story is a shame an' disgrace, an' is incompetent, irreverent, an' immaterial, an' not of record in this case.

Eh? Adds color to the—which? Narrative! Well, I d'n' know about that. I reely couldn't say as it does.

But mentionin' color, the thought of that little affair do make my face as red as a cow-town on pay-day. When I turn that tale loose we'll make a one-night stand of it by the grub-wagon. It comprises a shipper's pass to Sioux City, a sure-thing game in that moral town, which I win out by backin' my judgment with my Colt, an' a police court wherein the bank roll and my pile was rake-off for the court. Charge, gamblin'. All hands plead guilty. All correct says you, an' quite accordin' to the statues made an' pervided; an' so says I, ontil I casually picks up a paper in Belle Fourche, an' sees that it was a phoney police court, not only owned and controlled by the shell men, which wouldn't be surprisin', but privately installed as a sort of accident insurance on their other game.

"Hell hath no fury like a woman scorned," Mr. Elkins remarks to me one day, but all that is goin' to be changed when I ketch up with that police judge.

Ridin' the range makes a man talkative with the scenery, an' when I sees that Sioux City paper, I turns loose some remarks in the presence of a gentleman who subsequently turns out to be Mr. Elkins.

"Thanks," says he.

"When did you acquire any chips in this little solitaire blasphemy game?" says I, mad, as a man allus is if he's ketched solloloquisin' to himself.

"A man," says he, "with all the sidetracks filled with cars o' cattle an' more comin', an' no gang, is in, *ex proprio vigore*," says he, whatever that means, "anywhere where cuss-words is trumps."

He never smiled except back in his eyes, an' I, likin' his style, hires out to him, an' was third man on the J-Up-And-Down Ranch from the day the dogies begun to be unloaded, till James R. Elkins went to New York, with a roll that would choke a blood-sweatin' hippopotamus.

Third man, says I, an' if you think the first was the Old Man, J. R. E., you know, you've got another conjecture comin'. Number One was Mrs. Elkins, an' I reckon some of her New York friends'll enter into conniptions to know that, in lessn' a year, half the boys called her Josie—in their dreams, at least— an' some on 'em to her face; but none to her back, by a damsite! The Old Man—a lot of us called him Jim habitual—was a one-lunger when this dogie enterprise started, all mashed in body in the collapse of the boom at Lattimore; an' them as thinks I refer to any loggin' accident is informed that I mean the town-lot boom in the city of Lattimore, as is more fully set forth elsewhere, the same bein' made by reference a part hereof, marked "Exhibit A," which explains the broken bones aforesaid—

"If there's no objection," said Colonel Baggs, in a high court-room singsong, " 'Exhibit A' will be received in evidence. G'long, Aconite!"

Financially, he was millions worse than nothing, if you can understand that. Personally, I caint. Zero is the bottom of the spondulix scale fer me, although the thummometer seems to prove it ain't necessarily thus. Anyhow, the Old Man had Josie, an' any man from Sturgis to Dog Den Buttes would have shouldered all Mr. Elkins' shrinkages, especially the below-zero part, to've had her jest once smooth the hair off his beaded brow, let alone take charge of him like a Her'ford heifer does her fust calf. Which is sure the manner Josie took a-holt and managed the Old Man. But this hain't no love story. Quite the reverse. It's the "Tale of Ten Thousand Dogies."

I found out that when Mr. E. went into the bulb in a business way, this Wolf Nose Crick Ranch went around bankruptcy, instid of through it, becuz, mostly, nobody thought it wuth a—a thought. An' to them as think strange of ten thousand steers, even dogies, bein' bought by a busted boomer, I'll state that any man with the same range, an' not absolutely a convicted hoss-thief, could've got 'em by givin' the same cutthroat chattel mawgitch. Old Aleck Macdonald did sure sell 'em to Mr. Elkins reasonable, though, because James R. had made him a good deal of money in this boom, an' they was only dogies anyhow.

Now, this bein' my evenin' fer tellin' the truth, I'll state that ten thousand dogies is sure a complicated problem on the range. The distinction between them an' reg'lar native range cows lays in the lap o' luxury in which the dogies is dangled in the farmin' regions where they originate. The first little blizzard, they'll hump up an' blat fer home an' mother. They'll gaze fondly at a butte ten mile off, expectin' doors in it to slide open, an' racks full of clover an' timothy to pull out an' be forked out to 'em. They look grieved an' wring their jaws becuz water with the chill took off ain't piped to their stalls, an' they moan 'cause they ain't no stalls. I'd as soon run a Women's an' Babies' Home. You cain't get it into their heads where the water-holes is, an' it's allus an even break whuther they'll stan' an' freeze in their tracks, or chase after some bunch of 2:10 natives ontil their hooves drop off. That's why Macdonald talked as he did about 'em, as I'm informed.

"Take 'em," says he, "an' don't flatter yourself I'm donatin' anything. They's no feed fer 'em in their native Iowa at any livin' price, an' on the other hand, fifty per cent. of 'em'll die gettin' over their homesickness on the range. You'll have it in fer me fer stickin' you, when you know more about the cattle business. Fer the Lord's sake take 'em before they eat me out of every dollar I've got left!"

Some of this was straight goods, an' some stall; but that first winter was a special providence if they ever was one. So mild and barmy from September to March that the prairie-dogs forgot to hole up, an' Mrs. Elkins served Thanksgivin' dinner in the open air on the pizziazzy at the Ranch. An' she rode the range with Jim consecutively, an' said she'd found her 'finity in this cattle biz. As for him, the main thing the matter was that failure o' his a-millin' through his mental facilities. But this was their honeymoon, we found, an' that, an' no losses on the range, helped his case, an' by spring he begun to shoot the persiflage into the gang, an' set up an' reach for things to beat fours. As for the dogies, none of 'em had the faintest show fer a beller. The grass was like new-mown hay; every little snow was follered by a chinook; the water-holes was brimmin'; an' all went merry as a marriage bell.

"The fact is, Aconite," says Mr. Elkins, addressin' me, "I knew when I heard that burst of phonetic lava from your lips at Belle Fourche, that there'd be no fear of low temperatures if you could be induced to stay by the cows, and blow off once in a while."

He had the hot air under wonderful control, hisself, an' felt good at the way the stock was comin' on—March, April, May, an' fresh feed, ponds full o' ducks, cute little young wolves about the dens, an' every one o' the ten thousand dogies stretchin' to see hisself grow. But the fall—the fall was sure a bad one fer both feed an' water. The dogies, however, couldn't fairly be called such any longer, havin' recovered from what Jim called their acute nostalgia, an' bein' pret' near's good rustlers as natives. An' well it was fer 'em, fer grass was sca'ce, an' a son-of-a-gun of a while between drinks. After you got away from the crick—an' you jist *had* to git away f'r grass—it was a good day's ride to water, east, west, north, south, up'r down. On the hay-slews we had to prime the rake with old hay 'fore we could make a windrow. Laff if you want to, but they was whole outfits with less hay than some folks has gover'ment bonds. We had about enough to wad a shotgun, an' was merchant princes in the fodder line. The steers, lookin' like semi-animated hat-racks, as the Old Man said, come through the cold weather in a shrinkin' an' sylph-like way, so thin that you could throw a bull by the tail a dum sight furder'n I'd trust some folks, an' that's no dream!

By this time Mr. Elkins was a sure-enough cowman, president of the Association and the biggest man from Spearfish to Jackson's Hole. He knew some confounded joke on every man in the cow-country, an' not only called 'em all by their fust name, but had one of his own f'r most of 'em. Mrs. Elkins, havin' pulled him through his own dogy stage, dropped out of the cow business, an' devoted herself to kids. I knew that this dogy proposition was a sort of a straw that Jim Elkins grabbed at as he went under, an' it done me an' all the fellers good to see the percentage of loss so small, even if the brutes wasn't puttin' on weight as they orto, an' the price was away down, an' we knew we shouldn't be ready to sell when the mawgitch got ripe. Old Macdonald was Jim's friend, though, an' would sure extend the note when it come of age; an' fur's we could see, these dry seasons was only delayin' the clean-up.

So I thought, an' so thought the Elkins family, as peaceful as a Injun summer morn, an' as happy as skunks. But along in June of the third year, just in the last of the round-up, out comes what Elkins called our Nemmysis in the form of a jackleg lawyer with news of Macdonald's death, and papers to prove it, an' him appointed executioner of the estate of A. Macdonald, diseased. He wanted to see the cattle the estate had a mawgitch on. I was app'inted as his chaperon to show him the stock, an' it bein' a hurryin' time o' year, I exhibited to him ten 'r 'leven thousand head of mixed pickles, and called it square. He didn't know a cow-brand from one plucked from the burnin', an' credited us with a township or two of O-Bar-X cow stuff I run him into the first day out. I didn't feel that he was wuth payin' much notice to, if he hadn't had the say about the Old Man's mawgitch.

I gathered from him that he was goin' to rearlize on the outfit in the fall. I went so fur as to p'int out what a grave-robbin' scheme this was, an' how this dogy stuff had been kep' in the livin' skelliton department f'r two years by drouth an' a hell-slew of other troubles, an' couldn't possibly do more than pay off the mawgitch, an' leave us holdin' the bag in the wust country f'r snipe outside of the Mojave desert.

"They'll pay out," says he, "an' that's all I'm required to look out fer."

I swear, I was prospectin' f'r a good hole to plant him in all the rest o' the trip. I goes right to the ranch when we pulled in. The Old Man an' Josie was a-sittin' in the firelight, an' she had the baby, a yearlin' on her lap, and the boy, a long two-year-old, in the crib. Outside of a nest o' young wild ducks, I never seen anything softer and cuter. I reports an' asks instructions as to the best way of disposin' of Mr. Jackleg's remains.

"Quicklime," says he ruminatin'ly, "is a good and well-recognized scheme; but we haven't any, Aconite, have we? Or we might incorporate him into that burnin' lignite bed over in the butte. Boxin' him up an' shippin' him to fictitious consignees involves a trip to the railroad, an' creatin', as it does, a bad odor, an' stickin' a strugglin' railroad company for the freight, it never seemed to me quite the Christian thing. Don't you agree with me, Aconite?"

"Now, the God's truth is, I was speakin' parabolically about this projected homicide, but no man can bluff *me,* an' when the Old Man seemed to fall in with it in that heart-to-heart way, I made a lightnin' cat-hop, an' told him as sober as a Keeley alumnus that the lignite bed seemed most judicious to me, an' when should we load up the catafalque? Then Mrs. E. breaks in with a sort o' gugglin' laugh.

"Jim," says she, "you ought to be ashamed of yourself! Mr. Driscoll," addressin' me by my name, which never was Aconite, reely, "Mr. Driscoll, Mr. Elkins is not serious in his remarks."

"Neither'm I," says I.

"Of course not," says she. "We fully understand that."

"Sure," says the Old Man. "Let the lawyer take its course. Which will be assumin' possession of the ten thousand dogies; and I feel sure he'll want to leave you in charge of 'em. He's stuck on you, Aconite."

"See him in Helena fust," says I.

"But wait a minute," says Mr. Elkins. "Somebody's got to take charge of this stuff for the mortgagee, if he keeps on thinkin' as he does now. You're our friend. It'll be more agreeable in every way to have you than, say, Bill Skeels, of the O-Bar-X."

Of course I gets roped, throwed an' branded at last, an' Mr. Jackleg goes away takin' my receipt f'r ten thousand head, more or less, of steers branded "Jƒ" known in the cattle business as "J-Up-And-Down," the same bein' on the ranges at the headwaters of the Cheyenne, Moreau, Little Missouri, an' other streams, an' God knows where else, more definitely described in a certain indenture of mawgitch, and so forth and so on, till death comes to your relief. An' James R. Elkins was reduced to a few hundred white faces he'd put in as a side-line, an' I feelin' like a sheepman unmasked!

Mr. Jackleg—his real name turned out to be Witherspoon—give me his instructions from the buckboard as he prepares to pull out, in the presence of the Old Man an' Mrs. E.

"I was fetched up on a farm," says he, an' he looked the part, "an' I know a good deal about cattle. Every animal should hev water at least twice a day."

"I'll personally see to it," says I, winkin' at the

Old Man, "that every steer has a crack at the growler at least semi-daily."

"Another thing," says he; "I knew a herd-boy that run a bunch of fifty cows practically dry by holdin' 'em in too close a bunch on the prairie. Let 'em spread out so's to give 'em room to graze."

"Well, fer Gawd's sake!" says I, thinkin' of the feller's sanity; an' before I could finish my yawp, off he pelts, leavin' me gaspin'.

"Wake up," says Elkins, shakin' me by the shoulder. "If you git 'em all watered by bed-time, you'll have to git busy."

He sure is a good loser, thinks I, ontil I figgered that with Josie an' the kids counted in, he hadn't been pried loose from any great percentage of his holdin's after all.

Now, the idee was to round up an' ship about the first of December, so the estate could be wound up at the January term o' court. Pretty soon things seemed about as they was before. I went to the Old Man for orders, an' Mr. Jackleg's visit seemed, as Mrs. E. once said, like a badly-drawn dream. Every time I went to J. R. E. he says to me that I'm boss, an' to remember my instructions.

"Obey orders," says he, "if it busts owners."

Grass an' water was plenty ag'in, and the dogies was fattin' up. Round-up was drawin' on just as prospects f'r profit begins to brighten. It seemed a sort of a hash of midnight assassination, poisonin' water-holes, givin' away a podner, an' keepin' sheep, to ship them ten thousand then. An' all the time the Old Man was a-bearin' down about obeyin' orders, and beggin' me to remember Mr. Jackleg's partin' words, an' repeatin' that sayin' about obeyin' orders if it busted owners. The thing kep' millin' an' millin' in my brain till I got into the habit of settin' around an' sweatin' heinyous, ontil I'd come to with a start, in the middle of a pool of self-evolved moisture filled with wavin' rushes, an' embosomin' acres of floatin' water-lilies! That's the sort of sweater I am when a little worried. Fin'ly I turned on the Old Man like a worm—a reg'lar spiral still-worm.

"How in everlastin' fire," says I, not just like that, "am I to see that every dogy gits two swigs a day on these prairies, an' wherein am I to take any notice of that shyster's fool talk about rangin' wide?"

"Well," says he, "you know there's pools an' water-holes scattered from here to the Canada line, an' from the Missouri to the Continental Divide. A few head, dropped here an' there, handy to water, would be apt to live more accordin' to the hydropathic ideas of the executor of the will of A. Macdonald, diseased. At the same time you would be conformin' to his remarkable correct hyjeenic notions as to segregation."

"Hyjeenic y'r grandmother!" says I, f'r the sitiwation called f'r strong language. "They couldn't be rounded up in a year; an' it's damn nonsense, anyhow, to foller the so-called idees of a—"

"Oh, I see," says he, in a sort of significant way. "I see: it would be a slow round-up. Maybe my intrusts blinds me to those of the people you represent. A slow round-up wouldn't hurt me any! But, of course, you stan' f'r the mawgitchee's intrusts, an' are nat'rally hostyle—"

I set sort o' numbed f'r a minute. A new thing was a-happenin' to me, to wit, an idee was workin' itself into my self-sealin', air-tight, shot-proof, Harveyized skull. Talk about your floods o' light! I got what Doc calls a Noachian deluge of it right then.

"Sir," says I, " 'an' Madam, truly' "—quotin' from a pome Mrs. E. had been readin'—"I *think* I see my duty clear at last! If I fin'ly *hev* grasped it, my labors requires my absence," says I, "an' I'll see you later."

Mr. Elkins laughed a sort of a Van Triloquist's chuckle. Josie Elkins comes up, an' stannin' close to me in that maddenin' way o' hern, sort o's if she's climbin' into your vest pocket, she squose my hand, an' says she, "Mr. Driscoll, we know that you'll be true to any trust reposed in you! An' to your friends!" An' at the word "friends" she sort of made sunbeams from her eyes to mine, an' pressed my hand before breakin' away, as much as to say that, speakin' o' friends, the ones that had reely drunk from the same canteen an' robbed watermelon patches together from earliest infancy was her an' me. Holy Mackinaw! I went out into the wilderness givin' thanks an' singin' an' cussin' myself, at peace with all the world.

I flatter myself that the work done upon, or emanatin' from the J-Up-And-Down Ranch from that time, f'r a spell, stands in a class by itself in cow-country annuals. It begins with a sort o' quarterly conference of the punchers. I gives 'em a sermon something as follers:

"Fellers," says I, "it's been borne in upon me that these dogies need drivin' where they's fewer cows to the cubic inch o' water. Moreover, they're in too much of a huddle. Here's the hull ten thousand cooped up within twenty to thirty mile of the spot whereon we stand. You cain't swing a bob-cat by the tail," says I, "without scratchin' their eyes out. It vi'lates the crowded tenement laws. It corrupts the poor little innercent calves. It's a Mulberry Street shame. You are therefore ordered an' directed to disseminate these beeves over a wider expanse of the moral heritage. You, Doc, take Ole an' the Greaser, an' goin' south an' west with as many as you can round up, drop off a carload 'r so at every waterin' place an' summer resort up the Belle Fourche an' the North Fork, over onto the Powder, an' as fur as Sheridan. When yeh git short o' cows, come back f'r more. There ain't no real limits to yer efforts short o' the Yellowstone. We must obey Mr. Jackleg's orders about huddlin'. I'll give Absalom an' Pike the Little Missouri, the Cannon Ball and the Grand valleys. Git what help you need; I grant power to each of yeh to send f'r persons an' papers an' administer oaths, if necessary. I'll take my crew an' try to gladden the waste places along the Moreau an' Cheyenne an' White Rivers with dogies. Get your gangs, an' scatter seeds o' kindness an' long four-year-olds from hell to breakfast. For as yeh sow even shall yeh reap. If a critter smothers from crowdin' sev'ral to a township these hot nights, somebody's goin' to be held personally responsible to *me*. You hear, I s'pose?"

"Is this straight goods, Aconite?" says Doc.

"Am I a perfessional humorist," says I, "or am I the combined Fresh Air Fund, S. P. C. A., and Jacob A. Riis of these yere hills? Am I the main squeeze of this outfit, an' the head of a responsible gover'ment, or am I not? Hit the grit," says I, "an' begin irradiatin' steers."

Obedience is a lovely thing, fellers, an' a man poised in an air-ship a few thousan' feet above a given pi'nt som'eres in the neighborhood o' the Hay Stack Buttes, armed with a good long-range peekeriscope, might have observed a beautiful outbust of it, all that golding autumn, on the part of a class of men presumably onsubordinate—the ungrammatical but warm-hearted cow-boys. They preached a mixed assortment o' fair-to-middlin' steers unto all men. The Ten Thousand was absorbed into the landscape of four great states, like a ship-load o' Swedes into the Republican party. The brethren of the ranches heared gladly the gospel of obeyin' orders, an' wherever a wisp of cows amountin' to more than a double handful congregated together in one place, there was some obejient son of a gun in the midst of 'em, movin' 'em along towards the bubblin' springs, green fields an' pastors new of Mr. Jackleg's orders. It was touchin'. I never felt so good, so sort o' glory-hallelujahish in my life, as I did a-ridin' back to Wolf Nose Crick in the brown October weather, with the dogies off my mind an' the map, thinkin' of how Mrs. E. had squoze my hand, sort o' weepful on moonlight nights, but stronger'n onions in a sense o' juty well performed.

You can sort o' dimly ketch onto the shock it was to me, a-drillin' into camp at Wolf Nose Crick in this yere peaceful frame of mind, to find Mr. Jackleg there, madder'n a massasauga, an' perfec'ly shameful in his feelin's towards *me*.

"Where's these ten thousand head o'cattle, Driscoll?" he hollers on seein' me. "Here's your receipt for 'em; where's the stock?"

"Calm yourself," says I, droppin' my hand to my gun; "the dogies is all right. The dogies is out yan in the most unhuddled state of any outfit on the range, fur from the slums of Wolf Nose Crick an' their corruptin' influences, drinkin' at the pure springs o' four great American commonwealths, layin' on fat like aldermen, an' in a advanced state of segregation. Your orders," says I, tickled to think how I'd remembered langwidge so fur above my station in life, "your orders was to put 'em next to the damp spots, an' keep 'em fur apart, an' has been obeyed regardless."

Up to that time I had looked upon him with contempt; but the way he turned in an' damned me showed how sorely I'd misjudged him. As my respect fer him riz, it grew important not to let him go on so, f'r I couldn't let any reel man talk to me that-a-way, an' in less time than it takes to mention it, I had the boys a-holdin' me, and Mr. Jackleg stannin' without hitchin'.

"I may hev been hasty in my remarks," says he; "but I've been out with all the men I could git f'r two weeks, an' how many of our herd do you s'pose I have been enabled to collect?"

"Not knowin', cain't say," says I.

"Just a hundred an' fifty-seven!" says he.

"Good!" says I. "You've got no kick comin'. I couldn't have done better myself. But you won't git as many in the next two weeks! Cheer up; the wust is yet to come!"

An' at that he flies off the handle ag'in, an' lights out f'r the East, with the estate all unwound, I s'pose.

Now, everybody knows the rest of this story. Everybody knows how grass an' water an' winters favored the range-stuff f'r the next two years. Them dogies was as well off 's if they'd been in upholstered sheds eatin' gilded hay. When ol' Dakoty starts out to kill stock, she reg'lar Mountain-Medders-Massacres 'em; but when she turns in to make a feed-yard of herself, she's a cow paradise without snakes. The hist'ry of these dogies illustrates this p'int, an' shows our beautiful system of enforcin' honesty in marketin' range cattle whereby the active robbery is confined to the stock-yards folks and the packers, where it won't do no moral harm. As was perfec'ly square an' right, the brand inspectors at Omaha, Sioux City, Chicago an' Kansas City was on the lookout f'r J-Up-And-Down steers in the intrusts of Mr. Jackleg's mawgitch; an' after every round-up, some on 'em would dribble in with the shipments, an' be sold an' proceeds gobbled accordin' to Hoyle. An' when things got good—dogies about the size of Norman hosses, an' as fat as Suffolk pigs —the word goes out from Wolf Nose Crick to every ranch on the range, that the anti-slum crusade was off, an' J-Up-And-Down stuff was to be shipped as rounded up. F'r weeks an' months, I'm told, pret' near every car had some of 'em. Top grassers, they was at last, in weight an' price, an' when the half of 'em was in, the estate of A. Macdonald, diseased, was wound up, tight as a drum, intrust an' principal, an' Jim Elkins had left a little trifle o' five thousand beeves, wuth around a hundred apiece, free an' clear, an' the record of Aconite Driscoll, as a philanthropist, a humannytarian, an' a practical-cowpuncher, was once more as clear as a Christian's eye.

An' this is how Jim Elkins got his ante in this New York game he's a-buckin' so successful. An' so it was that my little meet-up with a Sioux City shell-man, which I'm lookin' fer yit, results in a reg'lar Pullman sleeper trip to Chicago, where I'm the guest of honor at a feedin' contest instituted by Mr. James R. Elkins, whereat Mr. Jackleg—Witherspoon, I mean, and dead game after all, if any one should inquire—makes a talk about the pleasure it affords all of us to see our old friend Elkins restored to those financial circulars where he was so well known, an' so much at home; an' alludin' to me as restorer-in-chief by virtoo of my great feet, **an'** losin' ten thousand dogies so that Pinkerton himself couldn't find 'em ontil the wilderness saw fit to disgorge 'em in its own wild an' woolly way. An' fin'ly I'm called on an' made to git up, locoed at the strange grazin' ground, but game to do my best, an' after millin' awhile, "I'm here," says I, "owin' to my eckstrordinary talent f'r obeyin' orders. I'm told to come hither, an' I at once set out to prove my effectiveness as a come-hitherer. As f'r losin' ten thousand dogies, I cain't see what that has to do with my great feet. An' right here," I says, "I wish to state that I onst lost something else, to wit, my val'able temper at something done 'r said by a gentleman now present, for all of which I begs pardon of Mr. Jackleg—Mr. Witherspoon, I means," says I, an' everybody hollers an' pounds, him most of all, but redder'n a turkey, "an' I wish to state that it does me good to feel that harmony and peace between him an' me is restored. Here in Chicago," says I, "him an' me can git together on the platform of feedin' in bunches, without dehornin'; with the paramount issue to go before the people on, however, that old plank o' his'n declarin' f'r frekent drinks!"

After that, I don't remember what eventuated—not quite so clear.

"I told you," said the Bride, as the party broke up for the night, "that we'd get some local color."

"Alas!" replied the Artist. "This is like the local color of Babylon and the Shepherd Kings—a tradition and a whisper borne on the night breeze, of things that were. O, Remington! Remington!"

CHAPTER VI

PROFESSOR BOGGS was in a brown study from the time his name emerged from the hat on starting from the Upper Geyser Basin, until the equipage of the Seven Wonderers, as the Poet called the party, reached the Thumb Lunch Station on Yellowstone Lake, nineteen miles to the east—which drive they made between breakfast and luncheon. The Colonel had telephoned ahead for a special banquet for the eight that night, at which Professor Boggs was to tell his story, and civilized life was to be resumed for the nonce—"To prevent," as the Colonel explained, "our running wild so that we'll have to be blindfolded and backed onto the cars when we get back to Gardiner." All up the pleasant Firehole Valley, the Professor worked at a packet of papers which he took from his bag.

"I'll bet he gives us an essay on some phase of rural education," challenged the Artist, with no takers.

Past the exquisite Kepler Cascade they went, after a stop which filled all except the Hired Man and the Professor with delight. When the party alighted for the walk of half a mile to the Lone Star Geyser, these two remained with the surrey—the Professor busy, the Hired Man lazily smoking. His mental film-pack was exhausted. Spring Creek Cañon proved another of those comforting features which relieve the strain of constant astonishment in the Park—the narrow and winding cañon, with its homelike rocks and cliffs, topped by inky evergreens, shut them in like some comforting shelter against the tempest of the marvelous. Down this wild glen tumbled a clear stream of cold water, bordered with ferns, willows and alders. The Bride scooped up a little of the water in her hand and drank it.

"Isn't it funny?" she asked.

"Isn't what funny?" asked the Groom.

"To find water actually cool and clear, and flowing down a glen of just rocks, with no steam, or rainbow colors, or anything but good earth and stones? I feel like one just out of some sort of inferno."

"The first feller to roam these here hollers," said Aconite, "was a guy named John Colter. He came out with the Lewis and Clark expedition, and stopped on the way back to trap. That was about 1807. He got into the Park some way, and when he emerged he told of it. And there was where the fust reppytation for truth an' veracity was blighted by the p'isenous exhalations of this region of wonders."

"Was he Jimbridgered?" asked the Artist.

"Was he whiched?"

"Jimbridgered; Marcopoloed; Münchhausened; Mandevilled; Driscolled; placed in the Ananias Club?"

"He shore was," replied Aconite. "W'y this place was called Colter's Hell from Saint Joe to Salt Lake by them as didn't believe in it. 'Whar'd this eventuate?' a puncher'd say to a feller that had seen something. 'In Colter's Hell' another would say, meanin' that it never did occur—an' if he didn't smile when he said it, there'd be gun play. An' hyar was all them marvels that Colter'd seen, and more, all the time!"

At Craig Pass, the cayuses were stopped so that all might feast their eyes on the little Isa Lake, frowned on by stern precipices, but smiling up into the blue, its surface flecked with water-lilies.

"An' hyar," said Aconite, "we hev a body of water that at one end empties into the Atlantic Ocean's tributaries, an' at the other waters the Pacific slope."

"Which is which?" asked the Colonel.

"The east end runs into the Pacific, and the west into the Atlantic," replied Aconite, quite truthfully.

"What's that!" exclaimed the Hired Man. "Do yeh mean to say we've got over on the coast by drivin' east—toward Ioway?"

"You've said 'er," said Aconite.

"I tell you," said the Hired Man, as the others began studying their maps to clear up this geographic anomaly, "I tell you that there ain't no way of understandin' the 'tother-end-toness of this place, except by sayin' that the hull thing is a gigantic streak of nature."

"The most rational explanation," said the Groom, "that I've heard. Mr. Hired Man sets us all right. Drive on, Aconite!"

Down Corkscrew Hill they volplaned, thrilled and somewhat scared by the speed of the cayuses, which flew downward in joyful relief at the cessation of the uphill pull to the pass. At the bottom there was a halt to afford a glimpse of Shoshone Lake, and far off to the south the exquisite Tetons, their summits capped with pearl. The visit to Shoshone Lake with its gorgeous geysers was to be postponed until after they should arrive at the thumb of Yellowstone Lake, and make camp.

An hour of steady driving succeeded. They drowsed in their seats, torpid from the early start and the days of strenuous sight-seeing. The road ran through a quiet forest, and there was something not unpleasant in the fact that the curtain of trees shut off the view—until suddenly at a turn in the highway, there burst upon their sight that most marvelous of inland seas, Yellowstone Lake. Straight away extended its waters, for twenty miles, to the dim shores of Elk Point, where the pines carried the wonderful landscape upward, their gloom cutting straight across the view, between the mirror-like sheen of the lake, to timber-line on the azure Absarokas, standing serenely across the eastern sky, their serrated summits picked out with snow against the blue.

A huge chalice lay the lake, reared to a height of a mile and a half above the dusty and furrowed earth where folk plow and dig and make their livings, the crown jewel of the continent's diadem, unutterably, indescribably lovely, filled with crystalline dew. The tourists caught their breaths. Aconite said nothing. For a long time they stood, until the horses began to move backward and forward, uneasy at the unwonted stay. The Bride was holding the Groom's hand, her eyes glistening with tears.

They passed the lovely little Duck Lake, unmindful of its prettiness, and drew up at the lunch station, where they remained unconscious of their hunger until the memory of the splendors of the lake were first dulled, and then obliterated by the scent of the bacon which Aconite was frying. The Hired Man ate valiantly, lighted his pipe, and sighed.

"That was all right," said he.

"Thanks," said Aconite. "It cost forty cents a pound, an' orto be good."

"I meant," said the Hired Man, "that view o' the lake from back yonder."

Night brought dinner, and that appetite for it which outdoors gives to healthy folk, at eight thousand feet above the sea. After the eating was well and thoroughly done, the Professor responded to the call for his story. He rose solemnly, bowed to the assemblage, arranged his papers, cleared his throat, and began.

A BELATED REBEL INVASION

THE PROFESSOR'S STORY

Unlike the rest of you, I am no mere seeker after pleasure. I am an outcast from my native Iowa. I have held high and honorable office, and I have been treated as was Coriolanus of old. I am the victim of the ingratitude of republics, as expressed in a direct primary in Stevens County, Iowa. I am on my way to the great new West, where I shall seek to serve newer communities where perfidy may not be so ingrained in the nature of the body politic. And I shall shun relations other than professional ones, with persons of youth, beauty, charm, and feminine gender. For by these I am a sufferer. I have with me my notes, and to you is given the first hearing of my side of a case which may become historic.

"The contest is unequal," says Epictetus, "between a charming young girl and a beginner in philosophy." Let this be remembered when I am blamed for the havoc wrought upon my political educational career in Stevens County, Iowa, by Miss

Roberta Lee Frayn of Tennessee. Not that I am a beginner in philosophy. The man who, at my age, has been elected county superintendent of schools is no mere tyro in the field wherein Epictetus so distinguished himself. But neither does the word "charming" adequately describe Miss Frayn, unless one trace back the word "charm" to its more diabolically significant root. I expect to write this, my *apologia*, and leave the verdict to posterity.

No citizen of Stevens County is likely to be ignorant of the manner in which Miss Frayn was deposited in my mother's farmyard by the wrecking of a railway train, or how her grandfather, Colonel Kenton Yell Frayn, died there in her arms and left the young girl penniless. Judge Worthington, hereafter to be mentioned, was on the train and doubtless assisted in extricating Miss Frayn and her grandfather from the wreckage, but I feel that my own efforts were more effective than was reported. We left the young woman in the care of my mother, and I took the judge with me in my buggy.

He was much distraught as we rode along. I tried to say something in the way of furthering my candidacy for the office I now hold; but he repulsed me.

"For God's sake, Oscar," I remember him to have

said, "don't try to electioneer me until I can get out of my mind the image of that poor young girl and her dying grandfather!"

I do not care to criticize the judiciary, but will say that Judge Worthington's early promotion to the bench and his undeniable comeliness of person have in a measure induced in him a certain arrogance.

I was triumphantly elected. I went to Boston and won recognition so far as to be placed on the sub-committee for the investigation of Tone-Deafness in the rural schools, in the superintendents' section of the National Teachers' Association.

"Gee!" ejaculated the Hired Man.

Feeling the growing breadth and fullness of life I returned and assumed my office. Then it was that the Frayn episode may be said to have begun, in a letter from my brother Chester, which I have here, and which runs, using an undignified diminutive:

"Dear Oc:
"We would like to see you. Mother and all are well, and glad you pulled through, even if you did run behind the ticket so. Am feeding three loads of steers, and they are making a fine gain. Middlekauff's look rough, and all the feeders think he'll lose money on them. He paid four cents for them. This is about all the news. Can't you appoint me

your deputy down here to examine Miss Frayn, whose grandfather got killed in that wreck? She wants to teach. She is a Southerner, but an awful nice lady, and just as smart as one of us. She dreads to go to Pacific City to be examined, as she won't let ma get her hardly any clothes. She is very sensitive about money matters, and I had to lie to her about the funds to bury her grandfather with, and tried to slip in $250 more, but she caught me at it and cried. I will be strict and make her write out the examination properly; so send along the questions, and the appointment.

"Yours truly, CHET.

"P. S.—Judge Worthington's office is so near yours, you might leave the appointment and the questions in there. The judge will bring them down. He comes down quite often now, because he says that the Boggses and the Worthingtons moved into Iowa in the same wagon train in an early day, and he thinks it strange that that accident that killed Colonel Frayn should have brought the families together again. He thinks that Miss Frayn will make a first-rate teacher, so you need not be backward about the appointment and the questions."

Not abating one jot or tittle of my official strictness, I informed Chester that Miss Frayn must appear and be examined as did others in the same situation. Chester is an Ames man, and a fine judger and feeder of cattle, but not fitted for responsibility in *belles-lettres*.

Professor Dustin, an elderly and myopic educator and the author of a monograph on the Grübe method, had charge of the examination when Miss Frayn appeared. I found Chester smoking a vile pipe in my lodgings when I came home.

"Say, Oc," said he, "this four-eyed old trilobite won't do. You've got to get in here and do business yourself."

Conjecturing that he meant Professor Dustin, I inferred that Miss Frayn's papers had been rejected. A glance justified the professor. She had given Richmond as the capital of the United States. A question in physiology called for a description of the iris, and Miss Frayn had answered that, further than that, "she" was a naiad, a dryad, or a nymph, and was pursued by Boreas, or Eolus, or Zephyrus until, turned into a flower, she could say nothing about Iris. The handwriting and drawing were beautiful; but the pages of mathematics were mostly blank, save for certain splashy discolorations presumably of lachrymatory origin, denoting lack of self-control and scholastic weakness.

"It is absurd," said I, "to think of certifying her. While she has a certain measure of intelligence—"

"A certain measure!" shouted Chester. "If you

weren't a natural-born saphead, I'd—! Come up to Aunt Judith's!"

I went with him, firm in that solid self-control which gives fixity of character to my nature. I saw in its true light the amiable weakness of my relatives which made them slaves to this girl. I felt as stern and austere as a public officer should, and looked it, I believe, for mother was quite in a flutter as she asked me to read a clipping from an eastern Tennessee paper describing the departure from that region of the Frayns.

From this I learned that Miss Frayn and the colonel had been the last of the Frayns, the family having been exterminated in the Frayn-Harrod feud. The colonel had been an engineer in Lee's army. He had given public notice on leaving that at noon he would nail to the front door of the court-house, with the revolver of Boone Harrod, the last enemy shot by the colonel, his version of the origin of the feud. He had carried out this parting piece of bravado with no disturbance except an exchange of shots as the train moved away from the station. I was horrified. Was a person in this barbarous state of culture asking me, Oscar Boggs, member of the National Sub-Committee on Tone-Deafness—!

"Okky," said my mother, from behind, "this is Miss Frayn!"

I looked at her, and was suddenly impressed with the non-existence of the material universe, except as centered in and consisting of eyes of a ruddy brown like those of fine horses, rufous hair surrounding the small head like a nimbus, and a fused mass of impressions made up of the abstract concepts of trimness, fire, elegance, and unconquerability. I have reported the matter to the society for psychical research, but have received no answer as yet. It was clearly abnormal.

She placed her arm about my mother's waist and looked most respectfully at me.

"You ah the great man," said she, "of the family Ah have so much cause to love." Here she stopped as if to regain self-control. "Ah wish mah po' papahs," she went on, "had—"

"There, there!" said my mother, patting her arm. "It'll be all right anyway, dear!"

I was considering what to say. Her skin was clear, white, daintily transparent, and of a delicacy our western girls seldom display (owing, I surmise, to climatic influences); she stood there on Aunt Judith's Persian rug, her petite figure with its rounded curves, half-levitated, like Atalanta upon the oat-heads—and there returned upon me the mental vertigo, the lack of cerebral coördination, and the obliteration of the material universe.

"Am Ah so igno'ant, really?" said she. "Ah'm fond of children; and Ah *must* find wohk!"

Why did I hate Dustin? Why could I not command my speech? I always rally at the crises, however, and did so in this instance.

"As for ignorance," said I, "Sir John Lubbock says: 'Studies are a means, not an end.' And Lord Bacon hath it: 'To spend too much time in studies is sloth.' I see that you have acted on these maxims. Professor Dustin's astigmatism and myopia rendered it impossible for him to see you."

I stopped in some returning confusion.

"Those dreadful cube roots and quadratics—" said she.

"The personality of the teacher," said I, "controls the matter."

I heard her laugh, a little delighted laugh, and found myself agreeing to the heresy that, after all, the chief thing is to train the girls to be gentle, and the boys brave! Then I gave her my arm in to dinner. Chester, who had never offered a girl his arm except at a dance or after dark, glared at me. Mother was uneasy at the stirring of the old brotherly antagonisms. I expanded, and told Miss Frayn that if all southern women were like the only one I had met, I didn't wonder at the feuds. Then seeing whither I was drifting, I asked her plans as to the school she would take, when I sent her her certificate. She said that "Mistah Chestah" was going to let her have the home school.

"A boy like Chester," said I, "will have little influence with Mr. Middlekauff, the director."

"Oh, cut it out, Oc!" burst in Chester. "I've got it all framed up to be elected director!"

"My political plans," said I, "will not allow of a breach between my family and Mr. Middlekauff."

"Well, mine do," retorted Chester. "You'll take your chances with the Middlekauffs, just as I do!"

It was not the occult influence, but a desire to benefit educational conditions, that led me to visit Miss Frayn's school the week Chester's insurgency placed her in it. My memory is hazy as to the matter, but my notes show that her weakness was in the matter of organization.

"Oh," said she, when I mentioned this, "do you all prefeh things so regulah and poky? It's so much mo' pleasant foh the little things to be free!" She called most of the little ones "Honey," and allowed much latitude in whispering and moving about. They crowded around her like ants to a lump of sugar. Some of them were beginning to evince a laxity of pronunciation, sounding the personal pronoun "I" like the interjection "Ah."

In a few days I went back—Chester sneered at me as I went by—to tell Miss Frayn of the necessity of teaching the effects of stimulants and narcotics according to the Iowa law. She was greatly surprised when I told her of this requirement.

"What, *daily*, Mr. Supe'intendent!" she exclaimed.

"Daily teaching," said I. "Our law requires it."

"It seems *so* unnecessa'y," she said in perplexity. "The young gentlemen will find out all about it in due time: and is it raght to expe'iment with the littlest ones? And wheiah shall I obtain the liquoh foh the demonstrations?"

I felt strangely overcome at this astounding speech, by an indescribable mixture of tender solicitude for her welfare, and horror at her fearful mistake; but I reproved her for jesting at the vice of drinking.

"Vice!" said she, with a bubbling laugh. "Why, down home we-all regyahd it as an accomplishment! But Ah reckon you ah jokin' about teachin' it. Youah jokes and use of the lettah 'ah' ah things Ah shall nevah get used to, Ah'm afraid; but Ah'm glad you don't mean that about the drinkin'."

Despairing of making her understand, I left her, again conscious of being under occult and abnormal control. I was astonished to see in the school several large boys who must have been greatly needed in the fields. They looked at each other sheepishly as I came in, but most of the time they gazed at the teacher, rather than at their books. Not having the gift of prophecy, I could not see in their presence the cloud that would soon overshadow my official life. I took their attendance as proof of the popularity of the school. I studied the philosophers, and sought calm of spirit. Learning from Epictetus that the earthen pitcher and the rock do not agree, and from Lubbock that love at first sight is thought by great minds actually to occur, I reëxamined my abnormal psychic symptoms in Miss Frayn's presence, and prudently refrained from seeking her society. Poise alone makes possible a consistent career, and this I had in large measure reconquered, when, like a bolt from the blue—or at least with much abruptness—into my quiet office burst a committee from the Teal Lake Township School Board, accompanied by a number of patrons of the Boggs school—all old neighbors of ours—headed by the defeated Mr. Elizur Middlekauff. This could mean but one thing —Miss Frayn! The rebel invasion was at the door.

"Mr. Middlekauff," said one, "is the spokesman."

"We've got a grievyance," said Mr. Middlekauff, "a whale of a grievyance in our deestrict; and we've come right to the power-house to fix it."

"It shall command my most careful consideration," said I. "Please state the case."

"That 'ere railroad wreck," said Mr. Middlekauff, who was a very forcible speaker at caucuses, "let loose on our people a scourge in caliker more pestilential than the Huns and Vandals. We come to you as clothed with a little brief authority, an' accessory after the fact to this scourge business."

"I fail," said I, "to catch your meaning."

"I mean," said he, growing loud, "that peaches-an'-cream invader from the states lately in rebellion that you've give a stiffkit, an' your brother Chet by stratagems an' spiles has got himself elected an' put into our school. That's what I mean!"

"I infer," said I, "some implied strictures upon the character or school management or educational qualifications of Miss Roberta Lee Frayn."

"W'l you infer surprisin'ly clus to the truth!" replied Mr. Middlekauff offensively. "We're a-complainin' of this schoolma'am with the rebil name; and of her onrivaled facilities f'r spreadin' treason an' emotional insanity! Try to git that through your hair!"

Like lightning a course of policy occurred to me.

"Are the defendant," said I, looking them over, "and Mr. Boggs, the director, among your numbers?"

"No," said Mr. Middlekauff. "This is kinder informal. An' besides, we'd crawl out right where we went in if she was here. I tell you she's a—a—irresistible force."

"It is elementary," said I, "that no *ex parte* investigation can have any validity."

"Now, see here, Oc Boggs!" hissed he, "I don't take any high-an'-mighty stand-off from a lunkhead that's stole my melons when he was a kid! You'll hear this complaint, see?"

I did not weaken, but I allowed his standing in the community and party to outweigh offensive orthoëpy, rhetoric, and manners. Unofficially, I took down the complaint, reserving my ruling. As the horrid tale was told I grew sick at the problem before me. I glean the details of the situation from my notes:

Miss Frayn (all these things are set down as *asserted*) had assigned William Middlekauff, whose father was a member of the G. A. R., the Confederate side of a debate on the comparative greatness of Washington and Robert E. Lee, and had said: "She reckoned Mr. William ought to have won, as he had the strong side." Complained of as against public policy, adhering to armed insurrection, and giving aid and comfort to the enemy. *Quære* (per O. B.): Is complaint good after forty years of peace, and Reconstruction?

All members of the committee said that every boy in the district of more than sixteen years of age was irresistibly attracted to her (exact language, "bedaddled over her," O. B.). Hence, her character must be "wrong" somehow. Two boys, each claiming an exclusive franchise to sweep out for her, had met in Allen's feed-lot to fight a duel, and been discovered in the act of firing and tied to the feed-rack by Allen's hired man, and spanked with the end-gate of his wagon. Clarence Skeen was poorly, and had been found kneeling before a bench calling it his darling Roberta and begging it to be his. Columbus Smith had turned somnambulist, and his father had lost ten tons of timothy which "Clumb" had failed to put up in cock. When sleep-walking Clumb had been heard by Vespucci, his brother (known as "Spootch"), to protest with sighs and groans that his heart was broken and to ask "Roberta" to shed one tear over his grave. Twitted of this by his young sister, Semiramis, Clumb had slapped her and, cursing profanely, had assaulted Spootch, who reproved him, and had fled to the Wiggly Creek woods with no subsistence but a loaf of salt-rising bread, a box of paper collars, and a book of poems. Letter from Mrs. Smith asking that this Jezebel's certificate be revoked before all should be lost.

Whipple Cavanaugh had been idle and "lawless" since attending school. Refused nourishment. Pillow wet with tears. Kissed Cavanaugh's mare, "Old Flora," on nose after Miss Frayn had patted her on said spot. Had written a poem to Roberta, and rather than have it read publicly by the hired girl, who had found it under his pillow, had eaten it, paper, ink, and all. Doctor Dilworthy called in; pronounced him in danger of gastritis and love-sickness with grave prognosis.

Names of fifteen boys given, known as "Frayn Mooners," who haunted the shrubbery about the home of Mrs. Jane D. Boggs, where the teacher boarded. Six fights were known to have occurred among them. Tension in the neighborhood was unbearable because of the loosing by Chester Boggs, "in violation of his official oath," of a bulldog which had bitten Albert Boyer, and thrown his mother into nervous prostration.

This epidemic of "worthlessness and sentimentality" was spreading outside the district, as evidenced by an excerpt found in the dog's possession, from the upper rear elevation of the Sunday trousers of Boliver Fromme, living in District No. 4. Progress in the studies of the boys confined to amatory poetry and pugilism, both unrelated to their life work. *Iowa, My Iowa,* Major Byers' stirring lyric, had been supplanted by *Maryland, My Maryland,* in school singing. Chester Boggs, the director, refused to receive complaints, and was condemned as equally affected with the disease, and probably a "Mooner" himself. There was a certificate of Doctor Dilworthy of Teal Lake as to the existence of many cases of "extreme mental exaltation accompanied by explosive and fulminant cerebral disturbances traceable to mediate or immediate association with one Roberta Lee Frayn, an individual seemingly possessed of an abnormal power in the way of causing obsessions, fixed ideas, aberrant cranio-spinal functionings, and cranial tempests, in those of her associates resembling her in the matter of age, and differing from her in social habits, hereditary constitution, and sex."

I sank back in my chair horrified, with a sinking in the region of the epigastric plexus.

"We kind o' thought, Oc," said Mr. Middlekauff, "that thet would hold yeh f'r a while."

I saw the muddled political relations with which this imbroglio teemed, and clung to delay as my sole hope.

"I am inexpressibly shocked," said I, "and as soon as we can meet with the defendant and the director—"

"What!" shrieked Mr. Middlekauff. *"Her* present! Arter what them papers says? And everybody follerin' her, if she jest smiles, like a caff arter salt! Why, dad ding me, if I'd trust *myself* f'r more'n a smile or two. She'll bamboozle the hull thing if she's there. I b'lieve *you've* got it, you conceited young sprout! No, sir; decide this thing now!"

"I regret the necessity," said I, "of asking time to get the opinion of the county attorney, and to—to—"

"Not by a dum sight!" roared Mr. Middlekauff. "We'll see what the court has to say on this. An' when you're up f'r election ag'in, come round, an' we'll consider it f'r a while—an' then you won't know you're runnin'!"

I was torn by conflicting emotions when they went away. I knew that Middlekauff was a man of influence. I was not averse to seeing Chester rebuked for his fatuous behavior, and for tempting me to a deviation from strict duty. I felt that in taking my stand with the "Mooners" I might be siding with the heaviest body of voters after all. By these whiffling winds of the mind was I baffled, finding no rest in my works on didactics and pedagogics, wondering what Middlekauff would do—until all doubts were settled by the filing of the case of The School Board of Teal Lake versus Frayn; and in a few days it came on for trial before Judge Worthington.

Chester telephoned, asking to see me. He came in looking thinner than I had ever seen him.

"Do you know," said he, "that this case old Middlekauff's got plugged up comes off this morning?"

"Having been summonsed by writ of subpœna," said I severely, "I am aware that your wilfulness in placing an untried importation in charge of our school, regardless of her unfitness, or of my political well-being, is this morning bearing its legitimate fruit in the hearing which comes *on*—not *off!* And I hope your lack of consideration for the welfare of the school system, so largely wrapped up in my career, will—"

That Chester was temporarily insane is clear. He flew at me, seized my trachea in his iron hands, compressed it so as greatly to impede respiration, and knocked my head against the wall, using incoherently certain technical terms he had learned at Ames.

"Shut up!" he cried. "You duplex—polyphase—automatic—back-action—compound-wound—multipolar *Ass!* Shut up!"

An anatomical chart on the wall preserved my head, and I retained my self-possession. When he let me down I took my station on the other side of a table and looked him in the eye, strongly willing that he quiet down.

"Forgive me, Oc," said he humbly, "I promised

myself eight years ago not to lick you any more! Pardon me."

I forgave him, and we have ever since remained reconciled. He explained that he wanted to consult as to methods of concealing from Miss Frayn the nature of the suit.

"Am I to understand," said I, "that she does not know that the relief sought is her expulsion from the school?"

"Of course she don't!" replied Chester. "Do you think I'd let her know? She thinks everybody loves her. Nobody ever dared tell her anything else, either here or down where she was raised. The boys down there always were in love with her. She don't see anything strange in it—and there isn't."

"A change," said I, "would be wholesome for her."

"She wouldn't know what to do," replied Chester. "And if she were to hear these charges—against herself! Why, I don't know what she might not do! She'd be absolutely desperate. She'd think she had no one to defend her—and you know the Frayn way."

"I shall not endeavor," said I, after consideration, "to reconcile medieval notions of honor and personal dignity with proceedings under the Iowa Code. Neither do I feel it prudent for me to see this person."

For a few minutes Chester sat grinding his teeth and gripping the desk, and then rushed from the office calling me a white-livered dub, and telling me to go plumb to some place the name of which was cut off by the door's slamming. I sat in the office feeling a sense of unrest, until the time for going to court, where I found Judge Worthington on the bench, Chester sitting at the defendant's table, and no Miss Frayn.

"Are both sides ready in the next case?" asked the judge, without looking at the calendar.

"We wish to put the defendant on the stand for a few questions," said Beasley, Middlekauff's lawyer. "I don't see her in court, your Honor."

"Call the witness!" said the judge; and the bailiff shouted three times: "Robert Lefrayne!"

"Has this man Lefrayne been subpœnaed?" asked the judge; "as he is defendant, I don't suppose you thought it necessary, Mr. Beasley."

We could all see that the mispronunciation of the name had misled the judge as to the identity of the defendant.

"To make sure," said Beasley, "we subpœnaed

the party. Here is the writ, your Honor, with proof of service."

"Mr. Clerk," said the judge, frowning sternly, "issue a bench warrant! Mr. Sheriff, attach this witness, and produce him at two. Some of these tardy witnesses will go to jail for contempt if this is repeated! Call your next!"

Chester was pale as a ghost, and accosted the bailiff as he went out with the warrant. Then he came back and listened with flushes of anger and clenched teeth to the reading of the pleadings, to which the judge seemed to pay no attention. At two, after the intermission, the bailiff, Captain Winfield, an old G. A. R. man, appeared with Miss Frayn on his arm. He was blushing and fumbling his bronze button, while she smiled up at him in a charming, daughterly way that brought back dangerous symptoms of relapse in my psychic nature.

"Call the witness Lefrayne!" cried the judge.

Light, airy, daintily flushed, she floated up to the bench. The fine for contempt died in Forceythe Worthington's breast, as he stared in a sort of delighted embarrassment.

"It was raght kahnd of you, Judge Wo'thin'ton," she said, looking up into his face, "to send Captain

Winfield to remahnd me of mah engagement hyah. Why, he was at Franklin, and Chickamauga, and knows Tennessee! And now, gentlemen, what can Ah do foh you-all?"

The judge stepped down from the bench and handed Miss Frayn to the witness chair like a lord chancellor placing a queen on her throne. Beasley looked at the witness as if fascinated. Middlekauff seized him by the lapel of his coat.

"Don't look at her, Beasley, more'n yeh c'n help!" he whispered. "I tell yeh, it's dangerous!"

And yet *I* am selected to bear blame for a momentary weakness of the prevailing sort!

"Proceed, gentlemen!" said Judge Worthington.

Beasley gathered up his papers. "Are you the defendant?" asked he.

"Ah don't quite gathah youah meanin' suh," said she, "but Ah think not, suh."

"You're the teacher of the Boggs School, in Teal Lake Township?"

"Oh, yes, suh!" said she. "Pahdon me! I thought you inquiahed about something else."

Judge Worthington started as if struck by a dart.

"Let me see the papers in the case," said he excitedly.

Beasley handed them up, and the judge examined them carefully. Then he handed them down, turned his back on Miss Frayn, and spoke in a low tone, like one greatly shocked.

"Proceed!" said he.

Something in his tone or in the turning of his back seemed to strike upon the senses of Miss Frayn as unpleasant or hostile. The few questions put to her by the lawyer to lay the foundation for some other bit of evidence did not appear to affect her at all; and when she took her seat between Chester and my mother, and was reassured by their whispered communications, she looked serene, save when she noted the judge's averted face. Chester's lawyer spoke insinuatingly of spite, prejudice, and unreasonable provincialism as being at the bottom of the case.

"And," he added, "I may add jealousy—jealousy, your Honor, of the defendant's charms of person, which, as a part of the *res gestæ,* are evidence in this case, if your honor only would observe them."

The judge started and blushed, but still looked steadily away. Mr. Middlekauff looked relieved. Miss Frayn fretted the linoleum with little taps of her toe, and her delicate nostrils fluttered. There was a mystic tension in the air.

"Mr. Chestah," said the girl, in a low voice, "he seems to be alludin' to—what does he mean?"

Judge Worthington rapped for silence. Miss Frayn's eyes grew bright, and her cheek showed a spot of crimson which deepened as the reading of the affidavit went on. As the legal verbiage droned through the story of the boys' infatuation, I looked at her, and knew that her indignation was swelling fiercely at she scarcely knew what. I began repeating to myself a passage from Seneca.

"Objected to," roared Chester's lawyer, "as incompetent, irrelevant, immaterial, impertinent, and grossly scandalous!"

Miss Frayn clenched her hands and held her breath as if at the realization of her worst fears. Then the judge spoke. "The affidavit," said he, "attributes to Miss Frayn a malign and corrupting influence over the whole neighborhood, and—"

"Suh!" she gasped.

Again did the judge rap for order.

"Ruling reserved," said he. "Proceed."

Triumphantly Beasley went on with the resolutions. At last Miss Frayn seemed to understand. She rose, stilled Beasley with a gesture, and in frozen dignity addressed the court.

"Judge Wo'thin'ton," said she, "Ah'm not quite ce'tain Ah get the full meanin' of this, but Ah feel that Ah cain't pe'mit it to go fu'thah. Ah desiah to say to you as a gentleman and an acquaintance, if not a friend, that these ah things that can not be said of a lady, suh!"

"The defendant," said the judge, after two or three ineffectual attempts to speak, "will be heard through her counsel—proceed!"

She was hurt and desperate as she sat down, and in a cold and livid fury. With her eyes level and shining like knife-points, she put off, with a look like a blow, Chester's efforts to comfort her. She sat, an alien in an inhospitable land, hedged about by a wall of displeasure at some formless insult, and at friends without chivalry. The judge began stating his decision, giving the argument for the one side and then for the other, as judges do.

"The evidence tends to prove," said he, "that Roberta Lee Frayn has a malign fascination over her pupils—the larger boys especially; that she has lured them into personal attendance upon her rather than to study; that she has incited young men to duels, brawls, breaches of the peace, and—"

I could see that she thought the phrase "it tends to

prove" an expression of his belief in the charges; and as he went on her face flamed red once more, and then went white as snow. She stepped back from the table as if to clear for action, one little hand lifted, the other in the folds of her dress.

"Suh!" she cried, in a passion of indignation which was splendid and terrible. "This must stop! If mah false friends lack the chivalry to protect me and mah good name, Ah'll defend mahself, suh!"

Chester half rose, as if to throw himself into the hopeless contest.

"The defendant does not understand," said the judge. "The defendant will resume her seat! The evidence tends to prove that—"

But the decision was never finished; for the girl drew a short, small pistol and aimed at him. We were frozen in horror. Judge Worthington looked unwaveringly into the muzzle.

"Roberta!" said he.

I then saw a rush by Captain Winfield to strike her arm; the pistol roared out in the court-room like a cannon; and as Miss Frayn sank back into my mother's arms, Judge Worthington stepped down with a rent across his shoulder, from which he withdrew his fingers stained red. From under the table, where irresistible force had thrown me, I saw him take her unresisting hand, and heard him whisper to her.

"Darling!" said he. "You don't understand! Let me explain, sweetheart, and then if you want the pistol back I'll give it to you, loaded!"

Then he stood up and took command.

"The bailiff," said he, "will remove the defendant and Mrs. Boggs to my chambers. I shall investigate this *in camera*. I am not hurt, gentlemen, more than a pin's prick, and am able to go on and take such measures as are necessary to protect the court. Remain here until I resume the trial!"

"I tell you," said Middlekauff, "we'll crawl out where we went in. Nobody can stand ag'in her at clus range like that!"

Captain Winfield's face bore a puzzled and mysterious smile as he emerged from the chambers.

"You can't subdue these Southerners, Oc," said he.

"The verdict of history," said I, "is otherwise."

"We just reconstructed and absorbed 'em," said he. "I was there, an' I know. The judge thinks we've got to handle this Frayn invasion the same way."

"I fail to get your meaning," said I.

"The way to absorb this rebel host," said the captain, "is to marry it. It's the only way to ground her wire and demagnetize her. I can't undertake the job, for reasons known to all. You're sort of responsible for her devastatin' course, an' I think it'll cipher itself down to Oscar Boggs as a bridegroom for the good of Teal Lake Township, and the welfare of the Boggs School."

My emotions were tumultuous. No such marriage could be forced on me, of course; but duty, duty! Marriage had been to me an asset to be used in my career, some time after my doctor's degree, like casting in chess. I thought of Miss Frayn's untamable nature; and then of her sweetly tender way with the little ones, how they clambered over her while she called them "honey."

"On the main point," said the captain, "the court had its mind made up when I came out. This marryin' has got to be did. Who's to do it is what they're figgerin' on!"

"Captain Winfield," said I, "if the public interests require it, if my constituents demand it, I will make the sacrifice! Doctor Johnson said that marriages might well be arranged by the Lord Chancellor, and

Judge Worthington is now sitting in chancery. I will marry the defendant, *pro bono publico!*"

"Oc," said the captain, in a properly serious manner, though some tittered, "you're a livin' marvel! I'll go back and report."

Almost immediately, as my heart-beats stifled me, they emerged from the chambers. My mother was in tears. Worthington bore Miss Frayn on his arm, and both looked exaltedly happy. Roberta, as I called her in my thoughts, shrank back bashfully, more beautiful than I had ever seen her. It was a great, a momentous hour for me. I felt that I had settled the case.

"I shall ask the plaintiff," said the judge, "to dismiss this case!"

"On what grounds?" interrogated Beasley sharply.

"Don't tell, Forceythe!" said Roberta, hiding her face on the judge's arm as I approached.

"Because the defendant," the judge replied to Beasley, "has resigned. She is about to be married!"

"Didn't I tell you, Oc," said Winfield, slapping me on the back—which in the delightful embarrassment of the occasion I did not resent—"that it was up to you?"

A boy in the audience—I think it was William

Middlekauff—caught the judge's statement, and ungrammatically shouted: "Who to?"

"The lucky man?" shouted the crowd. "Name him!"

As it seemed proper for me to do under the circumstances, I went forward to take Roberta's hand in anticipation of the announcement. Then all went dark before my eyes.

"I am happy," said Judge Worthington, "happy and inexpressibly honored to say that the defendant is to be married to me!"

The Hired Man was asleep as the Professor concluded his tale, and some of the rest were nodding. They rose to retire.

"I suppose," said the Groom, "that the only safe way is to let them entirely alone, Professor?"

The Professor, embarrassed by the presence of the Bride, could only bow.

"Gad!" said Colonel Baggs, taking his hand. "Your case goes into the hard-luck file with that of the Nez Percè victim, Mr. Cowan of Radersburg."

CHAPTER VII

"ON this lake," declaimed the Colonel, "farther from tide water than any other like body of water on this earth, could float our entire navy."

"Safest place in the world for it, too," declared the Groom.

"I know some awfully nice navy men," protested the Bride; "so don't be cattish about the navy."

They had spent many hours on Yellowstone Lake, and days in its vicinity. Paint pots, geysers, and iridescent springs were no longer recorded in the log-book; but when, at the Fishing Cone, the Hired Man came into camp asking for salt, with a cooked trout on his line, and the Bride learned that he had hooked the fish in cold water, and cooked it in hot without moving from the spot, wonder at the marvel was swallowed up in protest on the Bride's part, against such an atrocity.

"Oh, Mr. Snoke, Mr. Snoke!" said she, almost tearful. "How could you! How could you! How would you like to have a thing like that done to you —cooked alive. Oh!"

"Well," said Mr. Snoke. "If you put it that way, I wouldn't be very strong for bein' hooked, let alone cooked. After I'd been snaked out of the drink, I wouldn't care, Bride."

"Well, I move we don't cook any more of 'em until they have gasped out their lives slowly and in the ordinary mode," said the Artist.

"Shore," said Aconite, "no more automobiles de fe for the trout—hear that, Bill? An' speakin' of cookin' fish that-a-way," he went on, creating a conversational diversion. "Old Jim Bridger found a place out here som'eres, where the water was shore deep. At the bottom it was cold, and on the top hot —hot as it is in the Fish Cone over yon. He used to hook trout down in the cold water, and they'd cook to a turn while he was bringin' 'em to the surface an' playin' 'em."

"That sounds to me all right," assented the Colonel.

"The hot water," observed the Professor, "would naturally be at the surface; but as for the tale itself—"

"It would, eh?" queried Aconite. "Well, I've forded the Firehole where the bottom was hot, an' the top cold. An' Old Jim Bridger knowed of a place where the water of a cold spring starts at the top of a mountain, and slides down so fast that the friction heats the water hot—just rubbin' on the rocks comin' down. It's here in these hills som'eres, yet!"

The Artist, the Groom and the Colonel fished industriously for one day and then handed in a unanimous verdict that it was a shame to take advantage of the trout's verdancy. So the Hired Man and Aconite foraged for the frying-pan.

The change to boat from land carriage was so grateful, now, that they made wondrous voyages, first to the scenes reached by water. They photographed bears near camp and both deer and elk in the meadows and on their shore feeding-grounds. It was no longer a strange or startling thing to see a grizzly bear, and to stalk him with a kodak. The pelicans on the lake were to them as the swans on a private pond. The sense of ownership grew upon them. Here was their own pleasure-ground. It was theirs by virtue of their citizenship. They might not visit it often—though all declared their intention of coming back every summer—but, anyhow, it would be fine to know that here on the summit of the continent was this wonderland, owned by them and each of them.

They took saddle horses down the southern approach to Heart Lake, and voted it the loveliest lake in the park.

"That is," said the Bride, "it doesn't compare with the big lake up yonder in greatness; but it's just pure joy. Let's camp here for the night. Let's draw another romance from the library right now; and give the victim time to compose his thoughts while we go see that Rustic Geyser, with the stone logs around it."

Somehow they seemed farther from the haunts of men here than anywhere else in the Park. The stream of tourists seemed to sweep on past the Thumb Lunch Station, toward the Lake Hotel; and Heart Lake, with Mount Sheridan brooding over it, was theirs alone. And it was here that the Hired Man, with many protests that he wasn't really a member of the party, but only working his way, told his story—like another Ulysses returned from Troy and his wanderings.

FROM ALPHA TO OMEGA

THE HIRED MAN'S STORY

It narrows a man to stick around in one place. You broaden out more pan-handling over one division, than by watching the cars go by for years. I've been everywhere from Alpha, Illinois, to Omega, Oklahoma, and peeked over most of the jumping-off places; and Iowa is not the whole works at all. That's why I'm here now. Good quiet state to moss over in; but no life! Me for the mountains where the stealing is good yet, and a man with genius can be a millionaire!

I was in one big deal, once—the Golden Fountain Mine. Pete Peterson and I worked in the Golden Fountain and boarded with Brady, a pit boss. Ever hear of psychic power? A medium told me once that I have it, and that's why folks tell me their secrets. The second day Brady told me the mine was being wrecked.

"How do you know?" said I.

"They're minin' bird's-eye porphyry," said Brady, "purtendin' they've lost the lode."

"Maybe they have," said I.

"Not them," replied Brady, who never had had any culture. "I can show you the vein broad's a road an' rich as pudd'n'!"

I didn't care a whoop, as long as they paid regular; but Brady worried about the widows and orphans that had stock. I said I had no widows and orphans contracting insonomia for me, and he admitted he hadn't. But he said a man couldn't tell what he might acquire. Soon after, a load of stulls broke loose, knocked Pete Peterson numb, and in the crash Brady accumulated a widow. It was thought quite odd, after what he'd said.

The union gave him a funeral, and then we were all rounded up by a lawyer that insisted on being a pall-bearer and riding with the mourners, he and Brady had been such dear friends. The widow never heard of him; but unless he was dear to Brady, why did he cry over the bier, and pass out his cards, and say he'd make the mine sweat for this? It didn't seem reasonable, and the widow signed papers while he held in his grief.

Then we found he had awful bad luck losing friends. A lot of them had been killed or hurt, and he was suing companies to beat fours. We were going over our evidence, and another bunch was there with a doctor examining to see how badly they were ruined.

"Beautiful injury!" said the lawyer, thumping a husky Hun on the leg. "No patellar reflex! Spine ruined! Beautiful! We'll make 'em sweat for this!"

He surely was a specialist in corporate perspiration. I asked what the patellar reflex was, and the doc had Pete sit and cross his legs, and explained.

"Mr. Peterson," said he, "has a normal spine. When I concuss the limb here, the foot will kick forward involuntarily. But in case of spinal injury, it will not. Now observe!"

He whacked Pete's shin with a rubber hammer, but Pete never kicked. His foot hung loose like, not doing a blamed thing that the doc said it would if his spine was in repair. The doc was plumb dumbfounded.

"Most remarkable case of volitional control—" he began.

"Volitional your grandmother!" yells the lawyer. "Mr. Peterson is ruined also! He was stricken prone in the same negligent accident that killed dear Mr. Brady! He is doomed! A few months of progressive induration of the spinal cord, and breaking up of the multipolar cells, and—death, friend, death!"

The widow begun to whimper, and the lawyer grabbed Pete's hand and bursted into tears. Pete, being a Swede, never opened his face.

"But," said the lawyer, cheering up, "we'll make them sweat for this. Shall we not vindicate the right of the working-man to protection, Mr. Peterson?"

"Yu bat!" said Pete. "Ay bane gude Republican!"

"And vindicate his right," went on the lawyer, "to safe tools and conditions of employment?"

"Ay tank we windicate," said Pete.

"Nobly said!" said the lawyer and hopped to it making agreements for contingent fees and other flimflams. It was wonderful how sort of patriotic and unselfish and religious and cagey he always was.

We quit the Golden Fountain, and I got some assessment work for Sile Wilson. Pete wouldn't go. He was sort of hanging around the widow, but his brains were so sluggish that I don't believe he knew why. I picked up a man named Lungy to help. Sile's daughter Lucy kept house for Sile in camp, and in two days she was calling Lungy "Mr. Addison," and reproaching me for stringing a stranger that had seen better days and had a bum lung and was used to dressing for dinner. I told her I most always allowed to wear something at that meal myself, and she snapped my head off. He was a nice fellow for a lunger.

When I had to go and testify in the Brady and Peterson cases against the Golden Fountain, old Sile was willing.

"I'd like to help stick the thieves!" he hissed.

"How did you know they were thieves?" asked I.

"I located the claim," said he, "and they stole it on a measley little balance for machinery—confound them!"

"Well, they're stealing it again," said I; and I explained the lost vein business.

"They've pounded the stock away down," said the lunger. "I believe it's a good buy!"

"Draw your eighteen-seventy-five from Sile," said I; "and come with me and buy it!"

"I think I will go," said he. And he did. He was a nice fellow to travel with.

Well, the Golden Fountain was shut down, and had no lawyer against us. It was a funny hook-up. We proved about the stulls, and got a judgment for the widow for ten thousand. Then we corralled another jury and showed that Pete had no patellar reflex, and therefore no spine, and got a shameful great verdict for him. And all the time the Golden

Fountain never peeped, and Lungy Addison looked on speechless. Our lawyer was numb, it was so easy.

"I don't understand—" said he.

"The law department must be connected in series with the mine machinery," said I, "and shuts off with the same switch. Do we get this on a foul?"

"Oh, nothing foul!" said he. "Default, you see—"

"No showup at ringside," said I; "9 to 0? How about bets?"

"Everything is all right," said he, looking as worried. "We'll sell the mine, and make the judgments!"

"And get the Golden Fountain," said I, "on an Irish pit boss and a Swede's spine?"

"Certainly," said he, "if they don't redeem."

"Show me," said I; "I'm from Missouri! It's too easy to be square. She won't pan!"

"Dat bane hellufa pile money f'r vidder," said Pete when we were alone. "Ten thousan' f'r Brady, an' twelf f'r spine! Ay git yob vork f'r her in mine!"

"You wild Skandihoovian," said I, "that's *your* spine!"

"Mae spine?" he grinned. "Ay gass not! Dat legyerkin' bane only effidence. Dat spine bane vidder's!"

I couldn't make him see that it was his personal spine, and the locomotor must be attaxing. He smiled his fool smile and brought things to comfort Mrs. Brady's last days. But she knew, and took him to Father Mangan, and Pete commenced studying the catechism against the time of death; but it didn't take. The circuit between the Swedenwegian intellect and the Irish plan of salvation looks like it's grounded and don't do business.

"Very well said," commented the Groom. "I couldn't have put it more engenerically myself."

One night the lawyer asked me to tell "the Petersons," as he called them, that some New Yorker had stuck an intervention or mandamus into the cylinder and stopped the court's selling machinery. "We may be delayed a year or so," said he. Pete had gone to the widow's with a patent washboard that was easy on the spine, and I singlefooted up, too. And there was that yellow-mustached Norsky holding the widow on his lap, bridging the chasm between races in great shape. He flinched some, and his neck got redder, but she fielded her position in big league form, and held her base.

"Bein' as the poor man is not long f'r this wicked world," said she, "an' such a thrue man, swearin' as the l'yer wanted, I thought whoile the crather stays wid us—"

"Sure," said I. "Congrats! When's the merger?"

"Hey?" says Pete.

"The nuptials," said I. "The broom-stick jumping."

The widow got up and explained that the espousals were hung up till Pete could pass his exams with Father Mangan.

"Marriage," said she, "is a sacrilege, and not lightly recurred. Oh, the thrials of a young widdy, what wid Swedes, and her sowl, an' the childer that may be—Gwan wid ye's, ye divvle ye!"

Now there was a plot for a painter: the widow thinking Pete on the blink spinally, and he soothing her last days, all on account of a patellar reflex that an ambulance chaser took advantage of—and the courts full of quo-warrantoes and things to keep the Jackleg from selling a listed mine, with hoisting-works and chlorination-tanks!

I got this letter from Pete, or the widow, I don't know which [displaying a worn piece of paper], about the third year after that. Here's what it says:

"Ve haf yust hat hell bad time, savin' yer prisence, and Ay skal skip for tjiens of climit to gude pless Ay gnow in Bad Lands. Lawyer faller sell mine fer 10 tousan to vidder, an thin, bad cess to him, sells it agin to Pete fer 12000$ an git 2 stifkit off sheriff an say hae keep dem fer fees, an Ay gnok him in fess an take stifkit. Hae say hae tell mae spine bane O K all tem, an thrittened to jug Pete, an the back of me hand and the sole of me fut to the likes of him, savin' yer prisence, an Fader Mangan call me big towhead chump an kant lern catty kismus an marry me to vidder, an Pete, God bliss him, promised to raise the family in Holy Church, but no faller gnow dem tings Bfour hand, an Ay tank ve hike to dam gude pless in Bad Lands vun yare till stifkit bane ripe an Mine belong vidder an Ay bane Yeneral Manager an yu pit Boss vit gude yob in Yune or Yuly next, yours truely, an may the Blessid Saints purtect ye, PETER PETERSON.

"P. S. Vidder Brady mae vife git skar an sine stifkit fer Brady to lawyer faller like dam fool vooman trik an sattle vit him, but Ay tink dat legyerkin bane bad all sem an yump to Bad Lands if we dodge inyunction youre frend. PETE."

"So they got married," said Aconite.

Just the way I figured it.

Well, this lunger sleuthed me out when I was prospecting alone next summer.

"Hello, Bill," said he, abrupt-like. "Cook a double supply of bacon."

"Sure," I said. "Got any eating tobacco, Lungy?"

"Bill," said he, after we had fed our respective faces, "did you ever wonder why that Swede received such prompt recognition without controversy for his absent patellar reflex?"

"Never wonder about anything else," said I. "Why?"

"It was this way," said he. "The crowd that robbed Sile Wilson found they had sold too much stock, and quit mining ore to run it down so they could buy it back. Some big holders hung on, and they had to make the play strong. So they went broke for fair, and let Brady's widow and Pete and a lot of others get judgments, and they bought up the certificates of sale. D'ye see?"

"Kind of," said I. "It'll come to me all right."

"It was a stock market harvest of death," said Lungy. "The judgments were to wipe out all the stock. This convinces me that the vein is hidden and not lost, as you said."

"I thought I mentioned the fact," said I, "that Brady showed me the ore-chute."

"That's why I'm here," said he. "I want you to find Pete Peterson for me."

"Why?" I said.

"Because," answered Addison, "he's got the junior certificate."

"Give me the grips and passwords," I demanded; "the secret work of the order may clear it up."

"Listen," said he. "Each certificate calls for a deed to the mine the day it's a year old; but the younger can redeem from the older by paying them off—the second from the first, the third from the second, and so on."

"Kind of rotation pool," said I, "with Pete's claim as ball fifteen?"

"Yes," said he; "only the mine itself has the last chance. But they think they know that Pete won't turn up, and they gamble on stealing the mine with the Brady certificate. Your perspicacity enables you to estimate the importance of Mr. Peterson."

"My perspicacity," I said, giving it back to him cold, "informs me that some jackleg lawyer has been and bunked Pete out of the paper long since. And he couldn't pay off what's ahead of him any more'n he could buy the Homestake? Come, there's more than this to the initiation!"

"Yes, there is," he admitted. "You remember Lucy, of course? No one could forget her! Well, her father and I are in on a secret pool of his friends, they to find the money, we to get this certificate."

"Where does Lucy come in?" said I.

"I get her," he replied, coloring up. "And success makes us all rich!"

I never said a word. Lungy was leery that I was soft on Lucy—I might have been, easy enough—and sat looking at me for a straight hour.

"Can you find him for me?" said he, at last.

"Sure!" said I.

He smoked another pipeful and knocked out the ashes.

"Will you?" said he, kind of wishful.

"If you insult me again," I hissed, "I'll knock that other lung out! Turn in, you fool, and be ready for the saddle at sun-up!"

We rode two days in the country that looks like the men had gone out when they had the construction work on it half done, when a couple of horsemen came out of a draw into the cañon ahead of us.

"The one on the pinto," said I, "is the perspiration specialist."

"If he doesn't recognize you," said Lungy, "let the dead past stay dead!"

Out there in the sunshine the Jackleg looked the

part, so I wondered how we come to be faked by him. We could see that the other fellow was a sheriff, a deputy-sheriff, or a candidate for sheriff—it was in his features.

"Howdy, fellows!" said I.

"Howdy!" said the sheriff, and closed his face.

"Odd place to meet!" gushed the Jackleg, as smily as ever. "Which way?"

"We allowed to go right on," I said.

"This is our route," said Jackleg, and moseys up the opposite draw, clucking to his bronk, like an old woman.

"What do you make of his being here?" asked Lungy.

"Hunting Swedes," I said. "And with a case against Pete for robbery and assault. I hope we see him first!"

We went on, Lungy ignorantly cheerful, I lost-like to know what was what, and feeling around with my mind's finger for the trigger of the situation. Suddenly I whoaed up, shifted around on my hip, and looked back.

"Lost anything, Bill?" asked Lungy.

"Temporarily mislaid my brains," said I. "We're going back and pick up the scent of the Jackleg."

Lungy looked up inquiringly, as we doubled back on our tracks.

"When you kick a covey of men out of this sagebrush," I explained, "they naturally ask about anything they're after. They inquire if you know a Cock-Robin married to a Jenny-Wren, or an Owl to a Pussycat, or whatever marital misdeal they're trailing. They don't mog on like it was Kansas City or Denver."

"Both parties kept still," replied Lungy. "What's the answer, Bill?"

"Both got the same guilty secret," said I, "and they've got it the worst. They know where Pete is. So will we if we follow their spoor."

We pelted on right brisk after them. The draw got to be a cañon, with grassy, sheep-nibbled bottom, and we knew we were close to somewhere. At last, rolling to us around a bend, came a tide of remarks, rising and swelling to the point of roughhouse and riot.

"The widow!" said I. "She knows me. You go in, Lungy, and put up a stall to keep 'em from seeing Pete alone first!"

I crept up close. The widow was calling the Jackleg everything that a perfect lady as she was, you know, could lay her tongue to, and he trying to blast a crack in the oratory to slip a word into.

"I dislike," said Lungy, "to disturb privacy; but we want your man to show us the way."

"Who the devil are you?" said the sheriff.

"My name—" began Lungy.

"Whativer it is, sorr," said the widow, "it's a bether name nor his you shpake to—the black fardown, afther taking me man and lavin' me shtarve wid me babbies he robbed iv what the coort give! But as long as I've a tongue in me hid to hould, ye'll not know where he's hid!"

And just then down behind me comes Pete on a fair-sized cayuse branded with a double X.

"Dat bane you, Bill?" said he casual-like. "You most skar me!"

I flagged him back a piece and told him the Jackleg was there. He ran, and I had to rope him.

"You're nervous, Pete," said I, helping him up. "What's the matter?"

"Dis blame getaway biz," he said, "bane purty tough on fallar. Ay listen an' yump all tem nights!"

"How about going back for the mine?" I asked.

"Dat bane gude yoke!" he grinned. "Ay got gude flock an' planty range hare, an' Ay stay, Ay tank.

Yu kill lawyer fallar, Bill, an' take half whole shooting-match!"

"Got that certificate?" I asked.

It was all worn raw at the folds, but he had it. The Jackleg had an assignment all ready on the back, and I wrote Addison's name in, and made Pete sign it.

"Now," said I. "We'll take care of Mr. Jackleg, and you'll get something for this, but I don't know what. Don't ever come belly-aching around saying we've bunked you after Lungy has put up his good money and copped the mine. These men want this paper, not you. Probably they've got no warrant. Brace up and stand pat!"

So we walked around bold as brass. The widow was dangling a Skandy-looking kid over her shoulder by one foot, and analyzing the parentage of Jackleg. Lungy was grinning, but the sheriff's face was shut down.

"Ah, Mr. Peterson!" said the lawyer. "And our old and dear friend William Snoke, too! I thought I recognized you this morning! And now, please excuse our old and dear friend Mr. Peterson for a moment's consultation."

"Dis bane gude pless," said Pete. "Crack ahead!"

"This is a private matter, gentlemen," said Jackleg.

"Shall we withdraw?" asks Lungy.

"No!" yells Pete. "You stay—be vitness!"

"I wish to remind you, dear Mr. Peterson," said he as we sort of settled in our places, "that your criminal assault and robbery of me has subjected you to a long term in prison. And I suffered great damage by interruption of business, and bodily and mental anguish from the wounds, contusions and lesions inflicted, and especially from the compound fracture of the inferior maxillary bone—"

"Dat bane lie!" said Pete. "Ay yust broke your yaw!"

"He admits the *corpus delicti!*" yelled the lawyer. "Gentlemen, bear witness!"

"I didn't hear any such thing," said Lungy.

"Neither did I," I said.

"I figure my damages," he went on, "at twelve thousand dollars."

Pete picked a thorn out of his finger.

"Now, Mr. Peterson," went on the lawyer, "I don't suppose you have the cash. But when I have stood up and fought for a man for pure friendship and a mere contingent fee, I learn to love him. I would fain save you from prison, if you would so act as to enable me to acquit you of felonious intent. A prison is a fearful place, Mr. Peterson!"

"Ay tank," said Pete, "Ay brace up an' stand pat!"

"If you would do anything," pleaded the Jackleg, "to show good intention, turn over to me any papers you may have, no matter how worthless—notes, or—or certificates!"

Pete pulled out his wallet. Lungy turned pale.

"Take dis," said Pete. "Dis bane order fer six dollar Yohn Yohnson's wages. Ay bane gude fallar!"

"Thanks!" said the Jackleg, pious-like. "And *is* that long document the certificate of sale in Peterson *vs.* Golden Fountain, etc.?"

"Dat bane marryin' papers," said Pete. "Dat spine paper bane N. G. Mae spine all tem O. K. Dat leg-yerkin' bane yust effidence. Ay take spine paper to start camp-fire!"

It was as good as a play. Lungy turned pale and trembled. The lawyer went up in the air and told the sheriff to arrest Pete, and appealed to the widow to give up the certificate, and she got sore at Pete, and called him a Norwegian fool for burning it, and cuffed the bigger kid, which was more Irish-looking.

Pete dug his toe into the ground and looked ashamed and mumbled something about it not being his spine. The sheriff told Pete to come along, and I asked him to show his warrant. He made a bluff at looking in his clothes for it, and rode away with his countenance tight-closed.

Lungy and I rode off the other way.

That night Lungy smiled weakly as I started the fire with paper.

"Bill," said he, "I shall never burn paper without thinking how near I came to paradise and dropped plump—"

"Oh, I forgot," said I. "Here's that certificate."

Lungy took it, looked it over, read the assignment, and broke down and cried.

"How did it come out?" asked the Bride.

"Oh," said the Hired Man, "Lungy waited till the last minute, flashed the paper and the money, and swiped the mine. The company wanted to give a check and redeem, but the clerk stood out for currency, and it was too late to get it. He got the mine, and Lucy, and is the big Mr. Addison, now. No, me for where you can carry off things that are too big for the grand larceny statutes. This business of farming is too much like chicken-feed for me!"

CHAPTER VIII

"I CAME on this trip," said Colonel Baggs, "to rest my vocal organs, and not to talk. In this ambition I have been greatly aided by the willingness of Professor Boggs to assume the conversational burden in our seat. However, now that my name has been drawn from the hat, I shall have the pleasure, and honor, lady and gentlemen, to entertain you for a very few minutes—after which, thanking you for your very kind attention and liberal patronage, the hay—the hay, my friends, for me!"

At the Lake Hotel, to which they had come by boat, they found their tents pitched and their dinner awaiting them—for which they were indebted to the efficiency of Aconite and the Hired Man, who had come overland; and the latter of whom assured them that they had missed the greatest curiosity of the Park in failing to see the Natural Bridge.

"On your way, Bill!" said the Groom. "You didn't see the petrified sea serpent swimming off Gull Point, did you?"

"Dumb it all, no!" exclaimed Bill. "I never am around when anything good is pulled off!"

THE LAW AND AMELIA WHINNERY

THE TALE OF COLONEL BAGGS OF OMAHA

I was much interested (said the Colonel, beginning his story), in the tale told by my learned brother, Mr. Snoke. The story of the way Mr. Lungy Addison committed grand larceny in getting away with the Mortal Cinch mine is one that, falling from the mouth, as it does, of a person not learned in the law and its beauties, must be true. Nobody but a lawyer could have invented it—and I assure you that lawyers are too busy with the strange phases of truth to monkey—if I may use a term not yet laundered by the philologists—with fiction. The law is the perfection of human wisdom. Our courts are the God-ordained instruments by which these perfections are made manifest to the eyes of mere human beings. To be sure the courts are composed of men who were but even now lawyers—but that's neither here, there, nor yonder—when the anointment of their judicial consecration runs down their beard, as did the oil down that of Aaron, human imperfections are at end with them, and it's all off with frailty. And this brings me to the brief story which is my contribution to the Yellowstone Nights' Entertainment. I sing, my beloved, the saga of The Law and Amelia Whinnery.

I just got a decision over in Nebraska in the case of Whinnery *vs*. The C. & S. W. It shows that Providence is still looking out for the righteous man and his seed. Never heard of Whinnery *vs*. the Railway Company? Well, it may put you wise to a legal principle or two, and I'll tell you about it. I was ag'in' the corporations over there, as associate counsel for the plaintiff. Bob Fink, that studied in my office, was the fellow the case belonged to, and he being a little afraid of Absalom Scales, the railroad's local attorney, sent over a Macedonian wail to me, and said we'd cut up a fifty per cent. contingent fee if we won. I went.

Amelia Whinnery was the plaintiff. She was a school-teacher who had got hold of the physical culture graft, and was teaching it to teachers' institutes, making forty dollars a minute the year around.

"How much?" asked the Hired Man.

"I'm telling you what the record showed as I remember it," said the Colonel. "We proved that she was doing right well financially when the railroad put her out of business by failing to ring a bell or toot a whistle at the crossing coming into Tovala, and catching Bill Williams' bus asleep at the switch. Miss Whinnery was in the bus. When it was all over, she was in pretty fair shape—"

"Naturally," interpolated the Artist.

"Excepting that her nerves had got some kind of a shock and she was robbed permanently of the power of speech."

"How terrible!" exclaimed the Bride.

On the trial she sat in the court-room in a close-fitting dress, wearing a picture hat, and would give a dumb sort of gurgle when Scales would pitch into her case, as if to protest at being so cruelly assaulted while defenseless. It was pathetic.

Bob Fink shed tears, while he pictured to the jury in his opening, the agony of this beautiful girl set off from her kind for life, as the preponderance, the clear preponderance of the evidence showed she would be, by dumbness—"an affliction, gentlemen of the jury, which seals her lips forever as to the real facts, and stops the reply she could otherwise make to the dastardly attack of my honorable and learned friend, the attorney for this public-service corporation, which has been clothed with the power to take away your land, gentlemen of the jury, or mine, whether we want to sell it or not, and to rob us of our produce by its extortionate freight rates, and to run its trains into and through our cities, and over our busses, and to maim and injure our ladies, and bring them before juries of their peers, who, unless I mistake, will administer a stinging rebuke to this corporation without a soul to save or a body to kick, in the only way in which it can be made to feel a rebuke—in damages, out of that surplus of tainted dollars which its evil and illegal practices have wrung from the hard hands of toil as represented by the farmers and laborers who so largely compose this highly-intelligent jury."

"Good spiel," commented the Groom.

Bob was good until the other side had the reporter begin to take his speech down, so as to show appeals to passion and prejudice—and then he hugged the record close. The plaintiff sobbed convulsively. Bob stopped and swallowed, knowing that the reporter couldn't get the sobs and swallows into the record. The jurors blew their noses and glared at Scales and the claim-agent. I went over to the plaintiff and gave her a drink of water, and would have liked to take her in my arms and comfort her, but didn't.

"Too bad!" remarked the Poet.

Well, the jury found for us in about three hours for the full amount, ten thousand dollars and costs. They would have agreed earlier, only they waited so the state would have to pay for their suppers. A judgment was rendered on the verdict, and the railroad appealed. All this time Bob was getting more and more tender toward the plaintiff. I didn't think much about it until cards came for their wedding. I sent Bob an assignment of my share in the verdict for a wedding present—if we ever got it. Amelia promised to love, honor and cherish by nodding her head, and walked away from the altar with her most graceful physical culture gait, while the boys outside with their shivaree instruments ready for the evening, sang in unison, "Here comes the bride! Get on to her stride!" It was a *recherché* affair—but excessively quiet nuptials on the bride's side.

That evening Absalom Scales got in the finest piece of work that was ever pulled off in any lawsuit in Nebraska. The bridal party went away over the C. & S. W. Omaha Limited, and Amelia and Bob were there looking as fine as fiddles—Amelia a picture, they said, in her going-away gown. Scales had fixed up for a crowd of hoodlums to shivaree them as they went.

"Mighty mean trick, I should say," said the Hired Man, "for any one but a corporation lawyer."

"Wait, Brother Snoke," protested the Colonel, "until you are so far advised in the premises as to be able to judge whether the end didn't justify the means."

In addition to the horse-fiddles and bells and horns, Absalom had arranged some private theatricals. He had plugged up a deal by which Bill Williams, the bus man—who'd sold out and was going to Oregon anyway—came bursting into the waiting-room while they were waiting for the train —which was held at the water-tank by Scales' procurement and covin—and presented a bill for the damages to his bus by the accident which had hurt Amelia's oratorical powers. You see, he'd never been settled with, being clearly negligent. They tried to get off in Amelia's case on the doctrine of imputed negligence, but it wouldn't stick.

Well, Bill comes in with his claim against Amelia

and Bob for two or three hundred dollars for his bus. They disdainfully gave him the ha-ha.

"Then," says Bill Williams, "I will tell all, woman!"

Amelia flushed, and looked inquiringly at Bob. Bob walked up to Bill and hissed: "What do you mean, you hound, by insulting my wife in this way!"

"She knows what I mean," yelled Bill, turning on Amelia. "Ask your wife what she an' I was talkin' about when we was a-crossing the track that time. Ask her if she didn't say to me that I was the perfec'ly perportioned physical man, an' whether I didn't think that men an' women of sech perportions should mate; an' if she didn't make goo-goo eyes at me, ontil I stuck back my head to kiss her, an' whether she wasn't a-kissin' me when that freight come a pirootin' down an' run over her talkin' apparatus! Ask her if she didn't say she could die a-kissin' me, an' if she didn't come danged near doin' it!"

"How perfectly horrid!" gasped the Bride.

Well, Bob Fink was, from all accounts, perfectly flabbergasted. There stood Bill Williams in his old dogskin coat and a cap that reeked of the stables, and there stood the fair plaintiff, turning redder and redder and panting louder and louder as the enormity of the thing grew upon her. And then she turned loose.

Amelia Whinnery Fink, defendant in error, and permanently dumb, turned loose.

She began doubling up her fists and stamping her feet, and finally she burst forth into oratory of the most impassioned character.

"Robert Fink!" she said, as quoted in the motion for a reopening of the case that Scales filed—"Robert Fink, will you stand by like a coward and see me insulted? That miserable tramp—a perfect— If you don't kill him, I will. *I* kiss him? *I* ask him such a thing? Bob Fink, do you expect me to go with you and leave such an insult unavenged? No, no, no, no—"

"I don't blame her!" interjected the Bride.

I guess she'd have gone on stringing negatives together as long as the depot would have held 'em, if Bob hadn't noticed Ike Witherspoon, the shorthand reporter, diligently taking down her speech and the names of those present. Then he twigged, and, hastily knocking Bill down, he boarded the train with Amelia. He wired me from Fremont that it was all off with the judgment, as they'd tormented

Mrs. Fink into making a public speech. I answered, collect, bidding him be as happy as he could in view of the new-found liberty of speech and of the press, and I'd look after the judgment and the appeal.

"Well," said the Groom, "of course you got licked in the Supreme Court. It was clear proof that she'd been shamming."

"You're about as near right on that as might be expected of a layman," retorted the Colonel. "Just about. The law is the perfection of human reason. The jury had found that Amelia Whinnery couldn't speak, and never would be able to. A jury had rendered a verdict to that effect, and judgment for ten thousand dollars had been entered upon it. I merely pointed out to the Supreme Court that they could consider errors in the record only, and that it was the grossest sort of pettifogging and ignorance of the law for Absalom Scales to come in and introduce such an impertinence as evidence—after the evidence was closed—that the fair plaintiff had been shamming and was, in fact, a very free-spoken lady. The bench saw the overpowering logic of this, and read my authorities, and Bob and Amelia will henceforth live in the best house in their town, built out of the C. & S. W. surplus—and Amelia talking sixteen hours a day. It's locally regarded as a good joke on the railroad."

"But was it honest?" queried the Bride.

"Honest, me lady!" repeated the Colonel, *a la* Othello. "My dear young lady, the courts are not to be criticized—ever remember that!"

"That makes me think," said the Hired Man, "of the darndest thing—"

"In that case," said the Poet, "your name will be considered drawn for the next number. Save this darndest thing for its own occasion—which will be at our next camp. Oneiros beckons, and I go."

"In that case," said Aconite, "I'd go, you bet!"

CHAPTER IX

COMING in from the right as they took the open trail again, the Cody Road beckoned them eastward, as a side road always beckons to the true wanderer.

"What does it run to?" asked the Groom.

"Wyoming," responded Aconite. "It's nothing but scenery and curiosities."

"Let's follow it a little way," suggested the Bride, "and see how we like it."

Three miles or so on the way, the surrey halted at a beautiful little lake, which lay like a fragment broken off Yellowstone Lake, the shore of which lay only a stone's throw to the right. They walked over to the big lake to bid it farewell. A score of miles to the south lay Frank Island, and still farther away, shut off by the fringe of rain from a thunder shower, the South Arm seemed to run in behind Chicken Ridge and take to the woods. To the southwest stood Mount Sheridan, and peeping over his shoulder the towering Tetons solemnly refused even to glimmer a good-by.

"For all that," said the Bride, *"au revoir!* We'll come back one of these days, won't we, Billy?"

"Sure!" said Billy. "I'm coming up to put in a power plant in the Grand Cañon, one of these days. This scenery lacks the refining touch of the spillway and the penstock!"

Fifteen minutes' driving brought them to the second halt, a big basin of water, from which steam issued in a myriad of vents. Aconite suggested that they stroll down to the beach and take a look at the water. They found it in a slow turmoil, the mud rising from the bottom in little fountains of turbidity, the whole effect being that which might be expected if some mud-eating giant were watching his evening porridge, expecting it momentarily to boil.

"I don't care much for this," said the Bride.

"I'm not crazy about it myself," assented the Artist.

"What's the next marvel?" asked the Colonel.

"Wedded trees," said Aconite.

"Getting sated with 'em," said the Poet.

"Apollinaris Springs, Sylvan Lake, fine views of Yellowstone Lake and the mountains, bully rocks and things clear to Cody."

"And on the other hand," said the Professor, "what are the features on the regular road from which we have diverged?"

"Everything you come to see," responded Aconite. "Mud Volcano, with a clear spring in the grotto right by it; Mud Geyser, off watch for a year or more; Trout Creek, doubled around into the N. P. trade-mark; Sulphur Mountain—we can camp right near there, and see it in the morning, when we ought to see it—and on beyond, the Grand Cañon and everything. Besides—unless we go that-a-way, we'll never git back unless we come by the Burlington around by Toluca and Billings. Of course, it's all the same to me—I don't keer if we never go back or git anywhere. I'm havin' a good time."

"Turn the plugs around," said the Colonel.

In half an hour or so they were back on the great north road again. The horses seemed to feel the pull of the stable—still days ahead, for they trotted briskly along, while the tourists gazed with sated eyes on the beautiful Yellowstone River on the right hand, its pools splashing with the plunges of the great trout; and on their left the charming mountain scenery. Even the grotesque Mud Volcano, with its suggestions of the horrible and uncouth, failed to elicit the screams from the Bride, or the ejaculations of amazement from the men which characterized their deliverances earlier in the journey. Entering Hayden Valley, they were delighted at the sight in the middle distance of a dozen or more buffaloes, which held up their heads for a long look, and disappeared into the bushes. Not ten minutes later, fifty or sixty elk walked down to the Yellowstone to drink, crossing the road within a minute of the tourists' passage. Aconite pulled up in the shadow of Sulphur Mountain, the Hired Man, with the assistance of the party, soon had a fine fire blazing, and presently a pan of trout, hooked by the Bride, the Groom, the Artist and the Poet, and dressed by the skilful Aconite, were doing to a turn on the skillet.

The Hired Man, realizing that he was under obligation to tell his version of the "darndest thing" in his experience, was solemn, as befits a public performer. When the psychological moment was proclaimed by the falling down into a roseate pile of coals of the last log for the night, he discharged his duty and told this unimportant tale:

HENRY PETERS'S SIGNATURE

THE HIRED MAN'S SECOND TALE

The Colonel's story of how the law and the courts work, reminded me of what happened to old Hen Peters and his forty-second nephew, Hank. It all arose from a debate at the literary at the Bollinger school-house back in Iowa.

You see, old Hen's girl Fanny come home from the State Normal at Cedar Falls as full of social uplift as a yeast-cake, and framed up this literary. It was a lulu of a society, and nights when the sledding was good, the teams just surrounded the lot, and the bells jingled as uplifting as you could ask.

The night of the scrap Hank brought Fanny. The debate was on which was the most terrible scourge, fire or water. Hank was on the negative, and Fanny's father on the affirmative. Old Hen spoke of the way prairie fires deva*s*tated things in an early day, and read history, and gave a beautiful tribute to the Chicago fire and the O'Leary cow. Hank coughed with the dust kicked up when Hen sat down, but he got back with a rhapsody on the Hoang-Ho floods, and the wet season in Noah's time. He said that his honorable opponent ought to take a moment or two from time to time to ascertain the properties of water as a scourge, as an inward remedy, and as a lotion.

Now besides having an appetite for red-eye, old Hen was whiskery and woolly-necked, and handling lots of tame hay, he looked sort of unwashed. So the crowd yelled shameful and laughed; and when Hen got up to answer, he was so mad his whiskers stood out like a rooster's hackle, his words came out in a string like, all lapped on one another, and blurred, and linked together so you couldn't tell one from the other; and finally they reversed on the bobbin, and gigged back into his system, and rumbled and reverberated around in him like a flock of wild cattle loose in an empty barn; and the crowd got one of those giggly fits when every one makes the other laugh till they are sore and sick. Asa Wagstaff fell backward out of a window on to a hitching-post, and made Brad Phelps' team break loose. Old Hen stood shaking his fist at them and turning so red in the face that he got blue, and sat down without saying a syllable that any one could understand.

You could hear folks hollering and screaming in fits of that laughing disease going home, and getting out and rolling in the snow because they were in agony, and nothing but rolling would touch the spot. But old Hen Peters seemed to be immune.

Now, in a debate, no man is supposed to have friends or relations, and he floors his man with anything that comes handy, and Hank never dreamed that Hen would hold hardness when he got over his mad fit. Hank and Fanny had things all fixed up, and had been pricing things at the Banner Store, and sitting up as late as two o'clock; but the next Sunday night she met him at the door and told him maybe he'd better not come into the sitting-room till her pa cooled off. Hank was knocked off his feet, and they stood out in the hall talking sort of tragic until old Hen yelled "Fanny!" from the sitting-room, and they pretty near jumped out of their skins, and stood farther apart, and Fanny went in. In the spring there was a row over the line fence, ending in a devil's lane. Fanny looked pretty blue, only when she was fighting with her pa. Hen would lecture about the two Peters brothers that came across in 1720, and how all Peterses that were not descended from them were Nimshies and impostors.

"I despise and hate," says he, "a Nimshi and an impostor."

Then Fanny would shoot back a remark about the Iowa *Herald's* college, and when was her pa going to paint the Peters coat-of-arms on the hay-rake and the hog-house, using sarcasm that no man could understand after being out of school as long as her father had been. Sometimes the old man would forget the spurious registry of the Hank family in the Peters herd-book, and would argue that relations, even the most remote and back-fence kind, ought to be prosecuted if they even dreamed of marrying; and then Fanny would say that it is such a pleasure to know that folks are not always related when they claim to be. Hen would then cuss me for not taking care of my horses' shoulders or something, and things would get no better rapidly.

Young folks need to meet once in a while in order to keep right with each other, and Jim Miller and I often spoke of the way old Hen was splitting Hank and Fanny apart. Then an Illinois man come out and bought Hank out at a hundred an acre, and Hank wadded his money into his pocket, and bid good-by to the neighborhood for good and all. He never crossed the township line again. Fanny flirted like sixty, and cried when she was alone; but old Hen was as tickled as a colt.

It seemed like a judgment on Hen for driving as good a man as Hank to Dakota to have Fillmore Smythe begin yelping on his trail. His first yelp was a letter, asking Hen to call and pay a three-hundred-dollar note Fillmore had for collection. And here's where the law begins to seep into the story. Hen had Fanny type-write a scorching answer, saying that Hen Peters had discounted his bills since before Fillmore Smythe was unfortunately born, and didn't owe no man a cent; and Hen was so mad that he kicked a fifty-dollar collie pup, and hurt its feelings so it never would work, but went to killing young pigs and sheep the way a collie will if you ever sour their nature by licking them. Funny about collies.

One day old Hen come in from the silo, and saw Fillmore Smythe's team tied at the gate, and Fillmore sitting with Fanny on the stoop, reading *Lucile*.

"I hope I see you well, Mr. Peters," said the lawyer, kind of smooth-like.

"None the better for seein' you, sir," said Hen, jamming his mouth shut when he got through so his mustache and whiskers were all inserted into each other.

Now this was no way to treat a person from town, and Fanny began saying how wonderful the sunset was last night, and asking did he ever see the moon-vine flowers pop out in bloom in the gloaming, and to curb her neck and step high the way they do when they're bitted in college.

"Any partic'lar business here?" asked old Hen.

"Ah, yes!" said Smythe. "In addition to the pleasure of seeing you and your accomplished family, I desired a conference as to the curious way in which that little note—"

"Well, now that you've seen my accomplished family as much as I want you to," growled Hen, "you can git. I told you all I'm goin' to about what you call my note."

"But," said Fillmore, sort of like he was currying a kicking mule, "if you'd consent to look at it, I'm sure it would all return to your mind!"

Hen fired him off the place, though, and he sued Hen. The old man was affected a good deal like the collie pup, and mulled it over, and got sour on the world, especially lawyers that blackmailed and forged. He said he knew well enough that Smythe either did it or knew who did, and that every lawyer ought to be hung. I argued for imprisonment for the first offense for a no-account lawyer like Smythe, with a life sentence if it was proved that he knew any law, and the death penalty for good lawyers like Judge McKenzie; and Hen was so mad at me for what I said that he wouldn't let me have the top buggy the next Sunday night when I needed it the worst way.

The big doings come off when the case came up to be tried. I quit hauling ensilage corn, and went with Fanny and the old folks up to the county seat to give testimony that Hen never signed that note. Fanny stayed with Phœbe Relyea; but the rest of us stopped at the Accidental Hotel, where most of the jurors and others tangled up in court stayed too.

The lawyer in the case ahead of us was a newcomer, and strung it out day after day to advertise himself, and yelled so you could hear him over in the band-stand, to show his ability. Hen, all the time, was getting more and more morbid, and forgot his temperance vows, and tried to talk about the case to everybody. About half the time it would be a juryman he would try to confide in, and this made trouble on account of their thinking he was trying to influence them. One night Hen was owly as sin, drinking with Walker Swayne from Pleasant Valley Township; and when he cried into his beer because Fillmore Smythe was trying to swindle him and blast his good name, Walker slapped him for approaching him on a case he might be called to sit on. I put Hen to bed at the Revere House, and told Mrs. Peters he'd been called home. She 'phoned out to have him count the young turkeys, and the Swede second man had no more sense than to say he had not been there, instead of placing him where they had no telephone, as an honest hired man with any sprawl would have done. You couldn't trust this Swede as far as you could throw a thesaurus by the tail. I am not saying that he was corrupt; but he was just thumb-hand-sided and lummoxy, and blurted, "Hae ain't bane hare" into the transmitter with never a thought of the danger of telling the truth. Mrs. Peters didn't know what to be distressed about, and just because I'm paid the princely salary I get for saying nothing about such things, she jumped on me like a duck on a June-bug.

When Hen and I went to McKenzie's office the night before our case came up, the lawyer was worried. He asked us if we knew who was going to testify against us.

"No," snapped Hen; "an' I don't care. Nobody ever saw me sign that note, and it don't make any matter."

Then he went on to tell what great friends he and Judge Brockway used to be, when the judge used to shoot prairie-chickens in Hen's stubble, and Mrs. Peters cooked the chickens for the judge.

"Brockway thinks as much of me as a brother," said Hen. "He told me as much when he was running for judge. He won't see me stuck."

This didn't seem to impress Judge McKenzie much. He still looked worried, and said the other side had got every banker in town on their side as handwriting experts.

"I don't like the looks of things," said he.

Hen flew mad at the idea of his lawyer's hinting that any man could get stuck in such a case. The judge tried to explain, and Hen asked him how much the other side was paying him, and the judge threw up his job. Pretty soon, though, Hen got him to take a new retainer of fifteen dollars, and he opened a new account in his books. This made Hen feel good, for the judge was great with juries when he was sober. He was good and sober now, for he had just taken the drinking cure for the third time. We had lots of faith in Providence and McKenzie, but were scary as three-year-olds that night at any strange noise in the brush. You know how it is when you feel that way.

Things went wrong the next morning. So many of the jurors said that Hen had talked to them that Judge Brockway just glared at Hen, and said that the court was not favorably impressed by tactics of that sort.

Walker Swayne told how he had slapped Hen's chops to drive off his improper advances, and Judge Brockway said that he could not condone breaches of the peace; but a juror, like a woman, was justified if any one; and when old Hen asked Mac for the Lord's sake, were there any women sitting on this case, Brockway wilted Hen again with a look.

I asked Hen at recess if he thought Brockway would ask him as a friend and brother to sit up on the bench, and he flared up and said Brock was all right, but was disguising his feelings as a judge.

"He's got a disguise that's a bird," said I, and Hen said I might consider myself discharged; but wrote me a note after court took up, hiring me back.

The next juror up related another case of Hen's vile tactics, and the judge threatened to send him to jail if anything more bobbed up. Hen fell back into his chair limpsy, like dropping a wet string,—all spiral like,—and everybody looked at us in horror for our pollyfoxing with the jury. As a matter of fact, in his state of beer and overconfidingness, Hen would have wept on the breast of a wooden Indian that would have held still while he told of the octopus and its forgeries. In all the time I worked for him, he never tried once to destroy the jury system or his country's liberty.

Finally they found twelve men that didn't know anything about the case or anything, and had no opinions or prejudices for or against anything, and the lawyers told the jury what they expected to prove.

"The sacred system of trial by jury," said Fillmore Smythe, "has been saved from the attacks of the defendant by an incorruptible court. Placed on trial before this intelligent jury, what the defendant may do I can not even guess; but we have here in court his note, signed in his own proper person."

"'T ain't so!" busted out Hen, in his own improper person. "You hain't got no such note!"

"One more interruption of this sort," said the judge, peeking down at Hen, "and the example that I'll make of *you* won't soon be forgotten. Proceed, Mr. Smythe!"

"Concealing his love!" whispers I to Hen; and he put the leg of his chair on my foot and ground it around till I almost yelled.

When they had marked the note "Exhibit A" the way they do, Smythe said "Plaintiff rests," though they didn't seem near as tired as our side was, and the court let out for noon. They let McKenzie take the note with him to look at. There it was on one of those blanks that it cost me a good claim in Kansas once to practise writing on, and I never got to be much of a penman either; it was signed "Henry Peters" as natural as life.

"Well," questioned Mac, as Hen turned it over, "what do you say to it, Henry?"

I could feel that all the time McKenzie had had a hunch that Hen had really signed the note, and Hen felt it, too, and he threw to the winds the remains of his last conversion, and his fear that Mac would strike again, and talked as bad as if he was learning a calf to drink.

"Why, you scoundrelly Keeley graduate," he

yelled, "what did I tell you! That's a forgery, as any one but a half-witted pettifogger could see by lookin' at it!"

"I sever my connection with this case right now," said Mac, away down in his chest, and as dignified as a ring-master. "No inebriated litigant can refer to the struggle and expense I have incurred in lifting myself to a nobler plane of self-control, and then call for my skill and erudition in extricating him from the quagmire of the law in which his imprudences have immeshed him. Go, sir, to some practitioner so far lost to manhood as to be able to resist the temptation to brain you with his notary-public's seal. Leave me to my books!"

Mac went into the next room and shut the door, but did not lock it.

"I can see," said Colonel Baggs, "the wisdom of leaving it on the latch."

I took and apologized for Hen; but Mac stuck his nose in a book and waved me away. If Hen had been a little drunker he would have cried; and I went back to woo McKenzie some more. Finally, he agreed to come into the case again, on payment of another retainer fee of twenty dollars. Hen was game, and skinned a double-X off his roll without a flinch. Mac opened up a new account in his books, and Hen, for my successful diplomacy, raised my wages two dollars a month. It was a great lesson to me.

Of course I could see that it was not Hen's signature; for his way of writing was Spencerian, modified by handling a fork, shucking corn, and by the ink drying up while he was thinking. The name on the note was kind of backhand. Mac asked about other Henry Peterses, and Hen told him that there was a man that passed by that name in the county a year or so back, but that he never had credit for three hundred cents, never bought any such machinery, and had escaped to Dakota.

When old Hen testified, he had one of his spluttery spells of reverse English caused by his language getting wound on the shafting, and his denying the signature didn't seem to make much impression on any one. Smythe made him admit that he had bought the tools, and had no check-stub of the payment; and when he said he paid Bloxham in cash, Smythe laid back and grinned, and McKenzie moved that the grin be took down by the reporter, so he could move to strike it out.

Everybody just seemed to despise us but Mac;

and I was as ashamed as a dog. This Bloxham, the machine agent, was dead, and most everybody there had been to his funeral; but it took half an hour to prove his demise. Two jurors went to sleep on this, and one of them hollered "Whay! whay!" in his sleep, like he was driving stock, and Brockway pounded and glared at *us* for it. I wished I was back with Ole running the silage cutter.

All this time we kind of lost sight of Mrs. Peters and Fanny. Fanny sent some word over to the Accidental the second evening, and her mother went over to Relyea's, and came back kind of fluttery. I was sent to Fanny with a suit-case of dresses her mother had there, and Fanny was in the awfullest taking with blushing and her breath fluttering like a fanning-mill with palpitation of the heart that I couldn't think what was the matter with her. She had never blushed at seeing me before. I began to see what a pretty girl she was; but I couldn't think of tying myself down, even if she did. She came up close to me, shook hands with me, and bid me good-by when I came away. This was a sign she wanted to hold some one's hand or was going away; and I knew she wasn't expected to go away. It set me to thinking. Mac said he wouldn't want her testimony until the surrey-butter part, if then. I made up my mind I'd go up and talk with her once in a while, instead of sticking around down-town. But this trial absorbed my attention when the experts came on.

Smythe had had a magnification made of the name on the note, and the one on old Hen's letter, and every banker in town went on and swore about these names. John Smythe, Fillmore's half-brother, knew Hen's signature; and had had to study handwriting so hard in the bank that he had got to be an expert. He was always thought a kind of a ninny, but here's where he sure did loom up with the knowledge. He acted just as smart as those Chicago experts we read about, and living right here in the county all the time, and never out of the bank a day! A good deal of my ability comes from dropping into some big city like Fort Dodge or Ottumwa, or maybe Sioux City, or Des Moines every winter, and getting on to the new wrinkles and broadening out; but John Smythe was always behind that brass railing, like a cow in stanchions. And yet he was able to see that those two signatures just had to be made by the same man. This spiel was cutting ice with the jury, and Mac roared and pointed out where they were different; but Smythe hinted that it only seemed so because Mac was ignorant. He could just see the same man a-making them—the way the stem of the "P" was made, and the finish of the "y" like a pollywog's tail made it a cinch. Hen swore under his powerful breath that it was a dad-burned lie; but it looked awful plausible to me.

"You notice," said Fillmore, "that the name on the letter is more scrawly and uneven?"

"Yes," said John, "but that merely means that he used a different pen or was nervous. I think I see in the last the characteristic tremor of anger."

This looked bad to me, for if ever a man had a right to the characteristic tremor of anger, it was old Hen when he signed that letter. It showed Smythe knew what he was at.

Mac showed them a lot of Hen's real signatures, but the experts said they only made it clearer. Every one had a little curlicue or funny business that put Hen deeper in the hole; and he finally chucked the bunch, all the reporter didn't have, in the stove. Fillmore Smythe inflated himself and blew up at this; but Brockway, still concealing his love, said that while it looked bad, and the jury might consider this destruction of evidence as one of the facts, the papers belonged to defendant and the court didn't see fit to do anything. Our case looked as bad as it could, and I didn't see why Smythe hollered so about it. The jury looked on us as horse-thieves and crooks, and every time old Hen stepped, he balled things up worse.

Whitten, of the First National, was stronger than John Smythe. He said it was physically impossible for any man but the one that signed the letter to have made that note; and he was an expert from away back. He pointed out the anger tremor, too. Mac showed him how the check-signatures all looked like that on the letter, and not like the one on the note; but Whitten said a man was always calm when he made a note, and mad as a hatter when he drew a check. Knowing Hen, this looked plausible to me, and made a hit with the jury. The man that hollered "Whay!" wrote it down on his cuff.

Ole Pete Hungerford, the note-shaver, snorted disdainfully that there was no doubt that the note was genuine. He swore that a bogus check I made was genuine, too; and got redder than a turkey when he found I had made it, and said it was the work of a skilful forger. The man that hollered "Whay!"

looked at me in horror, and wrote some more on his cuff. I felt considerable cheap.

Every expert said the same thing. I believe that there was one while when Hen would have admitted he signed the note if they had called him and rawhided him enough. Hen had some hopes when Zenas Whitcher of the Farmers' Bank had some doubts about one signature; but he flattened out again when he found it was the one on the letter that had old Zenas guessing, and that he was dead sure the one on the note was a sure-enough genuine sig, only it looked as if he was trying to disguise his hand. Fillmore seemed to think pretty well of this, and had them all go back and swear about this disguise business. They could all see wiggly spots now and places gone over twice where Hen had doubled on his trail to throw pursuers off the track and disguise his hand. It begun to look to me like Hen was up to some skulduggery,—all these smooth guys swearing like that,—but Hen was paying me my wages and needed friends, and I stuck. He looked down his nose like an egg-sucking pup. When I came on to swear that it was not Hen's signature on the note, my mind was so full of curlicues and pollywogs' tails, and anger tremors, and disguises, and the gall of my swearing against these big men that had money to burn, that I went into buck fever, and was all shot to rags by Smythe's cross-examination, —any of you fellows would be,—so that I finally admitted that the note looked pretty good to me, and that I'd have probably taken it for Hen's note if I'd been a banker and had it offered to me. Mac threw up his hands, said that was all our evidence, then went at the jury hammer and tongs, and I looked at poor old Hen all collapsed down into his chair like a rubber snake, and I went and hid.

In the morning I crawled out, supposing that it would all be over, and wondering where I'd find Hen; but I heard Judge McKenzie's closing argument rolling out of the court-house windows like thunder. I didn't care for eloquence the way I was feeling, and was just sneaking away, when who should I run on to but Fanny walking with a fellow down under the maples. I was shocked, for she was hanging to his arm the way no nice girl ought to do unless it's dark. I trailed along behind to see who it was, when the fellow turned his head quick, and I saw it was Hank. They come up to me, Fanny still shamelessly hanging to his arm, looking excited and foolish, like they had just experienced religion or got engaged.

"Doc," said Hank, "we've just found out about it!"

"I've knowed it a long time," said I coldly. "What is it?"

"This lawsuit," said Hank—"is it over, or still running?"

"It's still running," I said. "Listen at the machinery rumble up there. It's all over but the shouting, and we've got a man hired to do that. Why?"

They never said a word, but scooted up the stairs. I strolled in and found Mac's machinery throwed out of gear by Hank's interruption. Hen was still collapsed, and didn't see Hank. Mac turned grandly to the judge, and told him that a witness he had been laboring to secure the attendance of from outside the jurisdiction had blowed in, and he wanted the case reopened. Smythe rose buoyantly into the air and hooted, but Brockway coldly reopened the case, and Hank was sworn. The juror that wrote on his cuff looked disgusted, but he wrote Hank's name and age with the rest of his notes.

"Where do you live?" asked Mac.

"South Dakota," answered Hank.

"Examine 'Exhibit A,'" said Mac proudly, handing Hank the note, "and tell the jury when if ever you have seen it before!"

"When it was signed," said Hank.

Old Hen kind of straightened up. Fanny sat down by him, and put her arm about him. She sure did look pretty.

"Who signed that note?" asked Mac, with his voice swelling like a double B-flat bass tuba.

"I did," answered Hank.

"I object," yelled Smythe, trembling like a leaf.

"Overruled," said Brockway in a kind of tired way.

"Do you owe this note?" asked Mac.

"You bet I do," answered Hank, "and got the money to pay it. I went to Dakota and forgot about the darned note. Bloxham shipped the machinery out there to me. It's my note all right; Hen Peters never saw it till Smythe got it."

The room was full of wilted experts. This did not appeal to them at all. McKenzie laughed fiendishly, as if he'd had this thing arranged all the time. The jury looked foolish, all but the one that hollered "Whay!" and he looked mad. I could see Hen reviving, and throwing off his grouch at Hank. Fillmore Smythe said he had a question or two in cross-examination.

"What kin are you to the defendant?" he asked.

"That's a disputed point," replied Hank. "I dunno 's I'm any by blood."

"Are you not related to him in any way?" asked Fillmore, prying into things the way they do.

"You bet I am," spoke up Hank, looking over at Fanny, and getting red in the face. "He don't know about it; but since night before last I've been his son-in-law."

CHAPTER X

IT was in camp at Sulphur Mountain that the Artist's fate overtook him. The gods pulled his name from the hat by the hard hand of the Hired Man. This mystic event overshadowed the visit to Sulphur Spring—though that was in every respect a success. It was timed so as to give them the last of the dawn—the splendid flood of rare light which precedes the first cast of his noose by the Hunter of the East—and both eye and camera caught beautifully the myriads of steam spirals ascending from the hill, each from its own vent. The spring itself, the Poet compared to the daily press, in that it made a mighty and unceasing pother and dribbled out a mighty small amount of run-off—and that the output stained everything with which it came in contact a bright yellow.

"No matter what it splashes," said he, "stick or stone, church, family or court, it yellows it."

"Speaking of courts," said the Artist, "and the

law—I think our friends the Colonel and Bill have dealt altogether too flippantly with them. I shall give you another view to-night."

"Do you notice," said the Bride, "how peaceful and sort of comforting the river is? It is as placid as a lake—or some deep river—like the Thames—made for pleasure boats and freighters."

"See the trout leap!" shouted the Colonel.

"Well," said Aconite, "you jest watch that river, an' it'll surprise yeh. It ain't reformed yit, if it hez sobered up. An' right here—Whoa!"

They were at the crossing of Alum Creek, and Aconite halted to point out matters of interest.

"Right hyar," said he, "or in this vicinity, took place one of the most curious things that ever happened to Old Jim Bridger. This crick is all alum, 'specially up at the head. Over yon"—pointing to the eastern bank of the Yellowstone with his whip—"is a stream named Sour Crick comin' in from the east. It's one or the other of these cricks, 'r one of the same kind, that Old Jim Bridger was obliged to go up f'r three days on his bronk, one time. It was a long trip. But on the way back he noticed that the crick had flooded the country, an' gone down ag'in, an' it seemed to him that he was makin' better time than goin' up. The hills that was low an' rounded when he went up, looked to him steeper, and higher, an' more clustered than they was. He didn't believe this could be, an' wondered how folks' minds acted when they was goin' crazy. Finely, he found his first camp, after he had been on the back track only half a day. He couldn't understand how he could 've made the distance in four hours that it took two days to cover comin' up, and begun to get the Willies. He come to a bottom that had scattered trees on comin' up, and it was timbered so thick now that he couldn't go through it— but it wa'n't furder through than a hedge fence. Then he noticed that his bronk was hobblin', and observed that his hooves was drawed down to mere points, but good-shaped hoss's hooves all the same —they was just little, like the hooves of a toy hoss. At last he come to a place whar there had been two great boulders that had been forty rods apart when he went up—he knowed 'em by marks he had made on 'em in his explorin' around—an' danged if they wasn't jammed up agin' each other so's they touched both stirrups when he rode through between 'em. 'An' there he was back whar he started from in a little more'n half a day. He got to studyin' it over, an' found that this crick of alum water had overflowed and jest puckered the scenery up, so that the distances to anywhere along its valley was shrunk up to most nothin'!"

The Hired Man looked away off to the east, and mentioned that the fish-hawks were thick this morning. The Bride giggled a very slight giggle—but the others were impassive. They seemed to be absorbing some of the taciturnity of the Indian. In the meantime the river did begin to surprise them. After miles of deep quiet, its valley walls began to crowd together.

"Somebody has been sprinkling alum on this scenery," suggested the Colonel—"eh, Aconite?"

Aconite clucked solemnly to the team.

The road was forced to the very edge of the bank. The river became mildly excited, as if in protest at the constriction. The road grew wilder and the landscape more rugged; and suddenly, the river, tortured by the pressure of the narrow trench provided for it, began raging and foaming, and sending up a hoarse roar, which grew upon them like an approaching tempest. The road trod first a narrow shelf above the terrific rapids, and then a bridge hung like a stretched rope over an awesome abyss. For half a mile the tumult below grew, until it seemed as if water could bear no more—when suddenly the river, just now ravening through a mere fifty-foot crack in the rocks, was gone. It turned abruptly away from the road, and fell away into space. They had passed the Upper Falls, where the Yellowstone, in a great spouting curve drops a sheer hundred and twelve feet in a curtain of white water, and sends up from the bottom of the cañon its hymn to liberty, in a cloud of mist.

They were no longer the tired sight-seers, with jaded senses; for this was new. They felt the thrill of power. And as they passed on, promising themselves a return when camp should be made, they cried out in delight as the Grand Cañon of the Yellowstone displayed the stupendous sluiceway into which the river had fallen. At their feet the lovely Crystal Falls of Cascade Creek played exquisitely, almost unnoted. The roar of the falls followed them to the Cañon Hotel near which they camped, and leaving the pitching of the tents to the men, they walked to the brink of the cañon, and gazed upon the most perfect scene, perhaps, that water, in its flow to the sea, has anywhere sculptured and painted to delight the eye of man. The Yosemite has greater heights; the Colorado offers huger dimensions, the Niagara or the Victoria possess mightier cataracts; but nowhere else is there such a riot of color, such dizzy heights, such glooming verdure, and such mad waters, united in one surpassingly splendid scenic whole.

They saw it all—that day, and subsequent days. They lingered as though unable to leave at all. They revisited the Upper Falls before seeing the lower, so as to view them in fairness and with no injustice to what seemed unsurpassable beauty.

"And now," said the Bride, "take me to the greater falls."

It was as if she had seen all but the Holy of Holies, and felt the exaltation suitable for higher things.

They were amazed at the tremendous plunge of more than three hundred feet which their river (as they now called it) made at the Lower Falls—even to the foot of which they descended. They looked from Inspiration Point, from Artist's Point, from Lookout Point. They watched the stream dwarfed by distance to a trickle, and strangely silent, as it wandered at the bottom of the gorge.

And at last the time came to leave. Early in the morning they were to start; and the last camp-fire was smoldering to ashes on that last night when the Artist found his audience collected, the demand for payment of his obligation presented; and without preface, save the statement that his was the story of a young fool, told his tale.

THE RETURN OF JOHN SMITH

THE STORY NARRATED BY THE ARTIST

His name was John Smith, but he was not otherwise unworthy of notice. Out of her vast, tempestuous experience Blanche Slattery admitted this as she swept into the offices and looked down at the boy, noting the curl in his hair which speaks of the hidden vein of vanity, the wide blue eyes which told of a stratum of mysticism, the unsubdued brawn of hand and wrist which reminded her more of harvests than of field-meets, the mouth closely shut in purposeful attention to one Mr. Thompson's *Commentaries on the Law of Corporations*.

He thought her the stenographer and kept his eyes on the page. She laid a card on his desk—a card at which he looked with some attention before rising to meet her eyes with his own, which dilated in a sort of horror, as she thought. Her cheek actually burned, though it grew no redder, as she turned aside with the crisp statement of her business.

"I want to see Judge Thornton," she said.

Without a word John Smith pushed a button and listened at a telephone. The judge took his time as usual, and John gazed at the Slattery person with the receiver pressed against his ear. She was powdered and painted; the full corsage of her dress glittered with passementerie; in her form the latest fad was exaggerated into a reminiscence of medieval torturing-devices. Through the enamel of her skin dark crescents showed under her great black eyes, the whites of which were mottled here and there with specks of red. The once sweet lips had lost their softness of curve with their vermeil tincture and had fallen into hard repose.

John knew her profession and how she dominated her world of saddest hilarity—a world which through all mutations of time and institutions persists as on that day when Samson went to Gaza. He felt that there emanated from her a sort of authority, like a sinister manifestation of the atmosphere surrounding men of power and sway—as though by dark and devious ways this soul, too, had carved out a realm in which it darkly reigned. She wondered, when he spoke, whether the softness in his voice were for her or whether it were merely a thing of habit.

"Judge Thornton is sorry that he can not see you this morning," he said. "Between ten and eleven to-morrow if it is convenient for you—"

"All right," she said. "I'll be here at half-past ten. Good morning!"

The perfume of her presence, the rustling of her departure, the husky depth of her voice haunting his memory, the vast vistas through which the mind of the country boy fared forth venturesomely, impelled by the new contacts of this town in which he had undertaken to scale the citadel of professional success—all these militated against the sober enticements of the law of corporations; and when Judge Thornton entered unheard, John Smith started as though detected in some offense.

"The law," said the judge, launching the hoary quotation, "is a jealous mistress."

John Smith blushed, but saw no lodgment for a denial where there was no accusation. He had been allowing his thoughts to go wool-gathering; but now he began questioning the judge on the doctrine of the rights of minority stock-holders. The judge condescended to a five-minute lecture which would have been costly had it been given for a client before the court. In the midst of the talk there bustled in a young man—a boy, in fact, who accosted the lawyer familiarly.

"Just a minute, Judge. About that mass-meeting Tuesday—I'm Johnson of the *News,* you know. Will you speak?"

"I don't think the readers of the *News* are lying awake about it," answered the judge, looking at the boy amusedly. "But my present intentions go no further than to attend the meeting."

"What about the movement for cheaper gas?" asked the reporter. "Will the meeting start anything?"

"The meeting," said the judge, "will be a law unto itself."

"Sure," replied Johnson of the *News*. "But a word from you as to the extortions of the gas company—"

"Will be addressed to the meeting—if I have any," said the judge. "I—"

"Oh, all right!" interrupted the boy. "That's what I wanted! Good-by!"

John Smith's amazement at the boy's self-possession and ready, impudent effrontery, passed away in a visualization of Judge Thornton's big, strong figure at the meeting, fulminating against oppression—the oppression of to-day—as did Patrick Henry and James Otis against the wrongs of their times. Now, as of old, thought John Smith, the lawyer is a public officer, charged with public duties, alert to do battle with any tyrant or robber. He flushed with pleasure at this conception of the greatness of the profession.

"As a science," said the judge, as though in answer to John's thought, "it's the greatest field of the intellect. It's the practice that's laborious and full of compromises."

"Yes," said John Smith, lamenting the interrupted lecture on the rights of minority stock-holders. Judge Thornton had donned his coat and his hat.

"I'm off for the day. Good day to you—oh, I almost forgot. Do you want to hear a paper on *King Lear* to-night? Nellie thought you might. Poor paper—but you'll meet people, and that's a part of the game."

"Oh, yes!" cried John. "I'd be glad to!"

"Come to the house about eight," said the judge, "and go with Nellie and me."

Ah, this was living! Why, at home he knew scarcely a person who had read more of Shakespeare than the quarrel scene in the Fifth Reader. Surely it was good fortune that had made his father and Judge Thornton playmates in boyhood. And to go with Nellie Thornton, too!

"Paint out that sign!" he heard some one say. "And what goes in the place of it, sir?" asked the painter. " 'Thornton & Smith,' " replied the judge's voice. "My son-in-law, Mr. Smith, has been taken into the firm."

The stenographer saw exaltation in his face as he closed the safe, bade her good night and went home.

As he sat beside Nellie that evening, he remembered the fancied colloquy between her father and the imaginary painter, and shuddered as he contemplated the possibility of thought-transference and of its ruinous potentialities. As a protection against telepathy he gave his whole attention to Judge Thornton's paper on *Lear*. The indescribable agony of the old king's frenzy, the whirling tempest of the tragedy in which he wandered to his doom clutched at the boy's heart. The wolfish Goneril and Regan, the sweet Cordelia, the bared gray head, the storm, the night— By some occult warning John Smith knew that Nellie was not pleased with his absorption, and that the discussion had begun.

"This treatment is *so* original," said the lady president. "Everybody must be full of questions. Now let us have a perfectly free discussion—don't wait to be called upon, please!"

To John Smith the lady president seemed enthusiasm personified; yet only a few people rose, and these merely said how much they had enjoyed the paper. John Smith could see himself on his feet pouring forth comment and exposition, but he sat close, hoping that no adverse fate might direct the lady president's attention to him. The discussion was dragging; one could tell that from the increasing bubbliness of the lady president's enthusiasm as she strove conscientiously to fulfil her task of imposing culture upon society.

"I'm sure there must be something more," she said. "Perhaps the most precious pearl of thought of the evening awaits just one more dive. Mrs. Brunson, can you not—"

"I always feel presumptuous," said Mrs. Brunson,

hoarsening her voice to the pitch she always adopted in public speaking, "when I differ from other commentators. But I also feel that the true critic must put himself in the place of the character under examination. Isn't there a good deal of justification for Goneril and Regan? I do not see, personally, how Lear could be supposed to need all those hundred knights, with their drinking and roistering and dogs and—and all that. I believe Lear's fate was of his own making, and—"

John Smith, the unsophisticated, was startled. The unutterable fate of "the old, kind king"—could this Olympian circle hold such treason?

"No, you unnatural hags,
I will have such revenges on you both,
That all the world shall—I will do such things—
What they are, yet I know not; but they shall be
The terrors of the earth. You think I'll weep;
No, I'll not weep:
I have full cause of weeping; but this heart
Shall break into a hundred thousand flaws,
Or ere I'll weep. O, fool, I shall go mad!"

The fiery denunciation rang in the boy's ears in answer to the words of this modern woman with her silks and plumes, standing here in a church and, in spite of the softening things of her heritage, sympathizing with these fierce sisters! Others rose and agreed with her. One read the words of Regan:

"O, sir, you are old;
Nature in you stands on the very verge
Of her confine: you should be ruled and led
By some discretion that discerns your state
Better than you yourself."

These, was the comment, were the really sane words regarding Lear.

"Oh, well!" said Judge Thornton as John broke his fast and the abstinence of a lifetime in the parlor, upon the cakes and wine served by Nellie. "It didn't surprise me a bit. Mrs. Brunson thinks she'd do as Goneril and Regan did with their father—and she would. She'd avoid the little peccadilloes with Edmund and so remain technically virtuous—the best people are the worst, in some things, John, never forget that. It will be useful to remember it. And the worst are nearly as good as the best—come into the office when that Slattery person comes in the morning, and you'll see what I mean. I'll give you some papers to draw for her."

The Slattery person swept into the private office with a rustle of stiffest silks, reminding the youth of the corn-husks at home in shucking-time, leaving behind her a whiff of all the Orient. John Smith walked into her presence, palpitating as at the approach to something terrible and daunting and mystically fateful to such as himself—as a sailor might draw warily near the black magnetic rocks, which, approached too closely, would draw the very nails from his ship and dissolve his craft in the billows. When Judge Thornton remarked by way of left-handed introduction that Mr. Smith would draw the papers, the woman paid John no attention other than to bow and look straight before her. The youth felt conscious of the same shuddering admiration for her that he might have felt for some gaudy, bright-eyed serpent.

"It's a simple matter, I guess," she said. "I want to make over some property so Abner Gibbs of Bloomington will get fifty dollars sure every month as long as he lives."

"Not so very simple," said the judge, "but quite possible. But why don't you remit it to him yourself?"

"I want to cinch it while I've the money. You see, it's this way. In—in my—business"—she looked into John Smith's girlish eyes and hesitated—"everything is uncertain. It's a feast or a famine. A wave of reform may strike the town to-morrow, and the lid goes on. The protection you pay for may be taken from you next week. You've no rights. You ain't human. So I fix the fifty a month for the old man while I can, see?"

"Gibbs—Gibbs!" said the judge. "Relation of yours?"

"In a way. Does it make any difference?"

"It goes to the consideration," said the lawyer. "Love and affection, you know."

"Well," said the Slattery person, "his son was my solid man—my side-partner—my husband. The last thing he said when he got his was, 'Blanche, old girl, take care of dad. You know his weakness. Don't let him starve!' And I ain't going to!"

"His weakness?" queried the judge. "What did he mean?"

"Drink," said the Slattery person. "It's in the blood. But he can't last long—and he's Jim's father!"

She looked out of the window and dabbed with a lace handkerchief at her bright eyes, which she dared not wipe for fear of ruin to the appliqué complexion. Suddenly she had, to the mind of the susceptible John Smith, become a woman, with a woman's weakness and yearning over the departed Jim— of the blackness of whose life John had no means of taking the measure. He felt all at once that this person had shown feelings so like those he would have expected from his mother that it startled him.

"Oh, we're all alike!" said the judge when she had gone. "These things are worth the lawyer's study. Human nature—human nature! We must get above it and study it! Just ponder on the contradictions in the bases of life involved in this Slattery person and Mrs. Brunson's feeling toward Lear. Here's a woman, that no one at the circle last night would touch with anything shorter than a ten-foot pole or lighter than a club, who is actually carrying out toward a drunkard in Bloomington a policy of love and humanity that would be beyond Mrs. Brunson. She'd say: 'Let him behave the way I say, and I'll take him in!' Any of us moral folks would do the same, too. No knights and roistering for us! Quite a study—eh, John?"

John sat silent, far afloat from his moorings. The judge was too deep, too ethically acute for him. Perhaps by long association he, John Smith, might grow in moral height and mental grasp, so as to—

"I don't know," said Judge Thornton, "which is the worse—sale of the body, or barter of the soul. I don't mean that the body can be sold without the soul going with it, though Epictetus seems a case in point in favor of the separable-transaction theory; but if it can, sale of the soul would seem the more ruinous. I—"

Judge Thornton was interrupted by the opening of the office door and the entrance of a brisk, capable-looking, Vandyke-bearded man who carried a cane and bore himself with an ease that seemed somehow at war with something of restraint—the ease on the surface, the embarrassment underneath, like a dead swell coming in against the breeze. There was a triumphant gleam in Judge Thornton's eyes, filmed at once with self-possession and inscrutable calm. "Come in, Mr. Avery," he said.

"Just a word with you," said Mr. Avery, "in—"

"Certainly!" said the judge. "Right in here, Mr. Avery."

Mr. Avery passed into the private office. Judge Thornton remained for a word with John Smith.

"This is the vice-president of the gas company," he said. "Don't mention his call and don't allow me to be disturbed."

John Smith was triumphant. The very might of Thornton's ability and power had brought the gas company to its knees! This crucial stage of the gas fight thrust entirely out of his mind the deep moral and ethical consideration of the relations of the Slattery person to the discussion of Lear. The law, as of old, was a great profession. Would any of the Boone County folk be able to believe that he, John Smith, was so near the heart of big things as to sit here while Judge Thornton won this great bloodless victory for the people?

Mr. Avery came out, cordially smiling upon Judge Thornton, who looked triumphant, pleased, uplifted. For a man who had just been throttled, Mr. Avery looked in rather good form.

"I'll send all the papers over to you, Judge," he said. "And I'm mighty glad we've got together. It ought to have been done before; but you know how it is when you leave things to subordinates."

"Oh, well," said the judge. "Of course I'm very glad; but the subordinates may have done the right thing. Maxwell and Wilson are good men, but local conditions may—"

They went out into the anteroom, and John Smith heard them go away together. He felt disquieted. The appearances were so different from what he had expected. Not that it was in the least degree his affair, but—

The newsboy threw in the evening paper. John Smith looked at once for the account of the gas fight.

"The anti-ordinance forces make no secret of their regret that Judge Thornton has seen fit to withdraw his promise to address the mass-meeting on Tuesday. Late this afternoon he told a *News* representative that he would not attend, and that in his opinion a study of the gas question will convince any business man that the illuminant can not be delivered at the meter at anything short of the rate now paid here. This is regarded by some as a reversal of Judge Thornton's position; but, as a matter of fact, in all his public utterances the judge has suspended judgment on the merits of the question. The outlook for a successful movement can not be regarded as bright to-day."

John Smith was looking at the paper as though it were some published blasphemy, some unspeakable profanation of all things good and holy, when Judge Thornton returned, whistling like a man at peace with the world and himself. The judge went into his private office and came out with a thin slip of paper folded in the palm of one smooth, strong hand.

"Too bad you're not a full-fledged lawyer, John, instead of a beginner. I could use you a good deal. My practice is getting more extensive. I've just been retained as the general counsel of the gas company. Oh, all you have to do is to wait and make yourself indispensable! *You'll* be getting plums like that one of these days. It's a great game! Good night."

Good night, indeed! There was no thunder and lightning like that on the heath when Lear went mad; but, to a boy whose world had suddenly tumbled into pieces, the snow which drove softly against his cheek and slithered hissingly along the asphalt was a natural feature to dwell in his memory for ever. He wandered out through the area of high buildings, past the residences, to where the snow rattled on the corn-husks that reminded him of the Slattery person's silks. He had confused visions of Mrs. Brunson, dressed in Judge Thornton's decent high hat, flaunting gaudy garments and painting her face for indescribable drinking-bouts. He came back past the Thornton home, where he paused in the gray dawn and looked at one lace-curtained window to murmur "Good-by." At the door of the office-building where his days had been spent since his coming to town, he went in from force of habit and pushed the button for the elevator. No sound rewarded the effort, and he pushed again impatiently. Then he laughed as he noted the elevator-cages about him, all shut down, all empty, like cells from which the lunatic occupants had escaped. A woman who had begun scrubbing the marble steps looked at him curiously as his mirthless laugh sounded through the empty building.

John Smith climbed flight after flight, opened the door which would never have "Thornton & Smith" on it, sat down at his desk and wrote:

"DEAR FATHER: I am quite well. Everything looks favorable for my studies. Judge Thornton says he wants to do all he can for me, and I think he does; but I guess I am not cut out for a lawyer. It isn't quite what I thought it was. If you are still willing to send me to the state college and give me that agricultural course, I believe I'll go. There's something about the farm that's always there; and you know it's there. I'll be home as soon as I can pack up.

"Your loving son,

"JOHN SMITH."

The party sat for a few moments motionless, as the Artist's voice became silent. Then the Colonel arose, bade them good night, and took the Artist's hand.

"As a legal Slattery person," said he, "I thank you for the tale of the young fool. Good night!"

CHAPTER XI

THE traveler who is wise, going from Grand Cañon Hotel to Tower Falls, will pass over Mount Washburn—and he starts early. He starts early that he may take with him the memory of the Upper and Lower Falls wrapped in the mist which they and night have wrought together, and which the nocturnal calm has perhaps left hanging wraith-like over the tremendous slot so filled with the roar of many waters. And he starts early, too, that he may make the ten-mile climb to Washburn's summit before the day-wind rises and sweeps the mountain's head with that gale which so tears the trees and twists them into a permanent declination, like vegetable dipping needles.

The Seven Wonderers pursued the way of wisdom, and so they startled deer and elk from their night beds along the road to Cascade Creek; and began the climb of Washburn before sunrise. The tops of Dunraven and Hedges Peaks were rosy with morning when the rested cayuses pulled over the first rugged spurs of these peaks, and it was morning with the perfect trees, that stood like spires about them, morning with the columbine and the larkspur, the forget-me-nots and the asters, the fleabane and the paint-brush—and all the wild flowers that enameled the wayside. For many days they had been in the heart of the Rockies, and yet the scenery had not seemed like real mountain scenery. Here for the first time, it became alpine. They threaded Dunraven Pass in the early forenoon, and took the high road straight over the summit. The team leaned hard into the squeaking collars, and frequent stops that the horses might breathe made the tourists glad. Every stop and every turn brought the eye new delights. The great lake came into view again, like a distant splash of silver; and as if for another good-by, away off to the south stood Mount Sheridan, with the three Tetons to the right of it, solemnly overlooking the Park of which they are a part to the eye only.

"Oh! Oh!" said the Bride, gasping. "There's the Grand Cañon, like a crack in the floor!"

"And," said the Poet, "there's the ghost of wasted

power, mistily brooding over the falls, just as when we left."

"Ghost of wasted power!" repeated the Groom. "That's not half bad, Poet."

Another turn, and the Absorakas notched the eastern horizon; and the whole huge valley, with titanic slopes as its farther wall, and the zigzag trench of the cañon as its central drain, lay at their feet. The air was cooler, now, and the breath came short, as lungs labored for more of the rare atmosphere. At their feet lay green meadows and open parks, on which they might have expected to see grazing herds of shaggy black Highland cattle.

Again a few starts and stops, and as if turned into view by machinery, came the northwest quarter of the Park, with all the country they had traversed —Electric Peak, in whose shadow they had entered upon their journey, Sepulcher Mountain, with its grave and the monuments at head and foot no longer to be made out, the valley of Carnelian Creek at their feet, and beyond it the jagged range, of which Prospect, Folsom and Storm Peaks are the culminations.

"That's something you don't always see," said

Aconite, pointing to something away off to the northwest. "That thing is the Devil's Slide."

"And we saw his Inkstand yesterday," said the Hired Man. "He seems to've preëmpted a lot of this here region."

"Well," remarked the Colonel sardonically, "isn't the Park dedicated to the enjoyment, as well as the benefit of the people?"

"It started as 'Colter's Hell,'" suggested the Groom.

"In Old Jim Bridger's time," said Aconite, "it rained fire up here in these hills one year."

"I don't doubt it," assented the Artist. "And we've either seen or are promised a view of Hell Roaring Creek, Hell Broth Springs, Hell's Half Acre, Satan's Arbor, and a lot of other infernal real estate."

"It's heavenly up *here!*" said the Bride.

Once at the summit the Park lay under their eyes like a map—all these and a thousand other features to be taken in by merely turning about. The land was sown with every variety of all that is wild and beautiful and strange; the sky was filled with peaks. Here they had mountains to spare. They looked, and looked, and grew tired of looking—and then gazed again. The wind blew up and whipped their faces; and the sun was far past the meridian, passing south through the silvery splotch of Yellowstone Lake, when Aconite literally loaded them into the surrey, and drove down the mighty flanks of Washburn, northwardly, until he found a place where a fire could be builded and luncheon prepared.

"You folks mustn't fergit," said he, "that scenery ain't so fillin' f'r them as looks it every little while, as it is f'r the tenderfoot."

The Professor was evidently pleased when his name came from the Stetson for the second time. He seemed to have something on his mind. Fully a mile short of Tower Falls, which they planned to visit in the early morning, they camped in dense forest, with a party of sight-seers just so far away as to seem neighborly without intrenching on privacy.

"This is the best camp we've had," said the Bride, hooking her hands over her knee, and gazing into the fire.

"Sure," said Billy. "Every camp is the best in life, for me, honey! Listen to the Professor, now—nobody heard!"

THE FEDERAL IMP COMPANY

THE PROFESSOR'S SECOND TALE

I can not bring myself to think lightly of devils and imps. Neither can I believe that the consensus of the opinions of so many millions of mankind associating eternal punishment with fire can be neglected by the student of ethnology or theology. These are filled with haunts of devils—if the opinions of those who named them are worth anything. In addition to those localities which have been mentioned, I have in my notes the following:

> The Devil's Frying Pan,
> The Devil's Slide,
> The Devil's Kitchen,
> The Devil's Punch Bowl,
> The Devil's Broiler,
> The Devil's Bath Tub,
> The Devil's Den,
> The Devil's Workshop,
> The Devil's Stairway,
> The Devil's Caldron,
> The Devil's Well,
> The Devil's Elbow,
> The Devil's Thumb,

and I know not how many of the members of His Satanic Majesty—all in this Park! And yet we say there is no devil, no brood of imps set upon the capture of human souls?

I shall tell you a story that seems worth considering as evidence on the other side. It is the story of something that occurred when I was journeying by a branch railway to take the main line to Washington, after a visit to the Boggses' ancestral farm in Pennsylvania. I had been at Boston as an attendant upon the sessions of the National Teachers' Association; with what recognition of my own small ability as an educator I have already mentioned. I boarded an old-fashioned, branch-line sleeping-car, and there met the being whose utterances and actions have so impressed me that I shall never forget them, never. I feel that this creature, so casually met, may be one of the actors in a series of events of the most appalling character, and cosmic scope.

When the porter came snooping about as if desiring to make up my berth, I went into the smoking compartment. I do not smoke; but it was the only place to go. I found there a person of striking appearance who told me the most remarkable story I ever heard in my life, and one which I feel it my duty to make public.

He had before him a bottle of ready-mixed cocktails, a glass, and a newspaper. With his bags and the little card table on which he rested his elbows, he was occupying most of the compartment. I sidled in hesitatingly, in that unobtrusive way which I believe to be the unfailing mark of the retiring and scholastic mind, and for want of a place to sit down, I leaned upon the lavatory. He was gazing fixedly at the half-empty bottle, his sweeping black mustaches curling back past his ears, his huge grizzled eyebrows shot through with the gleam of his eyes. He looked so formidable that I confess I was daunted, and should have escaped to the vestibule; but he saw me, rose, and with extreme politeness began tossing aside baggage to make room.

"I trust, Sir," said he with a capital S, "that you will pardon my occupancy of so much of a room in which your right is equal to mine! Be seated, I beg of you, Sir!"

I sat down; partly because, when not aroused, I am of a submissive temperament; and partly because he had thrown the table and grips across the door.

"Don't mention it," said I. "Thank you."

"Permit me, Sir," said he, "to offer you a drink."

"I hope you will excuse me," I replied, now

slightly roused, for I abhor alcohol and its use. "I never drink!"

"It is creditable to any man, Sir," said he, "to carry around with him a correct estimate of his weaknesses."

This really aroused in me that indignation which sometimes renders me almost terrible; but his fixed and glittering gaze seemed to hold me back from making the protest which rose to my lips.

"Permit me, Sir," said he, "to offer you a cigar."

It was a strong-looking weed; but although I am not a smoker, I took and lighted it. He resumed his attention to his bottle and paper.

"Will you be so kind," said he, breaking silence, "as to read that item as it appears to you?"

" 'Federal Improvement Company,' " I read. " 'Organized under the laws of New Jersey, on January 4th, with a capital of $1,000,000. Charter powers very broad, taking in almost every field of business. The incorporators are understood to be New York men.' "

" 'Imp,' " said he, "isn't it? not 'Improvement.' "

"I take it, sir," said I, "that the omission of the period is a printer's error, and that i-m-p means 'Improvement.' "

He leaned forward, grasped my wrist and peered like a hypnotist into my face.

"Just as badly mistaken," said he, "as if you had lost—as could be! It means 'Imp' just as it says 'Imp.' Have another drink!"

This time I really did not feel free to refuse him. He seemed greatly pleased at my tasting.

"Sit still," said he, "and I'll tell you the condemdest story you ever heard. That corporation means that we are now entering a governmental and sociological area of low pressure that will make the French Revolution look like a cipher with the rim rubbed out. In the end you'll be apt to have clearer views as to whether or not 'i-m-p' spells 'improvement'!"

This he seemed to consider a very clever play upon words, and he sat for some time, laughing in the manner adopted by the stage villain in his moments of solitude. His Mephistophelean behavior, or something, made me giddy. His manner was quite calm, however, and after a while we lapsed back into the commonplace.

"Ever read a story," said he, "named *The Bottle Imp?*"

"Stevenson's *Bottle Imp?*" I exclaimed, glad to

find a topic of common interest, and feeling that it could not be a dangerous thing to be shut into the same smoking compartment with any man who loved such things, no matter how Captain-Kiddish he might appear. "Why, yes, I have often read it. I am a teacher of literature and an admirer of Stevenson. He possesses—"

"Who? Adlai?" he said. "Did he ever have it?"

"I mean Robert Louis," said I. "He wrote it, you know."

"Oh!" said my companion meditatively, "he did, did he? Wrote it, eh? It's as likely as not he did—I know *Adlai*. Met him once, when I was putting a bill through down at Springfield: nice man! Well about this Bottle Imp. You know the story tells how he was shut up in a bottle—the Imp was—and whoever owned it could have anything he ordered, just like the fellow with the lamp—"

"Except long life!" said I, venturing to interrupt.

"Of course, not that!" replied my strange traveling companion. "If the thing had been used to prolong life, where would the Imp come in? His side of the deal was to get a soul to torture. He couldn't be asked to give 'em length of days, you understand. It couldn't be expected."

I had to admit that, from the Imp's standpoint, there was much force in this remark.

"And that other clause in the contract that the owner could sell it," he went on. "That had to be in, or the Imp never could have found a man sucker enough to take the Bottle in the first place."

The cases of Faust, and the man who had the Wild Ass's Skin seemed to me authorities against this statement; but I allowed the error to pass uncorrected.

"On the other hand," he went on, "it was nothing more than fair to have that other clause in, providing that every seller must take less for it than he gave. Otherwise they'd have kept transferring it just before the owner croaked, and the Imp would never have got his victim. But with that rule in force the price just had to get down so low sometime that it couldn't get any lower, and the Imp would get his *quid pro quo*."

"You speak," said I indignantly, for it horrified me to hear the loss of a soul spoken of in this light manner; "you speak like a veritable devil's advocate!"

"When I've finished telling you of this Federal Imp Company that's just been chartered," said he, "you'll have to admit that there's at least one devil that's in need of the best advocate that money'll hire!"

Here he gave one of his sardonic chuckles, long-continued and rumbling, and peered into the bottle of cocktails, as if the prospective client of the advocate referred to had been confined there.

"When it doesn't cost anything," he added, "there's no harm in being fair, even with an Imp."

I failed to come to the defense of my position, and he went on.

"Well," said he, "do you remember the Bottle Imp's history that this man Stevenson gives us? Cæsar had it once, and wished himself clear up to the head of the Roman Empire. Charlemagne, Napoleon, and a good many of the fellows who had everything coming their way, owed their successes to the Bottle Imp, and their failures to selling out too soon: got scared when they got a headache, or on the eve of battle, or something like that. It was owned in South Africa, and Barney Barnato and Cecil Rhodes both had it. That accounts for the way *they* got up in the world. Then the Bottle and Imp went to the Nob Hill millionaire who bought it for eighty dollars and sold it to Keawe the Kanaka for fifty. The price was getting dangerously low, now, and Keawe was mighty glad when he had wished himself into a fortune and got rid of the thing. Then, just as he was about to get married, he discovered that he had leprosy, hunted up the Bottle, which he found in the possession of a fellow who had all colors of money and insomnia, both of which he had acquired by purchasing the Bottle Imp for two cents, you remember, and was out looking for a transferee, and about on the verge of nervous prostration because he couldn't find one,—not at that price! Keawe became so desperate from the danger of going to the leper colony and the loss of his sweetheart, that he bought the Bottle for a cent, in the face of the fact that, so far as he knew, a cent was the smallest coin in the world, and the bargain, accordingly, cinched him as the Imp's peculiar property, for all eternity. I'll be—hanged—if I know whether to despise him for his foolishness or to admire him for his sand!"

"You recall," said I, "that his wife directed his attention to the *centime*—"

"Yes," said he, "she put him on. And they threw away one transfer by placing it on the market at four *centimes*. They might just as well have started it at five."

"I don't see that," said I.

"Because you haven't figured on it," said he. "You haven't been circulating in Imp circles lately, as I have, where these things are discussed. Listen! A *centime* is the hundredth part of a franc, and a franc is about nineteen cents. A cent, therefore, is a fraction more than five *centimes*. But they started it at four, the chocolate-colored idiots, after getting rid of their leprosy! When I think how that Bottle Imp has been mismanaged, I am driven—"

He illustrated that to which he was driven, by a gesture with the bottle on the table. He coughed, and took up his *résumé* of the story.

"Let that pass. They put it up at four *centimes,* and without Keawe's knowledge that she had anything to do with it, Keawe's wife got an old man to buy it, and she took it off his hands at three. The Kanaka soon found out that he was now carrying his eternal damnation in his wife's name, and he procured an old skipper or mate, or some such fellow in a state of intoxication, to buy it of her for two, on the agreement that he would take it again for one. Here they were, frittering away untold fortunes, each trying to go to perdition to save the other—it makes me tired! But the old bos'n or whatever he was, said he was going, you know where, anyhow, and figured that the Bottle was a good thing to take with him, and kept it. And there's where the Kanakas got out of a mighty tight place—"

"And the Bottle disappeared and passed into history!" I broke in. I was really absorbed in the conversation, in spite of a slight vertigo, now that we had got into the field of literature where I felt at home.

"Passed into—nothing!" he snorted. "Passed into the state of being the Whole Thing! Became It! Went on the road to the possession of the Federal Imp Company as the sole asset of the corporation. Folks'll see now pretty quick, whether it passed into history or not! Yes, I should say so!"

"Who's got it now?" I whispered. I was so excited that I found myself sitting across the table, and us mingling our breaths like true conspirators. He had a good working majority in the breaths, however.

"Who's the Charlemagne, the J. Cæsar, the Napoleon of the present day?" he whispered in reply, after looking furtively over his shoulder. "It don't need a Sherlock Holmes to tell that, does it?"

"Not," said I, "not J. P.—"

"No," said he, "It's John D.—"

But before he finished the name he crept to the door and peered down the aisle, and then whispered it in my ear so sibilantly that I felt for a minute as I used to do when I got water in my ear when swimming. But I noticed it very little in my astonishment at the fact he had imparted to me. I felt that I was pale. He rose again and prowled about as if for eavesdroppers. I felt myself a Guy Fawkes, an Aaron Burr, an—well, anything covert and dangerous.

"He bought this Bottle Imp," my companion went on, resuming his seat, "of the old sailing-master, or whatever he was—the man with the downward tendency and the jag. What J. D. wanted was power, just as Cæsar and Napoleon wanted it in their times. But the same kind of power wouldn't do. Armies were the tools of nations then; now they are the playthings. Now nations are the tools of money, and wealth runs the machine. This emperor of ours chose between having the colors dip as he went by, and owning the fellows that made 'em dip. He gave the grand-stand the go-by, and took the job of being the one to pull the string that turned on the current that moved the ruling force that controlled the power back of the power behind the throne. D'ye understand?"

"It's a little complex," said I, "the way you state it, but—"

"It'll all be clear in the morning," he said. "Anyway, that's what he chose. And what is he? The Emperor of Coin. He was a modest business man a few years ago. Suddenly the wealth of a continent began flowing into his control. It rolled in and rolled in, every coin making him stronger and stronger, until now the business of the world takes out insurance policies on his life and scans the reports of his health as if the very basis of society were John D. You-Know-Who. Emperors court his favor, and the financial world shakes when he walks. You don't think for a minute that this could be done by any natural means, do you?"

"But the price of the bottle was one *centime!*" said I, my altruism coming uppermost once more. "One *centime:* and he is no longer young!"

"Exactly," he answered, "and he's got to sell it, or go to— Well, he's just about got to sell it!"

"But how?" I queried. "What coin is there smaller than a *centime*—what he paid?"

"All been figured out," said he airily. "Who solved the puzzle I don't know; but I guess it was Senator Depew. Know what a mill is?"

"A mill? Yes," said I. "A factory? A pugilistic encounter? A money of account?"

"Yes," said he, "a 'money of account.' Never coined. One-tenth of a cent. *One-half a centime!* Have you heard of Senator Aldrich's currency bill, S. F. 41144? It's got a clause in it providing for the coinage of the mill. And there's where I come in. I'm an unelected legislator—third house, you know. Let the constructive statesman bring in their little bills. I'm satisfied to put 'em through! S. F. 41144 is going to be put through, and old J. D.'ll sell his Bottle, Imp and all. Price, one mill. When this grip epidemic started in, he got a touch of it, and I'll state that a sick man feels a little nervous with that Imp in stock. So they wired for me. It's going to be a fight all right!"

"Why, who will oppose the bill?" said I. "No one will know its object."

"Lots of folks will oppose it," said he. "Every association of clergymen in the country is liable to turn up fighting it tooth and nail. There are too many small coins now for the interests of the people who depend on contribution boxes. The Sunday-schools will all be against it. And the street-car companies won't want the cent subdivided. Then it'll be hard to convince Joe Cannon; he's always looking for a nigger in the fence, and there *is* one here, you understand. But the mill's going to be coined, all the same!"

"But," said I, "who will buy the diabolical thing for a mill? If Keawe and his wife had such trouble selling it for a *centime*, it will be impossible to dispose of it for a mill, absolutely impossible! It's the irreducible minimum!"

"I take it, Sir," said he, with a recurrence of the capital S, "that you are not engaged in what Senator Lodge in our conference last night called 'hot finance'?"

"No," I admitted, for in spite of the orthoëpic error, I understood him. "No, I am not—exactly."

"I inferred as much from your remark," said he. "When there's anything to be done, too large for individual power, or dangerous in its nature, or, let us say, repugnant to some back-number criminal law, or, as in this case, dangerous to the individual's soul's salvation, what do you do? Why you organize a corporation, if you know your business, and turn the whole thing over to it—and there you are. The Federal Imp Company will take over the Bottle Imp at the price of one mill. Mr. R. won't own it any more. His stock will be non-assessable, and all paid up by the transfer of the Imp, and there can't be any liability on it. He can retain control of it if he wants to—and you notice he generally wants to, and can laugh in the Imp's face. We've got all kinds of legal opinions on *that*. And whoever controls that company will rule the world. That Imp is the greatest corporate asset that ever existed. All that's needed is for the president of the corporation to wish for anything, or the board of directors to pass a resolution, and the thing asked for comes a-running. The railways, steamships, banks, factories, lands—everything worth having—are just as good as taken over.

Why it's the Universal Merger, the Trust of Trusts! The stock-holders of the Federal Imp Company will be the ruling class of the world, a perpetual aristocracy; and the man with fifty-one per cent. of the stock, or proxies for it, will be Emperor, Czar, Kaiser, Everything!"

"But this is stupendous!" I exclaimed: for, being a student of political economy—"economics," they call it now—I at once perceived the significance of his statements. "This is terrible! It is revolution! It is the end of democracy! Can't it be stopped?"

"M'h'm," said he quietly, evidently assenting to my rather excited statement; and then in reply to my question, he added with another chuckle, "Stop nothing! Federal injunction won't do it: presidential veto won't do it: nor calling out the militia: nor anything else. For the Imp controls the courts, the president, *and* the army; and J. D. R. runs the Imp —fifty-one per cent. of the Imp stock! The socialists will go out campaigning in favor of the government's taking over the Federal Imp Company, but the Imp controls the government—and the socialists, too, when you come down to brass nails. Oh, it's a cinch, a timelock, leadpipe cinch! The stuff's off with everybody else, if we can get this bill through!"

I was shocked into something like a cataleptic state, and sat dazed for a while. Either this or the strong cigar, or something, so affected me that, as he passed the flask to me for the fourth time, the smoking compartment seemed to swim about me as the train rolled thunderously onward through the night. To steady myself I gazed fixedly at my extraordinary fellow traveler as he sat, his now well-nigh empty bottle before him, peering into it from time to time as if for some potent servant of his own. Suddenly he leaned back and laughed more diabolically than ever.

"Ha, ha, ha!" he roared. "You ought to have been with us last night in his library! Aldrich and Depew and some of the others were there, and we were checking over our list of sure votes in the House. The old man had the grip, as I said a while ago, and privately, I'll state I think he's scared stiff; for every fifteen minutes we got a bulletin from his doctors and messages from him to rush S. F. 41144 to its passage, regardless, or he'd accept a bid he'd got for the Bottle Imp from Sir Thomas Lipton, who wants it for some crazy scheme regarding lifting the Cup. All the while, there stood the Bottle with the Imp in it. When the grip news was coming in there was nothing doing with his Impship. But whenever we began discussing his transfer to the Company, the way business picked up in that bottle was a caution! Why, you could hear him stabbing the stopper with his tail, and grinding his horns against the sides of the bottle, and fighting like a weasel in a trap, in such a rage that the Bottle glowed like a red-hot iron. It was shameful! One of the lawyers took the horrors, and had to be taken home in a carriage—threw a conniption fit every block! Ha, ha, ha! Ha, ha, ha! Oh! it was great stuff!"

"I don't see—" I began.

"No? Don't you?" he queried, between the satanic chuckles. "Well, by George, the Imp saw, all right! He saw that modern financial ingenuity has found a way to flimflam the devil himself. He saw, Sir (here his voice assumed an oratorical orotund, and the capital S came in again), that our corporation lawyers have found a spoon long enough so that we can safely sup with Satan! Why, let me ask you once, what did the Imp go into the Bottle deal for in the first place? To get the aforesaid soul. You can see how he'd feel, now that the price is down to the last notch but one, to have it sold to a corporation, with no more soul than a rabbit! If—that—don't beat the—the devil, what does?"

It all dawned upon me now. The reasonableness

of the entire story appealed to me. I reached for the paper. There it was: "Federal Imp Company: Charter powers very broad, taking in almost the entire field of business." I looked at the lobbyist. He had dropped asleep with his head on the table beside the empty cocktail bottle. Again things seemed to swim, and I lapsed into a state of something like coma, from which I was aroused by some one shaking me by the shoulder.

"Berth's ready, suh," said the porter, and passed to my companion.

"Hyah's Devil's Gulch Sidin', suh," said he, rousing the slumbering lobbyist. "You get off, hyah, suh!"

He passed out of the door with a Chesterfieldian bow and good night. I passed a sleepless and anxious night. The shock, or something, made me quite ill. I have not yet recovered my peace of mind. An effort which I made to place the matter before Doctor Byproduct, the president of the university of which I am an alumnus, led to such a stern reproof that I was forced to subside. The doctor said that the story was a libel upon a great and good man who had partially promised the university an endowment of ten millions of dollars. I am ready, however, to appear before any congressional committee which may be appointed to investigate the matter, or before the Interstate Commerce Commission, and to testify to the facts as above written, if it costs me my career.

"By gad, sir!" shouted the Colonel, breaking a long silence. "That infernal scheme would work!"

The party went one by one to their tents. Soon no one but the Colonel and the Hired Man were left.

"It sounds to me," remarked the Hired Man oracularly.

CHAPTER XII

"IF these lovely little waterfalls," asserted the Bride, as she gazed upon the graceful Tower Falls, "could only have a fair chance, they would win fame—but they are overshadowed here—and they don't seem to care."

Undine Falls, the Virginia Cascade, Mystic Falls, Kepler Cascade and Crystal Falls were in the mind of the Bride; but she might have mentioned many more, which in their incursion into the Park they had not seen.

"This," said the Artist, "is no place to look at, and leave—it is a region for the artist to live in, to study, to make a part of his life, and finally, to understand."

"I reckon," said the Hired Man, "that he'd git homesick f'r the corn country after a winter or so."

Some competent judges think Tower Falls the most beautiful cascade on earth. Perhaps it is. Certainly no fault has ever been found with it as a picture. The Seven Wonderers spent a day near their pretty camp, resting, exploring, and renewing their acquaintance with the gorge of the Yellowstone, and forming that of the Needle, slender as a campanile, and three hundred feet high, marking the end of the Grand Cañon. Junction Butte, which they crossed the New Bridge to see, standing where many roads and rivers meet, seemed to the Bride another monument placed there by the gods with manifest intention. Why otherwise, she queried, could not the Needle be anywhere else, just as well as at the lower end of the Grand Cañon, or Junction Butte, in any other place as easily as in this cross-roads of highways and waters?

"Why, indeed?" assented the Groom. "When you find a stone stuck on end at the corner of a parcel of land, you know that the stone was placed there to mark the corner, don't you?"

"Reminds me of the providential way that rivers always run past cities, just where they are needed," carped the Colonel.

"It isn't the same thing," said the Bride hotly. "You're getting mean, Colonel!"

"Honing for the wrangle of the courts, Bride," said he. "I apologize."

"Well," said Aconite, "there's a lot of bigger mysteries than them in these regions. Here's the Petrified Trees, over here in a ravine just off the road. If we don't see the petrified forest up Amethyst Crick way, maybe you'd like to look at these an' tell me how trees ever turned to stone that-a-way."

There they stood, splintered by the elements, indubitably the stubs of trees, and unquestionably stone. The Professor began an explanation of the phenomenon of petrifaction, but nobody paid him any attention.

"Old Jim Bridger," said Aconite, "discovered the Petrified Forest, up in the Lamar Valley; an' back in the mountains som'eres he found a place where the grass, birds an' everything else was petrified. Even a waterfall was petrified, an' stan's thar luk glass."

"And the roar of it is petrified, and the songs of the birds, and the sunlight, and the birds singing their petrified songs in the petrified air, in which they are suspended for ever, by reason of the petrifaction of the force of gravity, which otherwise would bring them down!"

Thus the Poet. Aconite looked at him in surprise. "Either you've been here before," said he, "or you've knowed some one that has been!"

Time refused to serve for an exploration of the regions northeast of the New Bridge, though the road invited, and the Artist strongly argued for the trip. He wanted to see the Fossil Forest, and Amethyst Falls, Amethyst Creek, Amethyst Mountain and Specimen Ridge. But they turned their backs on these, on Soda Butte and its wonderful cañon, and that of the Lamar, on the piscatorial delights of Trout Lake, the mystery of Death Gulch, and the weirdnesses of the Hoodoo Region. The Bride and Groom were due to take train from Gardiner, and on to San Francisco. At Yancey's the Bride invited them to a parting dinner when they should reach Mammoth Hot Springs Hotel, and when Aconite and the Hired Man failed to recognize themselves as included, the Bride assured them that the occasion would be ruined if they did not attend—and they promised.

They reached Yancey's early in the afternoon, but the Bride was so enraptured by its beauties as a camping place that they made camp for the night, and drawing from the hat the name of Aconite as the entertainer for the evening, and the Poet for the dinner at the Hotel, each found himself feeling like one who has sent his luggage to the station, and awaits the carriage to bear him from home; or like sailors who have their dunnage ready for the dock at the end of the voyage.

Their relationship had grown to something very like intimacy in something more than half a month. And they were about to go their several ways, like ships that pass in the night. It was their great good fortune to have so met and acted that every member of the party felt the companionship a tolerable thing to contemplate as a permanency—that should they be in any mysterious—though scarcely improbable—interposition of glass barrier, or fiery lake, or gulf filled with deadly vapor, shut into this marvelous region, they could be good friends and good fellows. And they listened respectfully as Aconite, under the trees at Yancey's, spun the yarn of his love affair with an Oberlin College girl, his connection with a Rosebud beef issue fraud, and the tragedy that resulted from the mixture thereof.

THE JILTING OF MR. DRISCOLL

ACONITE'S SECOND TALE

This here doctrine of Mr. Witherspoon's about lettin' cattle range wide, has some arguments of a humane nature back of it. But his openin' of it up in the instructions f'r runnin' the ten thousand dogies, was the same kind of a miscue the Pawnees made when they laid fer an' roped the U. P. flyer—which Mr. Elkins described as a misapplication of sound theory to new an' unwonted conditions; as the rattler said when he swallered the lawn hose. Principles has their local habitats the same as live things; an' nothin' is worse f'r 'em than to turn 'em loose where they don't know the water-holes an' wind-breaks. Principles that'll lay on fat an' top the market in Boston, 'll queer the hull game in a country where playin' it is tangled up with Injuns, gold mines, 'r range-stuff. In the short-grass country, dogy principles are sure a source of loss, until they get hardened up so's to git out and rustle with the push. Now, this Humane-Society-Injun-Relief-Corps form of doin' good—harmless, you'd say, as we set here by the grub-wagon; but I swear to Godfrey's Gulch, the worst throw-down I ever got in a social way growed out of a combination of them two highly proper idees with a Oberlin College gal I met up to Chamberlain.

This was the way of it: The "O. M." Mr. Elkins, I mean, of the J-Up-An'-Down Ranch, was called to Sioux Falls as a witness in a case of selling conversation-water to the Injuns, an' casually landed a juicy contract with Uncle Sam f'r supplyin' beef-issue cattle over on the Rosebud. The Pierre firm of politicians he outbid, havin' things framed up pretty good, as they thought, on the delivery, at once hops to him with a proposition to pay him I d'know how much money an' take it off his hands. Havin' a pongshong f'r doin' business on velvet, the O. M. snaps 'em up instantaneous, an' comes home to Wolf Nose Crick smilin' like he'd swallered the canary, an' sends me to Chamberlain to see that the contract is carried out as fer as proper.

"Go up, Aconite," he says, "an' remember that while the J-Up-An'-Down outfit don't feel bound to demand any reforms, its interests must be protected. Any sort of cattle the Pierre crowd can make look like prime steers to the inspector, goes with us.

But," he goes on, "our names and not theirs are on the contract. These inspectors," says he, "bein' picked out on their merits at Washington, to look after the interests of the gover'ment an' the noble red, it would be unpatriotic if not *Lee's Majesty* to cavil at their judgment on steers, especially if it coincides with that of Senator Whaley's men at Pierre. Therefore, far be it from us to knock. But be leery that we don't get stuck for non-performance: which we can't afford. See?"

It was purty plain to a man who'd matrickelated as night-wrangler, an' graduated as *it* on the J-Up-An'-Down, an' I went heart-free an' conscience clear, seein' my duty perfectly plain.

Now at Chamberlain was this Oberlin College lady, who had some kind of an inflamed conscience on the Injun question, an' was dead stuck on dumb animals an' their rights. She was one of the kind you don't see out here—blue eyes, you know, yellow hair, the kind of complexion that don't outlive many hot winds; an' she had lots of pitchers around her, of young folks in her classes, an' people with mortarboard hats an' black nighties, 'r striped sweaters. She was irrupting into the Injun question *via* Chamberlain. Her thought was that the Injuns was really livin' correct 's fur as they had a chance, an' that we orto copy their ways, instid of makin' them tag along after our'n.

"Maybe that's so," says I, "but I've took the Keeley cure twice now, an' please excuse me!"

She looked kinder dazed f'r a minute, an' then laffed, an' said somethin' about the sardonic humor of the frontier.

I had been asked to give a exhibition of broncho bustin' at the ranch where she was stayin' an' she was agitatin' herself about the bronks' feelin's. I told her that it was just friendly rivalry between the puncher an' the bronk, an' how, out on the ranch, the gentle critters 'd come up an' hang around by the hour, a-nickerin' f'r some o' the gang to go out an' bust 'em.

"It reminds me," she says, "of my brother's pointers begging to go hunting."

"Same principle," says I.

It seemed to ease her mind, an' feelin' as I did toward her, I wouldn't have her worry f'r anything. Then she found out that I was a graduate of the high school of Higgsville, Kansas, an' used to know what quadratics was, an' that my way of emitting the English language was just an acquired mannerism, like the hock-action of a string-halted hoss, an' she warmed up to me right smart, both then an' after, never askin' to see my diploma, an' begun interrogatin' me about the beef-issue, an' discussin' the Injun question like a lifelong friend. Whereat, I jumped the game.

But, for all that, about this time I become subject to attacts of blue eyes an' yellow hair, accompanied by vertigo, blind-staggers, bots, ringin' in the ears— like low, confabulatin' talk, kinder interspersed with little bubbles of lafture—an' a sense o' guilt whenever I done anything under the canopy of heaven that I was used to doin'. Can yeh explain that, now? Why this Oberlin proposition should make me feel like a criminal jest because the pony grunted at the cinchin' o' the saddle, 'r because I lammed him f'r bitin' a piece out o' my thigh at the same time, goes too deep into mind science f'r Aconite Driscoll. O' course, a man under them succumstances is supposed to let up on cussin' an' not to listen to all kinds o' stories; but you understand, here I was, conscience-struck in a general an' hazy sort of way, mournin' over a dark an' bloody past, an' thinkin' joyfully of death. It was the condemnedest case I ever contracted, an' nothin' saved me to be a comfort to my friends but the distraction of the queer actions of that inspector.

I never had given him a thought. Senator Whaley an' his grafters was supposed to arrange matters with him—an' I'm no corruptionist, anyway. Of course, the cattle wasn't quite up to export shippin' quality. The senator's gang had got together a collection of skips an' culls an' canners that was sure a fraud on the Injuns, who mostly uses the cattle issued to 'em the way some high-up civilized folks does hand-raised foxes—as a means of revortin' to predatory savagery, as Miss Ainsley says. Ainsley was her name—Gladys Ainsley—an' she lived som'eres around Toledo. The p'int is, that they chase 'em, with wild whoops an' yips over the undulatin' reservation until they can shoot 'em, an' I s'pose, sort of imagine, if Injuns have imaginations, that time has turned back'ard in her flight, an' the buffalo season is on ag'in. Whereas, these scandalous runts of steers an' old cow stuff was mostly too weak or too old to put up any sort of a bluff at speed.

But, under my instructions, if they looked good to the inspector, they looked good to me; an' bein' sort of absent-minded with gal-stroke, I rested easy, as the feller said when the cyclone left him on top o' the church tower.

The inspector was a new man, an' his queer actions consisted mostly of his showin' up ten days too soon, an' then drivin' 'r ridin' around the country lookin' at the stock before delivery. This looked suspicious; fer we s'posed it was all off but runnin' 'em through the gap once, twice 'r three times to be counted. Whaley's man comes to me one day, an' ast me what I thought of it.

"I'm paid a princely salary," says I, "fer keepin' my thoughts to myself. This here's no case," I continued, "callin' f'r cerebration on my part. If thinkin's the game, it's your move. What's Senator Whaley in politics fer," says I, "if a obscure forty-a-month-an'-found puncher is to be called on to think on the doin's of a U. S. inspector? What's he in this fer at all, if we've got to think at this end of the lariat?"

"He was talkin' about cavvs," said the feller, whose name was Reddy—a most ungrammatical cuss. "He was a-pokin' round with the contrack, a-speakin' about cavvs. Wun't you go an' talk to him?"

"Not me!" says I, f'r the hull business disgusted

me, an' my guilt come back over me shameful, with the eyes an' hair an' things plenteous. Whaley's man rode off, shakin' his head.

Next day the inspector hunted me up.

"Mr. Driscoll?" says he, f'r I'd been keepin' out of his way.

"Correct," says I.

"You represent the Elkins' interests in the matter of supplying for the issue, do you not?" says he.

"In a kind of a sort of a way," says I, f'r I didn't care to admit too much till I see what he was up to. "In a kind of a sort of a way, mebbe I do. Why?"

"Did you have anything to do," says he, unfoldin' a stiff piece of paper, "with procuring the cattle now in readiness for delivery?"

"Hell, no!" I yells, an' then seein' my mistake, I jumped an' added: "You see, the top stuff f'r the Injun market is perduced up around Pierre. So we sub-contracted with this Pierre outfit to supply it. It's their funeral, not ours. It's good stock, ain't it?"

"I am assured by Senator Whaley's private secretary," says he, "who is a classmate of mine, that there would be great dissatisfaction among the Indians, owing to certain tribal traditions and **racial peculiarities**—"

"You bet!" says I, f'r he seemed to be gettin' wound up an' cast in it, "that's the exact situation!"

"Would be dissatisfaction," he went on, "if cattle of the type which in the great markets is considered best, were furnished here. And I have great confidence in his judgment."

"So've I," I says. "He's one of the judgmentiousest fellers you ever see."

"So let that phase of the question pass," says he, "for the present. But there's a clause in this contract—"

"Don't let that worry you," says I. "There's claws in all of 'em if you look close."

He never cracked a smile, but unfolded it, and went on.

"Here's a clause," says he, "calling for a hundred and fifty cows with calves at foot, for the dairy herd, I presume."

"Cavvs at what?" says I.

"At foot," says he, p'intin' at a spot along toward the bottom. "Right there!"

"It's impossible!" says I. "They don't wear 'em that way."

He studied over it quite a while, at that, an' I begun to think I'd won out, but at last he says:

"That's the way it reads, an' while I shall not insist upon any particular relation of juxtaposition in offspring and dam—"

"Whope!" says I, "back up an' come ag'in pardner."

"It seems to be my duty to insist upon the one hundred and fifty cows and calves. Now the point is, I don't find any such description of creatures among the—the bunches in seeming readiness for delivery."

"O!" says I, "that's what's eating yeh, is it? W'l don't worry any more. The cow kindergarten's furder up the river. We didn't want to put the tender little devils where they'd be tramped on by them monstrous big oxen you noticed around the corrals. This caff business is all right, trust us!"

Whaley's man was waitin' fer me down at the saloon, an' when I told him about the cavvs, he shrunk into himself like a collapsed foot-ball, an' wilted.

"Hain't yeh got 'em?" says I.

"Huh!" says he, comin' out of it. "Don't be a dum fool, Aconite. This is the first I understood of it, an' whoever heared of an inspector readin' a contrack? And there ain't them many cavvs to be got by that time in all Dakoty. Le's hit the wires f'r instructions!"

The telegrams runs something like this:

To Senator Patrick Whaley, Washington, D. C.:
   Contract calls for a hundred and fifty cows with calves at foot. What shall I do? REDDY.

To Reddy Withers, Chamberlain, S. D.:
   Wire received. Calves at what? Explain, collect.
WHALEY.

Hundred and fifty cows and calves. What do you advise? REDDY.

See inspector. WHALEY.

Won't do. Inspector wrong. REDDY.

Fix inspector or get calves. WHALEY.

I'd got about the same kind of a telegram to Mr. Elkins, addin' that the Whaley crowd was up in the air. I sent it by Western Union to Sturgis, and then up Wolf Nose Crick by the Belle Fourche and Elsewhere Telephone Line. The O. M., as usual, cuts the melon with a word. His wire was as follows.

Take first train Chicago. Call for letter Smith & Jones Commission merchants Union Stock Yards.
ELKINS.

This was sure an affliction on me, f'r I had fixed up a deal to go with Miss Ainsley an' her friends on a campin' trip, lastin' up to the day of the issue. She'd been readin' one of Hamlin Garland's books about a puncher who'd scooted through the British aristocracy, hittin' only the high places in a social way, on the strength of a gold prospect an' the diamond hitch to a mule-pack. She wanted to see the diamond hitch of all things. There orto be a law ag'inst novel-writin'. I got Reddy to learn me the diamond hitch so I could make good with Gladys, an' here was this mysterious caff expedition to the last place in the world, Chicago, a-yankin' me off by the night train.

I went over to tell her about it. First, I thought I'd put on the clo'es I expected to wear to Chicago, a dandy fifteen dollar suit I got in town. An' then I saw how foolish this would be, an' brushed up my range clo'es, tied a new silk scarf in my soft roll collar, an' went. Here's my diagram of the hook-up: Any o' them mortar-board-hat, black-nightie fellers she had pitchers of, could probably afford fifteen dollar clay-worsteds; but it was a good gamblin' proposition that none of 'em could come in at the gate like a personally-conducted cyclone, bring up a-stannin' from a dead run to a dead stop 's if they'd struck a stone wall, go clear from the bronk as he fetched up an' light like a centaur before her, with their sombrero in their hand. Don't light, you say? Wal, I mean as a centaur would light if he took a notion. You'd better take a hike down to see how the steed's gettin' along, Bill, 'r else subside about this Greek myth biz. It helps on with this story—not!

The p'int is, that gals and fellers both like variety. To me, the "y" in her name, the floss in her hair, the kind of quivery lowness in her voice, the rustle of her dresses as she walked, the way she looked like the pitchers in the magazines an' talked like the stories in 'em, all corroborated to throw the hooks into me. An' I s'pose the nater's-nobleman gag went likewise with her. Subsekent happenin's—but I must hold that back.

We sot in the hammock that night—the only time Aconite Driscoll ever was right up against the real thing in ladies' goods—an' she read me a piece about a Count Gibson a-shooting his lady-love's slanderers so full o' holes at a turnament that they wouldn't hold hazel-brush. They was one verse she hesitated over, an' skipped.

I ast her if she thought she—as a supposed case—could live out in this dried-up-an'-blowed-away country; an' she said the matter had really never been placed before her in any such a way as to call for a decision on her part. Purty smooth, that! Then she read another piece that wound up with "Love is best!" from the same book, an' forgot to take her hand away when I sneaked up on it, an'—Gosh! talk about happiness: we never git anything o' quite that kind out here! I never knowed how I got to the train, 'r anything else ontil we was a-crossin' the Mississippi at North McGregor. Here the caff question ag'in unveiled its heejus front, to be mulled over till I reached the cowman's harbor in Chicago, the Exchange Building at the Yards, an' found Jim Elkins' instructions awaitin' me. They read:

"Dear Aconite:

"The Chicago stockyards are the nation's doorstep for bovine foundlings. New-born calves are a drug on the market there, owing to abuses in the shipping business which we won't just now take time to discuss, to say nothing about curing 'em. What is done with 'em is a mystery which may be solved some day; but that they perish in some miserable way is certain. Two carloads of them must perish on the

Rosebud instead of in Packingtown—in the Sioux soup kettles, instead of the rendering tanks, if you can keep them alive to reach Chamberlain—and I have great confidence in your ability to perform this task imposed upon you by the carelessness of Senator Whaley's men either at Washington or at the range. I have heard that one or two raw eggs per day per calf will preserve them, and it looks reasonable. Smith and Jones will have them ready loaded for you for the next fast freight west. I hope you'll enjoy your trip!"

Well, you may have listened to the plaintive beller of a single caff at weanin' time, 'r perhaps to the symferny that emanates from the pen of three 'r four. Furder'n this the experience of most don't go. Hence, I don't hope to give yeh any idee of the sound that eckered over northern Illinois from them two cars o' motherless waifs. The cry of the orphan smote the air in a kind of endless chain o' noise that at two blocks off sounded like a chorus of steam calliopes practicin' holts at about middle C. Nothin' like it had ever been heared of or done in Chicago, an' stockmen, an' reporters, an' sight-seers swarmed around wantin' to know what I was a-goin' to do with the foundlin's—an' I wa'nt in any position to be interviewed, with the Chicago papers due in Chamberlain before I was. I'd 'ave had a dozen scraps if it hadn't been f'r the fear of bein' arrested. But with the beef issue comin' on a-pacin', I had to pass up luxuries involvin' delay. I sot in the caboose, an object of the prurient curiosity of the train-crew ontil we got to Elgin 'r som'eres out there, where I contracted eight cases of eggs an' one of nervous prostration.

Here it was I begun ministering to the wants of my travelin' orphan asylum. They was from four hours to as many days old when the accident of birth put 'em under my fosterin' care. I knowed that it was all poppy-cock givin' dairy 'r breedin' herds to them Injuns, an' that these would do as well f'r their uses, 'sif they had real mothers instid o' one as false as I felt. But to look upon 'em as they appeared in the cars, would 'ave give that consciencious but onsophisticated inspector the jimjams. Part of 'em was layin' down, an' the rest trampin' over 'em, an' every one swellin' the chorus o' blats that told o' hunger an' unhappiness. I took a basket of eggs an' went in among 'em, feelin' like a animal trainer in a circus parade as the Reubens gethered around the train, an' business houses closed f'r the show. I waited till the train pulled out, an' begun my career as nurse-maid-in-gineral.

"How cruel!" said the Bride.

"Thanks," said Aconite. "It shore was!"

Ever try to feed a young caff? Ever notice how they faint with hunger before you begin, an' all at once develop the strength of a hoss when you stand over 'em an' try to hold their fool noses in the pail? Ever see a caff that couldn't stand alone, run gaily off with a two-hundred-an'-fifty-pound farmer, poisin' a drippin' pail on his nose, an' his countenance a geyser of milk? Well, then you can form some faint idee of the practical difficulty of inducin' a caff, all innercent o' the world an' its way o' takin' sustenance, to suck a raw egg. But nothin' but actual experience can impart any remote approach to a notion o' what it means to incorporate the fruit o' the nest with the bossy while bumpin' over the track of a northern Iowa railroad in a freight car, movin' at twenty-five miles an hour. I used up two cases of eggs before I was sure of havin' alleviated one pang of hunger, such was the scorn my kindly offers was rejected with. The result was astoundin'. Them cars swept through the country, their decks slippery with yaller gore, an' their lee scuppers runnin' bankfull, as the sailors say, with Tom-an'-Jerry an' egg shampoo. An' all the time went on that symferny of blats, risin' an' fallin' on the prairie breeze as we rolled from town to town, a thing to be gazed at an' listened to an' never forgot; to be side-tracked outside city limits f'r fear of the Board of Health and the S. P. C. A., an' me ostrichized by the very brakey in the caboose as bein' unfit f'r publication, an' forced to buy a mackintosh to wrap myself in before they'd let me lay down on their old seats to sleep. An' when my visions reverted back to the Oberlin people, I couldn't dream o' that yaller hair even, without its seemin' to float out, an' out, an' out into a sea of soft-boiled, in which her an' me was strugglin', to the howlin' of a tearin' tempest of blats.

"And next when Aconite he rides," remarked the Poet, "may I be there to see!"

At last we arrived at Chamberlain. An' here's where the head-end collision of principles comes in, that I mentioned a while ago. Here's where Aconite Driscoll, who for days had been givin' a mother's care to two hundred cavvs, was condemned f'r cruelty; an' when he'd been strainin' every nerve an' disturbin' the egg market to keep from bustin' a set of concealed claws in a gover'ment contract, he was banished as an eggcessory to the crime of bilkin' poor Lo. This tradegy happens out west o' the river at the Issue House.

Reddy had a string of wagons with hog-racks onto 'em waitin' in the switch-yards when we whistled in, an' the way we yanked them infants off the cars and trundled 'em over the pontoon bridge, an' hit the trail f'r the Issue House, was a high-class piece o' teamin'. We powdered across the country like the first batch of sooners at a reservation openin'. Out on the prairie was Reddy an' his punchers, slowly dribblin' the last of his steers into the delivery, too anxious f'r me an' the cavvs to be ashamed of their emaciation. Out behind a butte, he had concealed a bunch of cow-stuff he'd deppytized as mothers *pro tem* to my waifs. The right way t've done, o' course, would've been to incorporated the two bunches in a unassumin' way at a remoter place, an' drove 'em gently in as much like cattle o' the same family circles as yeh could make 'em look. But they wan't time. The end-gates was jerked out, an' the wagons ongently emptied like upsettin' a sleigh comin' home from spellin' school. Most all the orphans could an' did walk, an' I was so tickled at this testimonial to the egg-cure f'r youthful weakness, that we had 'em half way to the place where the knives o' their owners-elect was a waitin' 'em when I looked around an' seen Miss Ainsley, an' the Chamberlain lady she was a-stayin' with, standin' where they must 'a' seen the way we mussed the cavvs hair up in gettin' of 'em on the ground.

Gladys' eyes was a-blazin', an' they was a red spot in each cheek. She seemed sort o' pressin' forwards, like she wanted to mix it up, an' her lady friend was tryin' to head her off. I saw she didn't recognize me, an' I didn't thirst f'r recognition. I knew that love ain't so blind as she's been advertised, an' that I wouldn't never, no, never, be a nater's nobleman no more if she ever tumbled to the fact that the human omelette runnin' this caff business was A. Driscoll. It was only a case of sweet-gal-graduate palpitation o' the heart anyhow, an' needed the bronzed cheek, the droopin' mustache, the range clo'es, the deadly gun, the diamond hitch, and the centaur biz to keep it up to its wonted palp.

An' what was it that was offered to the gaze o' this romantic piece o' calicker? Try to rearlize the truth in all its heejusness. Here was the aforementioned Driscoll arrayed in what was once an A1 fifteen-dollar suit of clay-worsteds, a good biled shirt, an' a new celluloid collar. But how changed from what had been but three short days ago the cinnersure of the eye of every sure-thing or con-man on South Halsted Street? Seventy-five per cent. of eight cases of eggs had went billerin' over him. The shells of the same clung like barnacles to his apparel. His curlin' locks was matted an' muci-laged like he'd made a premature getaway from some liberal-minded shampooer; an' from under his beetlin' brows that looked like birds' nests from which broods had just hatched, glared eyes with vi'lence an' crime in every glance. Verily, Aconite was a beaut! An' here, a-comin' down upon him like the angel o' the Lord on the Assyrian host, come a starchy, lacey, filmy, ribbiny gal, that had onst let him hold her hand, by gum! her eyes burnin' with vengeance, an' that kinder corn-shucky rustlin' that emanated mysterious from her dress as she walked, a drawin' nearer an' nearer every breath.

"Gladys! Gladys!" says her lady friend. An' as Gladys slowed up, she says, lower: "I wouldn't interfere in this if I were you, dear!"

"I must!" says Gladys. "It's my duty! I can't permit dumb animals to be treated so without a protest. It is civic cowardice not to do disagreeable things for principle. I wish to speak to the man in charge, please!"

I kep' minglin' with the herd, not carin' to have disagreeable things done to me for principle, but she cuts me out, an' says, says she, "Do you know that there's a law against cruelty to dumb animals?"

"They ain't dumb," says I, trying to change my voice, an' officin' up to Reddy to shove 'em along to their fate while I held the foe in play. "When you've associated with these cute little cusses as long an' intermately as I have, ma'am, you'll know that they have a language an' an ellerquence all their own, that takes 'em out of the pervisions o' that law you speak of, an'—"

Here's where I overplays my hand, an' lets her get onto the genuyne tones of my voice. I ortn't to done this, f'r she'd heared it at close range. An' to make a dead cinch out of a good gamblin' proposition, I looked her in the eyes. It was all off in a breath. She give a sort of gasp as if somethin' cold had hit her, an' went petrified, sort o' slow like.

"Oh!" says she, turnin' her head to her friend. "I understand now what it was your husband was laughing about, and his odious jokes about fooling the inspector; and the bearing of the article he showed us in the Chicago paper! O, Mr. Driscoll, you to be so cruel; and to impose these poor motherless creatures upon those ignorant Indians, who are depending upon their living and becoming the nucleus of their pastoral industry; and the first step to a higher civilization! I don't wonder that you look guilty, or try—"

"I don't!" says I, f'r I didn't, as fer as the stock was concerned. "It's these here eight cases of eggs that make me look so. It's a matter o' clo's. An' the reds'll never raise cattle," says I, "or anything but trouble, in God's world. An' if these cavvs had as many mothers as a Mormon kid," I went on, "they'd be no better f'r stew!"

"Mr. Driscoll," says she, "don't ever speak to me again. I shall expose this matter to the inspector!"

I tried to lift my hat, but it was stuck to my hair; an' the sight of me pullin' desperately at my own head had some effect on her, f'r she flees to her friend, actin' queer, but whuther laffin' 'r cryin' I couldn't say, an' I don't s'pose she could. It's immaterial anyway, the main p'int bein' that her friend's husband, a friend of the senator's, persuaded her from havin' us all pinched, when she found that Reddy'd beat her to it with the cavvs, the last one of which was expirin' under the squaws' hatchets as she hove in sight of the issue, an' the soup-kittles was all a-steamin'. It reely was too late to do anything, I guess.

That night I slep' in Oacoma jail. You naturally gravitate that way when fate has ground you about so fine, an' you begin to drift with the blizzard. I could 'a' stood the throw-down, but to be throwed down in a heap with eggs an' dirty clo'es, was too much. I took that suit an' made a bundle of it, an' out on the pontoon bridge I poked it into the Missouri with a pole. They're usin' the water to settle coffee with, I'm told, as fur down as Saint Joe, to this day—'s good as the whites of eggs, the cooks say. Then, havin' wired my resignation to Elkins, feelin' that the world held no vocation f'r me but the whoop-er-up business, I returned to the west side of the river as the only place suited to my talons, an' went forth to expel the eggs an' tender memories from my system with wetness. I broke jail in the mornin' but in a week I come to myself ag'in on the same ol' cot in the same prehistoric calaboose, an' Mr. Elkins was keepin' the flies off me with one o' them brushes made of a fringed newspaper tacked to a stick.

"I've come," says he, "to take you home, Aconite."

"All right," says I, "but can you fix it up with the authorities?"

"I'm just going over to get your discharge," replies he. "They seem quite willing to part with you, now that they discover that none of your victims have anything deeper than flesh wounds. I've give bonds not to let you have your guns this side of the Stanley County line. I'll be back in half-an-hour with the horses."

An' here's where I had a narrow escape. I wouldn't have faced her, the girl, you know, f'r no money; but as Jim went away, right at the door I seen through a little winder a shimmerin' of white and blue. It was her, herself! She must have met Jim before, f'r I heared her speak his name an' mine. He seemed to be perlitely arguin' with her; an' then she went away with him. I breathed easier to see her go; an' then set down an' cried like a baby. A feller'll do that easy, when he's been on a tear, you know.

Jim an' I rode all that day sayin' never a word.

But when we'd turned in that night I mentioned the matter.

"Mr. Elkins," says I, "she sure has got it in f'r me pretty strong, to foller me to jail to jump on me!"

"Aconite," says he, "I'll not deceive you. She has. Forget it!"

"Good night, Aconite," said the Bride. "I forgive you—and I think I know just how that girl felt toward you!"

CHAPTER XIII

THE Bride's luggage came down from Gardiner, that she might be arrayed in her purple and fine linen—and silks, satins, ribbons, laces and fallals—for the dinner. And then her heart failed her; and she took counsel of the Groom.

"Wear 'em!" said he. And she did. She floated into their banquet room in a costume that would have been the envy of every woman in the room if the function had been at one of the mansions along the Sheridan Road or the Lake Shore Drive, instead of at the Mammoth Hot Springs Hotel. Aconite gasped, wrenched for a moment at his new silk neckerchief of the sort whose local color had won for him the Bride and Groom as fares, and bowed as he backed into a corner, where the Hired Man joined him. But after the Groom, the Artist and the Poet had made their appearance in their outing suits, and the Colonel in nothing more formal than a black frock, they gradually recovered, and were soon in the group which hung about the Bride paying homage to those twin gods of all our adoration, Beauty and Millinery. From soup to nuts they discussed their adventures, and re-trod their marvelous road. As the Bride rose to withdraw when the coffee and cigars were served, there was a loud adverse *vivâ voce* vote. The Bride must stay; she had stayed at the camp-fire, and she should not leave them in the banquet hall. So it was an unbroken circle that listened to the last of the Yellowstone Nights' tales, as it fell from the Poet's lips. The story was suggested, as most of its predecessors had been, by the events of the day. They had seen antelope and elk and deer as they drove in from Yancey's, and had talked of hunting adventures and accidents. The Poet began by speaking of the way in which men are sometimes the hunters, sometimes the hunted—quoting the lines from Hiawatha,

> "The fiery eyes of Pauguk,
> Glare upon him in the darkness."

"Pauguk," said he, "is Death. And I will tell you the true story of how a man stalked Pauguk through the Minnesota woods."

THE STALKING OF PAUGUK

THE POET'S SECOND STORY

This story has been told elsewhere, and has been blamed for its lack of a moral. People seem to expect one so to put to the rack the facts in the case that they will shriek out some well-tried message. Some have behaved as if they thought the moral here, but faulty. Colonel Loree of the Solar Selling Company, however, thinks the affair rich in the *hic-fabula-docet* element. So does Williamson, soliciting-agent for the Mid-Continent Life; and so—emphatically so—does the Mid-Continent itself. Trudeau, the "breed" guide, has had so few years in which to turn it over in his slow-moving mind as he has lain rolled in his blankets while the snow sifted through the moaning pines, that he has not made up his mind. As for Foster Van Dorn and Gwendolyn, their opinions—but the story itself is not long.

Williamson says that when he left Van Dorn's office with the application, he was as near walking on air as insurance men ever are. People had been so slow in writing their autographs on the dotted line—and here was a six-figure application, with a check. These, accompanied by the wide-eyed Williamson, exploded into the mid-December calm of the agency headquarters like the news of a Tonopah strike in the poker-playing ennui of a Poverty Flat.

"What's that, Williamson?" ejaculated the cashier. "Five hundred—you don't mean *thousand?*"

"Why, confound you," sneered Williamson, "look at that application!"

"Let me see it!" panted the manager, bursting in. "'Foster G. Van Dorn;' half a million! Holy cat, Williamson; but this will put you and the agency in the lead, for— Is he good for it, Williamson?"

"Why don't you see that *check?*" inquired the lofty solicitor. "I tell you, fellows, there's always a way to land any man. Why, for a year, I've—by George! I'm forgetting to send Doctor Watson over to make the examination. Van Dorn's going on a hunting trip, and we've got to hustle, and get him nailed before he goes!"

The manager stood by Williamson during the telephoning. "Who is Mr. Van Dorn?" he asked, as the agent hung up the receiver.

"President of the Kosmos Chemical Company," replied Williamson. "Son-in-law and enemy of Colonel Loree of the Solar Selling Company, you know," said the cashier.

"Oh-h-h-h!" replied the manager, as if recalling something. "I remember the 'romance' in the newspapers; but I thought the young fellow was poor. Fixed it up with the colonel, I suppose—the usual thing."

"Not on your life!" replied Williamson. "Loree would kill him if he dared—old aristocrat, you know; but Van Dorn's too smart for him. You remember he was an engineer for Loree's company, and met the daughter on some inspection trip. Love at first sight—moonlight on the mountains—runaway and wedding on the sly—father's curse—turned out to starve, and all that."

"I remember that," answered the manager; "but it doesn't seem to lead logically up to this application."

"Well," went on Williamson, "Van Dorn turns up with a company formed to work a deposit of the sal-ammoniac, or asphaltum, or whatever the stuff the Solar Company had cornered may be, and began trust-busting. The colonel swore the new deposit really belonged to his company because Van Dorn found it while in his employ, and called him all sorts of a scoundrel. But the young man's gone on, all the same, floating his company, and flying high."

"I heard that Loree was sure to ruin him," interposed the cashier.

"Ruin nothing!" said Williamson. "It was a case of the whale and the swordfish. Van Dorn's got him licked—why, don't you see that check!"

"That does look like success," replied the manager. "I hope his strenuous life hasn't hurt his health—Watson is fussy about hearts and lungs."

"That's the least of my troubles," replied Williamson. "Van Dorn's an athlete, and a first-class risk. There's nothing the matter with Van Dorn!"

And yet, Trudeau the guide, far up in the Minnesota woods, looked at the young man and wondered if there wasn't something the matter with Van Dorn. They had come by the old "tote-road" to the deserted lumber-camp armed and equipped to hunt deer. Most young men in Van Dorn's situation were keen-eyed, eager for the trail and the chase—at least until tamed by weariness. But Van Dorn was like a somnambulist. Once Trudeau had left him behind on the road, and on retracing his steps to find him, had discovered him standing by the path, gazing at nothing, his lips slowly moving as if repeating something under his breath—and he had started as if in fright at Trudeau's hail. He had been careful to give Trudeau his card, and admonished him to keep it; but he seemed careless of all opportunities of following up the acquaintance. Most of these city hunters were anxious to talk; but what troubled Trudeau, was the manner in which Van Dorn sat by the fire, wrote in a book from time to time, and gazed into the flames. Now that they had reached the old camp, Trudeau hoped that actual hunting would bring to his man's eyes the fire of interest in the thing he had come so far to enjoy.

"I'll fix up camp," said he. "If you like, you hunt. Big par*tie* Chicageau men ove' by lake—keep othe' way."

"How far to their camp?" asked the fire-gazer.

" 'Bout two mile," answered Trudeau.

"Chicago men?" queried Van Dorn. "How many?"

"Mebbe ten," answered Trudeau; "mebbe six. She have car on track down at depot. Big man—come ev'ry wintaire. Jacques Lacroix guide heem, Colonel Lorie—big man!"

"Colonel Loree! From Chicago?" cried Van Dorn.

"*Oui,* yes!" replied Trudeau. "You know heem?"

"No," said Van Dorn.

The man who did not know Loree went to his knapsack and took out a jacket made of deerskin tanned with the hair on. It was lined with red flannel. He held it up and looked at it fixedly. Trudeau started as it met his gaze, and he came up to Van Dorn and pointed to the garment.

"You wear zat?" asked he.

"Yes," said the other. "It is a good warm jacket."

"A man w'at wear deerskin zhaquette," said Trudeau, "in zese wood', in shoo*ting* sea*sone,* sartaine go home in wooden ove'coat—sure's hell!"

"Oh, I guess there's no danger!" said Van Dorn, his lips parting with a mirthless smile.

"*Non?*" queried Trudeau. "You ben in zese wood' before?"

"Oh, yes!" replied Van Dorn. "Lots of times!"

"Zen you know!" asserted Trudeau. "Zen you are zho*king* wiz me. Zese huntaire sink brown cloth coat, gray coat, black coat, anysing zat move—she sink zem every time a deer. Las' wintaire lots men killed for deer. Pete St. Cyr's boy kill deer, hang heem in tree, and nex' morning take heem on back an' tote. A city huntaire see deer-hide wiz hair on mov*ing,* an bim! sof'-nose bullet go thoo deer, thoo

Pete St. Cyr's boy's head! Zat zhaquette damn-fool thing!"

"It goes either side out," said the hunter. "I can turn it, you know."

"*I* turn heem! *I* turn heem!" said Trudeau, suiting the action to the word. "Red is bettaire, by gosh —in zese wood'."

Trudeau watched his companion as he made his laborious way through the cut-over chaos until he disappeared; but he did not see him pause when out of sight of camp, and turn toward the lake.

"I would rather it were any one else," said Van Dorn, as if to something that walked by his side; "but what difference does it make? Why not let him finish his work?"

The sheer difficulty of the country brought back to Van Dorn something like the forester's alertness. The lust for lumber had ravaged the spiry forest, and left, inextricably tangled, the wrecks of the noble trees—forest maidens whose beauty had been their destruction; only the crooked and ugly having escaped. So deep and complex was the wreckage that it seemed like the spilikins of a giants' game of jack-straws—gnarled logs, limbs like *chevaux-de-frise*, saplings and underbrush growing up through chaos. And spread over and sifted through all was the snow, as light as down.

Van Dorn must have told the truth as to his former visits; for he went on like one used to this terrible maze. Nowhere could he take three steps straight forward: it was always climbing up, or laping down, or going around, or crawling under. Here thick leaves upheld the snow, and in the dry pine straw on the ground he could hear the forest mice rustle and scurry. There a field was smoothed over by the snow, as a trap is hidden by sand, covering débris just high enough to imperil the limbs of the pedestrian. Yonder was a tamarack swamp too thick to be pierced: and everywhere it was over and under and up and down, and desperately hard, for miles and miles, with no place for repose.

He gazed away over the strange abomination of desolation, blindly reflecting upon man's way of coming, doing his worst, and passing on with sated appetite, leaving ruin—as he had done here. He wondered why that tall tract of virgin pine over at the right had been allowed to escape, standing against the sky like a black wall, spiked with tall rampikes. He stared fixedly at the snow, the blue shadows, the black pines, somnambulistic again.

To the something that seemed to walk by his side, he spoke of these things, as if it had been visible. Strange actions, strange thoughts for the president of the Kosmos Chemical Company, the great antagonist of Loree of the Solar Selling Company, the David to Loree's Goliath, the swordfish to the colonel's whale! Think, however, of David, with all the stones spent against the giant's buckler, and cowering within the lethal reach of that spear like a weaver's beam; or of the swordfish, with broken weapon, hunted to the uttermost black depths by the oncoming silent yawning destruction. And in Van Dorn's case, the enemy was an avenger as well as a natural foe.

Poor little Kosmos Chemical Company with its big name, its great deposits of "a prime commercial necessity"—see prospectus—its dependence on railways with which Loree was on terms of which Van Dorn never dreamed, its old and wily foe, skilled to snatch victory from the jaws of defeat, raging for the loss of his ewe lamb, whom, notwithstanding his giantship, he had loved for twenty years to Van Dorn's two, and had dreamed dreams and committed crimes for! Not very strange after all, perhaps, that the man went on muttering somnambulistically.

They say that one gripped in the lion's mouth is numb and filled with delusions.

Suddenly, putting life into the dead scene, a bounding form came into view past a thicket—a noble buck with many-pointed antlers, moving with great deliberate leaps among the giants' spilikins. The delicate, glassy hoofs, the slender, brittle limbs and horns, fragile as china, seemed courting destruction in those terrific entanglements. Yet the beautiful animal, as if by some magic levitation, rose lightly from a perilous crevice between two logs, turned smoothly in mid-leap, struck the four pipe-stem limbs into the only safe landing-place, shot thence with arrowy spring between two bayonet-like branches to another foothold, and so on and on, every rod of progress a miracle.

He stopped, snuffing the air. Instinctively the hunter leveled his rifle; and then came into view the buck's retinue, two does, one large and matronly, the other a last summer's fawn. The sleep-walker's eyes softened, the rifle swung downward from the point-blank aim, snapping a twig in its descent, and with swift, mighty bounds, the deer vanished, putting a clump of bushes between themselves and the foe with unerring strategy.

"Toward the lake," said the hunter. "I'll follow!"

There came the report of a distant rifle from the direction of the deer's flight, then another and another. Some one was working a repeater rapidly. The hunter stopped, took off his deer-skin jacket, turned it hair side out, and like a soldier making for the firing-line, pressed forward after the deer.

Trudeau saw his man halt on the edge of the firelight that evening, turn his jacket, and come wearily into camp. Trudeau sat and thought that night, while the other slept heavily. Next morning there was a raging storm, and the guide was puzzled that the hunter refused to brave its dangers. It was not sure then that monsieur desired the wooden overcoat? He told Van Dorn many stories of death in these storms, and watched for the effect.

"W'en man is lost in bliz*zaird,*" said Trudeau, "ze vidow mus' wait an' wait, an' mebbe nevaire know if he is vidow or not."

"It would be better," said the other reflectively, "to have the proof ample—ample!"

Trudeau, pondering over this, watched his charge putting names in a book opposite amounts in figures; but he did not know that here was the lost fortune of an old aunt, there the savings of a college chum.

Van Dorn looked them over calmly as if it had been a bills-payable sheet to be paid in the morning. Then the strange pleasure-hunter began writing a letter to a sweetheart to whom he seemed to be able to say only that he loved her better than life, that she must try to love his memory, and to train up the baby to respect his name, that the right thing is not always easy to discern, that sometimes one has only a choice of evils, that when a man has made a mess of it which he can straighten out by stepping off the stage, he might as well do it—and that he had had his share of happiness since she had been with him anyhow, and was far ahead of the game! Trudeau could not know what a foolish, silly, tragic letter it was, this product of insane commercialism. He thought life and the woods enough, and wondered at the shaking of the man's shoulders, and was amazed to see the tears dropping through his fingers as he bowed his head upon his hands—a man with a fifty-dollar sleeping-bag!

Over at the Loree headquarters there were roaring fires, fresh venison, a skilful chef, jolly companions, and the perfection of camp-life. The storm cleared. That strong old hunter, Loree, declaring that his business was to stalk deer, marched off in the solitary quest which is the only thing that brings the haunch to the spit in the Minnesota cut-over forest. He was bristly bearded, keen of eye and vigorous, handled his gun cannily, and craftily negotiated the fallen and tangled timbers, his glance sweeping every open vista for game. There was no time to think of anything but the making of his way, and of the chase. Troubles and triumphs retired to the outer verge of consciousness. Primeval problems claimed his thoughts, and the primeval man rose to meet them. It was in this ancient and effective wise that he had sharpened his weapons, set his snares, and hunted down Foster Van Dorn—and left him in the money-jungle, apparently unhurt, but really smitten to the heart and staggering to his fall. It was the Loree way. As an old hunter, he knew just where his shaft had struck, and how long the quarry could endure the hemorrhage. Had he not said that the fellow should be made to rue the Loree displeasure?

Like a flash these half-thoughts became no thoughts, as a dark blotch caught his eye, far off on the snow, beyond a little thicket.

"What is that?" he said to himself. It is a little hard to say, but the matter is worth looking into.

Just the color of a deer! Just where a deer would rest! We must work up the wind a little closer, for some men are so foolish as to wear those duns and browns; but that!—that *is* a deer's coat. It won't do to jump him and trust a shot as he goes—those firs will hide him at the first leap. A long shot at a standing target—there! He moved! There's not a second to lose!

A long shot, truly; but that graceful rifle thinks nothing of half a mile. There are many intervening bushes and saplings; but the steel-jacketed bullet would kill on the farther side of the thickest pine, and even a soft-nosed one will cut cleanly to this mark. The colonel's practised left hand immovably supported the barrel; the colonel's keen eye through the carefully adjusted sights saw plainly the blotch of deerskin down the little glade; and the colonel's steady forefinger confidently pressed the lightly-set trigger. Spat! The colonel felt the rifleman's delicious certitude that his bullet had found its mark, threw in another shell, and stood tensely ready to try the bisecting of the smitten deer's first agonized bound—but the blur of fur just stirred a little, and slipped down out of sight.

Panting in the killer's frenzy, Loree struggled

over the débris to reach his game. How oddly the deer had fallen! Heart, or brain, likely; as it went down like a log. Here was the thicket, and on the other side—yes, a patch of reddened snow, and the body of—no, not a deer, but a man, dead, it seemed, clad in a deerskin jacket, a rifle by his side and in his hand a note-book full of figures, its pages all stained and crumpled!

There was a shout in the far distance, but Loree heard it not. He knew his solitude, and never looked for aid. The white strangeness of the face of the man he had shot overcame the sense of something familiar in it; and the colonel, after a moment's scrutiny of it, addressed himself frantically to the stanching of the blood. A deep groan seemed to warrant hope; and stooping beneath the body Loree took it up and began bearing it toward the camp. He had an overwhelming consciousness of the terrible task before him; but the realization of the human life dashed out, some home blasted, some infinity of woe, and the bare chance of rescue rolled sickeningly over him, and he set his teeth and attacked the task like an incarnate will.

Logs and boughs and dead-wood held him back; countless obstacles exhausted him. He felt like crying out in agony as he realized that his age was telling against him. He felt strangely tender at this meeting with death in its simple and more merciful form. He clenched his teeth hard, felt his heart swell as if to burst, his lungs labor in agonized heavings—and when Trudeau the guide overtook him, he found him a frenzied man, covered with dark streaks and splashes of blood, unconquerably hurling upon his impossible task his last reserves of strength, with all that iron resolution with which he had beaten down resistance in his long battle with a relentless world.

"For God's sake," he panted hoarsely, "help me get him to camp! We've got a doctor there!"

"How's the colonel?" said the doctor, when he had done all he could for the colonel's victim.

"Knocked all to pieces," answered a young man. "Wants to know if we've found out who the man is."

Colonel Loree was interrogating Trudeau; surprised that he did not know the name of the wounded man.

"*Non*," answered Trudeau, "she tell me his name, and give me *carte*, but I lose heem an' forget firs' day. Remember wood', remember trail, remember face ver' well—but name; she I forget. She write lettaire an' cry, an' all time put fig' in book. Zis is heem; mebbe *she* tell name!"

The smutched names were strange to the colonel; but on another page there were some inexplicable references to Kosmos Chemical affairs; and on the cover were dim initials that looked like "F. V. D."

"I know something is wrong," went on Trudeau; "for I tell her it ben *très dangéreuse* to wear deerskin zhaquette in zese wood' in shoo*ting* sea*so*ne. I turn zhaquette red out. She go toward your camp. I watch. I see her turn heem hair out. I tell you, messieurs, zat man want to go home in wooden ove'coat. She have hungaire to die."

"Here's a letter we found in his pocket," said the young man. "Look at it, Colonel."

The colonel looked, saw his daughter's name, remembered the familiar look in the white, agonized, pitiful face; and saw the whole situation as by some baleful flash-light.

"Good God! Good God!" he cried. "It's Van Dorn! Get things ready to carry him in his bed to the car—quick, Johnson! And get to the wire as soon as you can. Have Tibbals bring Gwennie— Mrs. Van Dorn—to Duluth. Wire the hospital there! You know what's needed—look after things right, Johnson, for I think—I think—I'm going mad, old man!"

Mrs. Van Dorn ran into her father's arms in the hospital anteroom. Through mazes of frenzied anxiety she felt an epoch open in her life with that embrace from the father who had put her out of his life for ever, as they thought.

"Dear, dear papa!" she whispered, "let me go to Foster, quick!"

"Not just now, Gwennie, little girl," said he, patting her shoulder. "He's asleep. Did you bring the —the baby?"

"No, no! I thought—but Foster?" cried Gwendolyn. "Will he—will he—"

"He'll live, by Heaven!" cried the colonel. "I fired one fool for hinting that he wouldn't; and now they're all sure he'll pull through. Why, he's got to live, Gwennie!"

The colonel reached for his handkerchief, much hampered by Gwendolyn's arms.

"And when he's well," said he, "I want your help —in a business way. I'm too old to fight a man like Foster. He's got me down, Gwennie—beaten me to earth. If he won't come in with me, it's all up with the Solar. He's a fine fellow, Gwen—I—like him, you know—but he don't know how hard he hits. You'll help your old dad, won't you, Gwennie?"

To this point had the appeal of concrete, piteous need brought Colonel Loree, the ferocious, whose heart had never once softened while he did so much more cruel things than the mere shooting of Van Dorn. It broke Gwendolyn's heart afresh.

"Oh, don't papa!" she cried. "I can't sta-stand it! He sha'n't use his strength against you! I'll be on your side. He's generous, papa—he wanted to name baby Loree—and, oh, I must go to him, papa! I can't wait!"

The cigars had burned out, and the coffee cups and their saucers were messy with ashes. The Hired Man nodded in his chair. Aconite was slowly formulating some comment on the Poet's story—when the Bride rose.

"You've all been awfully nice to me," said she, "and I feel almost weepy when I think of never seeing you again. So I am not going to think of it. I shall hope to meet you," said she to Aconite, "in the stories which my friends bring back from the

Park—for I'm going to tell them all to come, and to ride with you, and learn about Old Jim Bridger. And you, Mr. Bill, I shall see when I pass through the corn country sometime—I feel sure of it. You will be plowing corn, and I shall wave my hand from the car window as you look up at the speeding train. I shall always see a friend in every plowman now. And you, sir, I shall watch for in the Poet's Corner of the Hall of Fame; and you in the Artist's alcove. And, Colonel, I know I shall see you sometime, for every one passes through Omaha sooner or later. Good-by, and God bless you, every one! We have made a continued story of our trip—for that, thanks to all, and now let us close the book, after writing

THE END